PALM BEACH BROKE

A CHARLIE CRAWFORD MYSTERY (BOOK 7)

TOM TURNER

TRIBECA PRESS

JOIN TOM'S AUTHOR NEWSLETTER

Get the latest news on Tom's upcoming novels when you sign up for his free author newsletter at **tomturnerbooks.com/news**.

PROLOGUE

IT REMINDED THORSEN PAUL OF WHEN HE USED TO SMUGGLE girls up to his bedroom in his parents' house in Greenwich. Except now he and his lady friend were in the guesthouse of his parents' house in Palm Beach and it was twelve years later. His parents had stopped trying to catch him in the act a long time ago.

The only real danger was the boyfriend of the woman he was in bed with. The guy's name was David Balfour and he had a nasty temper. Thorsen and Bree had just made love and were lying next to each other naked and sweaty, the top sheet up to their waists. It was one o'clock in the afternoon and Bree had to get back to the gallery on Worth Avenue where she worked.

"I love our little nooners," Bree said, getting up out of bed.

Paul grabbed her arm gently. "Do you have to go?"

She pulled her arm away. "Sorry, gotta get back. You know, another day, another Picasso to sell."

"Really?"

"I wish," Bree said, sliding into her panties. "Don't you have to go see your bankers and lawyers?"

Thorsen groaned. "Just my lawyer. And it's not going to be fun."

Bree pulled up her short white silk skirt over her hips and buttoned it. Then she lifted her black spaghetti strap shirt over her head and pulled it down.

"I love women who don't wear bras," Paul said, a lustful look in his eye.

Bree walked over to the bed and leaned down and kissed him. "You love *all* women." She put a finger up to his lips. "Bye, my love."

"Hurry back."

She walked toward the back door, opened it and left.

Thorsen Paul looked at his watch. He had two hours until he had to see his lawyer.

Five minutes later he was sound asleep.

THE SECOND-FLOOR DOOR SUDDENLY FLEW OPEN AND TWO people burst in. One had a Glock and the other, a short, heavily tattooed man, brandished a long knife.

"Don't say a word," said the one with the Glock. "Get out of bed."

"But—"

"*Now.*"

Two days later.

CHARLIE CRAWFORD AND MORT OTT, THE FULL COMPLEMENT of Palm Beach's homicide department, were on their way back from lunch in West Palm Beach. The radio was tuned to a local news station.

Former billionaire and twenty-eight-year-old founder of NextRed Corporation, Thorsen Paul, has been reported missing by his attorney. The San Francisco resident and son of Palm Beach philanthropist, Roderick Paul, was last seen at his parent's home yesterday afternoon by a source who asked to remain anonymous. The family has requested that if anyone has any knowledge of Mr. Paul's whereabouts, to please contact...

The news anchor provided a phone number identified as that of Mr. Paul's attorney.

Ott nodded. "NextRed was that company that went from being worth billions to worthless in about five minutes, right?" he asked as he drove their Crown Vic over the middle bridge from West Palm to Palm Beach.

"It was a little more than five minutes, but yeah, it got totally crushed," Crawford said. "I read somewhere that Paul declared personal bankruptcy and was like...close to homeless."

Ott shook his head. "Poor bastard," he said. "Not to be a downer, but you think maybe the guy offed himself?"

Crawford shook his head. "Jesus, Mort, you just heard this and already you got the guy dead and buried."

ONE

CHARLIE CRAWFORD GOT THE CALL FROM DISPATCH THE SAME day, a few minutes after 8 p.m. Dead woman ID'd as Adriana Palmer, had been shot four times, at 897 North Ocean Boulevard. He drove quickly from his West Palm Beach condo, and reached the Palm Beach residence a few moments before Mort Ott arrived.

Ott rumbled in behind the wheel of his tricked out 1969 Pontiac GTO Judge Ram Air IV, a car their boss, Chief Norm Rutledge, thought inappropriate for a homicide cop. Ott slid his two-hundred-fifty-pound frame past the steering wheel, got out, and looked over at Crawford.

"Just when I was all hunkered down, ready to binge out on *Bosch*," he said, referring to the TV show.

"Maybe we can solve it quick," Crawford said. "Get you right back there."

"When does that ever happen?"

"Yeah, true."

Three uniforms were there already. One of them, Bob Shepley, introduced Crawford and Ott to the victim's twin sister, Amanda Palmer, who was sitting in her sister's living room. Shepley explained that a next-door neighbor said she'd heard several loud pops and called the police.

Amanda, who lived in a house on the other side of her sister, had told Shepley that she had just arrived home, heard sirens and seen the flashing lights of arriving police cars. She was a medium-height, fit-looking blonde who had mascara pooling below her eyes, and a splotchy red nose. She wore tight jeans and a blue T-shirt with *St. Barth's* on it.

"We're sorry about your loss, Ms. Palmer," Crawford said, showing her ID. "I'm Detective Crawford and this is my partner Detective Ott. Can we ask you a few questions? We want to find who did this as soon as possible."

"Yes, sure," she said, wiping her eyes on the short sleeve of her blouse. "What do you want to know?"

It turned out Amanda and her sister owned The Max, an exclusive fitness club that Crawford had heard of a few times. She said Adriana had left work at a little before six and that she had left around seven-thirty. Amanda said her sister had told her she needed to run a few errands before she headed home.

Amanda shrugged. "Sorry, I wish I could tell you something really helpful."

"Are you aware of any recent burglaries in the neighborhood, Ms. Palmer?" Crawford asked. Theft wasn't Mort's or his beat.

Amanda shrugged. "No, not that I'm aware of."

"Did your sister ever mention anyone she was afraid of?" Ott asked. "Anyone who may have threatened her, possibly?"

Amanda shook her head. "No, and I would certainly know about that."

"Nobody at all?" Ott pressed.

Amanda shook her head

Crawford nodded. "Okay, well, thank you. We're going to look around your sister's house, if that's okay. Then I'm sure we'll have more questions. You'll be here for a while, right?"

Amanda nodded and sniffled.

As they walked out of the living room, Crawford and Ott each donned a pair of vinyl gloves.

They walked through the living room and out to an enclosed sun porch.

Ott pointed at a window, opened a crack. He and Crawford walked over to it.

"Remember when there was that string of burglaries? Houses on the beach?" Ott said.

"Yeah, just before I came down," Crawford said. "A gang from Miami, right?"

"Yeah, Cuban guys, in a Donzi." A so-called *go-fast* boat. "Took a while to get 'em, but eventually they did."

"So that's what you're thinkin'?"

"Just that it's a possibility," Ott said. "Not necessarily by boat, but houses on the ocean are easier to hit. Just walk down the beach."

Crawford nodded as he looked around for anything else out of place.

"Plus, most people who live on the ocean have expensive shit," Ott said.

"You've made a study of that?"

"Yeah, you name it: jewelry, flat screens, furs, silverware, hell of a lot nicer here than in my neighborhood."

Crawford nodded.

"Not that someone's gonna drag a flat screen out of here. But all that other stuff's pretty portable."

"Yeah," Crawford said. "I'm gonna go out to the car. Get my Maglite and look around out back."

Ott nodded and they both went and retrieved Maglites from their cars, then walked through the house and out the French doors, which led to a big stone terrace and a pool beyond.

Outside, they shined their Maglites on the ground below the open window. The beams illuminated a large shoe print in the dirt, pointed away from the house, toward the ocean.

"Bingo," Ott said.

Crawford crouched and studied it. "Should be able to get a good impression." He pointed at the print. "Tread looks like a sneaker."

Ott nodded. "About a nine or ten," he said, looking around for more prints but seeing only the one.

Walking in a straight line, four feet apart, they walked toward the ocean, then back to the house, covering a small grid pattern.

"Hey, check this out," Ott said, his Maglite pointing at something in the grass. It was a string of pearls.

Crawford reached down to pick up the pearls with a vinyl-clad hand.

They spent the next half hour scouring the beach but found nothing more. At the water's edge, they walked along the sand, looking for any sign of a boat having landed on the beach or been pushed off from it. But the tide had recently come in, so if there had been any footprints or signs of a boat, they'd been washed away.

They walked back up to the house. "Let's check the security system," Crawford said, and they went into the foyer and found the keypad. It looked expensive and state-of-the-art. Not surprising. But what *did* surprise them was...it was off.

"Why would you ever turn it off?" Ott asked.

Crawford shrugged. "Damn good question. Let's go talk to the sister."

Ott nodded and they turned and walked toward the living room.

"You know anything about The Max?"

"Just that it's a little out of my budget."

Ott chuckled. "I heard they get like a grand a month."

"Make that way out of my budget."

AMANDA PALMER WAS SITTING IN THE LIVING ROOM, HAVING A glass of wine. Bob Hawes, the medical examiner, had arrived, along with two crime-scene techs. Crawford was disappointed that neither of them was Dominica McCarthy, with whom he shared a special relationship. He also believed she was the best tech in the department—but, then, he might have been a little biased.

Crawford and Ott approached Amanda Palmer. "Mind if we ask you a few more questions, Ms. Palmer?"

"Sure, whatever I can do to help," she said, gesturing toward the couch opposite her. "Have a seat."

Crawford and Ott sat as Crawford pulled out the pearl necklace from his jacket pocket. "Is this your sister's?"

Amanda nodded, wide-eyed. "It sure is. Where'd you find it?"

"On the lawn out back," Crawford said. "Our theory is your sister may have walked in on a burglary. Could have tried to resist the burglar, or burglars, with the pepper spray found in her possession, and was shot."

"Oh, my God," Amanda said. "Did you find anything else?"

"We found a well-preserved footprint just below where we believe the suspect entered and exited the house," Crawford said.

"Can you track someone down with a footprint like that?"

"It's not easy," Crawford said. "But it's a start." He remembered the keypad. "Do you know why your sister's security system was turned off?"

Amanda shrugged. "No, sorry. That seems odd."

"That's what we thought."

"On another note," Ott said, "was Adriana going out with anyone, seeing someone?"

"Yes," Amanda said, "a man named Ed Bertoli."

Crawford heard footsteps from the foyer. A tall man in blue jeans and a polo shirt burst into the living room. "Oh, my God," he said, running up to Amanda. "I just heard. Are you all right, honey?"

Amanda stood, threw her arms around the man, and started to sob. "I—I just can't," she started. "I can't even comprehend it."

The man kissed her. "I am so damned sorry."

"These nice men are Detective Crawford and...sorry I forgot—"

"Detective Ott," Ott said with a smile.

"I'm Ted Bartow," he said. "Amanda's boyfriend. Do you have any idea how it happened?"

"It's too early to know for sure," Crawford said. "We think Adriana may have walked in in the middle of a burglary."

Bartow looked back at Amanda. "I'm so sorry, honey," he said again, putting an arm around her shoulder.

"Thank you." Amanda wiped her eyes, spreading mascara. "I think I want to go home unless you have some more questions," she said to Crawford.

"We'll make it brief," he assured her. "I'm assuming your sister had people who worked at the house on a regular basis. Like a cleaning lady? Pool cleaners? Landscapers, probably?"

"All the above," Amanda said. "Plus, she had a man come and detail her car every two weeks."

"Do you use the same people your sister used?" Crawford asked.

"Yes," Amanda said. "We vetted them all pretty thoroughly. They've all been working for us"—she thought for a second— "for over five years."

"Why?" Bartow asked Crawford. "Were you thinking it might be an inside job? One of them decided to rob the place?"

Crawford nodded. "We've seen it before," he said, then to Amanda. "But you never had any kind of problem with anything disappearing before?"

Amanda shook her head. "No. Nothing like that."

Crawford glanced over at Ott, who was taking notes in his old leather-bound notepad. His partner looked up and shrugged.

"Well, I guess that'll do it for now," Crawford said, reaching for a card in his wallet. "If you think of anything else, please call me." He handed cards to Amanda and Bartow. "In the meantime, we'll be in touch and keep you up to speed on our investigation."

"Thank you very much," Amanda said.

Crawford nodded.

"Again, sorry for your loss," Ott said.

Amanda gave the detectives a pained smile, still clinging tightly to Bartow.

Crawford and Ott walked to the foyer, where the ME and the two crime-scene techs were still studying the body and the area surrounding it.

"Perp came in through a window in the sun porch," Crawford said. "It's on the other side of the living room."

"And there's a good footprint outside below the window," Ott added. "Perp exiting the house."

Crawford asked Hawes, "Can you measure it, and let me know what its size is?"

Hawes nodded. "For you, Charlie, anything."

"We also found this string of pearls owned by the vic out in the lawn behind," Crawford said, handing it to Hawes, who promptly bagged and tagged the necklace.

"So, burglary gone wrong, huh, Charlie?" the ME said.

"Maybe."

"What do you mean, maybe?"

Crawford looked at Ott, then back to Hawes. "'Cause, having done this for a while, I've seen my share of curve balls."

Ott nodded. "Yeah, especially in this town."

TWO

CRAWFORD AND OTT DROVE THEMSELVES BACK TO THE STATION
from the crime scene and met in Crawford's office: a bare-bones,
medium-sized room without the usual pictures of wives, kids, and
dogs, because Crawford had none of the above. He had a *former* wife.
And a beloved Labrador retriever that his former beloved wife had
ended up with. No kids.

He did keep a framed poster of the original Twin Towers in New
York City. Crawford had been working for the NYPD on 9/11, and
the memory remained as raw as ever.

He sat behind his desk and Ott in one of the two chairs facing it—
the one he claimed was "permanently molded to the shape of my ass",
even though it was made of wood.

"I'm pretty sure Rose belongs to that gym, The Max," Crawford
said, referring to his friend-with-benefits and real estate agent
nonpareil Rose Clarke.

"Gym? Are you kidding me? I hear that place is a goddamn
palace," Ott said. Despite his ample girth, Ott could bench press his
weight, and one time even out-sprinted Crawford, who'd lettered in
both football and lacrosse in college. Ott logged five hours or more

every week at his gym—quaintly named Lou's Sweat Shop— which was a far cry from The Max. Think of a large dingy room with low ceilings that smelled of sweat instead of the fresh-cut flowers at The Max, and had racks and racks of free weights, barbells, and a few well-worn medicine balls.

Kettlebells and brightly colored exercise balls? Not a one in sight.

Ott, at forty-eight, was a refugee from the mean streets of Cleveland, while Crawford had moved down from New York City four years back, six months after Ott's arrival in Palm Beach. Physically, Crawford and Ott were polar opposites. Crawford was a rangy six-three, had big blue eyes, and dirty blond hair he wore a little on the long side. When Crawford first met Ott, he saw a pronounced resemblance to his high school janitor. A fact that he never shared with Ott, a roly-poly five-eight and about five dozen follicles short of bald.

"So, what are you waiting for?" Ott asked.

"What do you mean?"

"Rose. Give her a call. Find out what she knows about the sisters."

"Way ahead of you, bro," Crawford said. "Meeting her for breakfast tomorrow morning."

"Brunch at the Breakers?"

Crawford laughed. "You know me better than that. The five ninety-nine special at Green's."

"Can't beat it."

Green's Pharmacy was a combination knick-knack store that sold everything from flip-flops to nineteen-dollar Foster Grant sunglasses, plus an actual pharmacy that filled prescriptions, but it was known most famously for its eighty-two-seat old-style luncheonette that served the best breakfast and lunch within a hundred-mile radius. The one possible exception being Harry and the Natives up in Hobe Sound.

Crawford and Ott spent the next two hours going through Palm Beach County's Sheriff's Office's most-wanted profiles as well as convicted-felon profiles, paying particular attention to burglars. At

11:30 that night, Ott went home, too tired even for *Bosch*. A half-hour later Crawford got in his car and headed back to his condo in West Palm Beach.

———

EIGHT HOURS LATER, CRAWFORD WAS SITTING AT A TABLE AT Green's, looking at a menu, though he already knew what he was going to have: two big sweaty sausages, a mushroom omelet, and rye toast slathered with raspberry jam.

Rose Clarke sat across from him, a tall, beautiful blond who endured daily sessions with a Svengali male trainer, leaving her gym-trim and tight with absolutely no droops or jiggling body parts.

"How do you get away with it?" Rose asked, as their orders showed up ten minutes later.

"Get away with what?"

"That hard body of yours," Rose said. "All you eat is junk."

Crawford looked offended. "Junk? How can you say that? This is an All-American breakfast."

"Yes, exactly. Which is why all of America is so damned fat."

"Don't get on your high horse, girl. Besides, I had a salad last week...or maybe the week before."

Rose laughed. "Wow, Charlie. You're almost a vegetarian." She pointed at his sausage. "You know what's in those things?"

Crawford pushed down on one of the sausages with his fork. Bubbly liquid oozed out. "No, can't say I do. But it sure smells good."

Rose frowned. "Yuck. Whatever it is, it's disgusting."

Crawford pointed at Rose's fruit platter. "Beats the hell out of bananas, strawberries, and blueberries any day of the week."

"You forgot the kumquats," Rose said, pointing.

"That's because I had no idea what they were."

Rose could only shake her head.

"Speaking of health, I want to ask you about your health club, The Max."

"Nice segue, Charlie. I thought we might get around to that. You usually spend a little more time on the foreplay. Anyway, it was really sad what happened to Adriana. She was kind of a head case, but I got along with her."

Rose stabbed at a piece of banana, then a slice of strawberry.

"What do you mean head case?"

"Tell you exactly," Rose said. "A damn good Pilates instructor. Ran a good Zumba class, too. But always seemed to be going in ten different directions at once. And as a businesswoman?" Rose shook her head. "Neither of them were."

"Why, what happened?"

"It's just kind of chaos half the time. They keep raising the prices, saying they're going to get a new top-of-the-line this or that. But the new this or that never showed up. Yes, they've got a lot of fancy state-of-the-art stuff, but half of it doesn't work. That's an exaggeration, but like the saltwater pool, all the pipes are corroded. And a few of the elliptical machines have out-of-service signs on them. I heard they had plans to franchise them all over the country. How can you do that if you can't run the first one right?"

Crawford shrugged. "I had no idea. I thought it was top-of-the-line everything. Do you know where they got the money to start it?"

"I heard they had a rich daddy. Set 'em up but had to keep feeding the dragon."

"He live around here?

"No clue. This is just locker-room gossip." She put her fork down. "I heard her murder was probably a burglary gone bad. Is that right?"

"Maybe."

Rose cocked her head. "Well, what else could it have been?"

Crawford smiled. "I don't know. That's part of the reason I'm here with you. The main reason, of course, is just to be in your orbit while at the same time gleaning some of your brilliant insights."

Rose laughed. "You're so full of it."

Crawford patted her hand.

"But I do love flattery," Rose said as she speared a kumquat and downed it. "Just so happens, I have a few thoughts for you."

"Let's hear 'em."

"You should talk to a couple guys who went out with Adriana. One of them, come to think of it, was going out with her when she was killed. Name's Ed Bertoli. Owns a restaurant in West Palm."

"Yeah, I heard about him. And who else?" Crawford had his iPhone out to take down the next name.

"A nice guy who's the tennis pro at the Racquet & Beach club. She dated him for a couple of years."

"What's his name?"

"Peter Georgescu."

Crawford took the last bite of his squishy sausage. "The boyfriends may not be able to shed any light on this. I mean if it was, in fact, a robbery gone bad."

Rose put her coffee cup down in the saucer. "Wait a minute, aren't you the guy who told me it's never quite what it seems in that wonderful world of murder and mayhem of yours?"

Crawford thought for a few moments, then nodded. "I am that guy," he said, "and you're right, time to go have a little chat with Ed and Pete."

THREE

CRAWFORD WENT BACK TO THE OFFICE AFTER BREAKFAST WITH Rose. He wanted to know everything he could possibly learn about Amanda and Adriana Palmer. Their father, too. Google was where he always started. There were quite a few search results about the sisters, including the fact that they had both graduated from Princeton in 2001. Their father's name was Norman Bobrow. Crawford Googled Bobrow and learned that he had been a senior vice president of Eastman Kodak in Rochester, New York, for fifteen years and died back in 2014. Right after the real estate crash in 2008, he had bought a house and two lots in Palm Beach. He'd built homes for each daughter on the lots, and lived in a house on Pendleton Avenue from October through the middle of May every year, presumably, going north each summer.

It was weird how he'd died. Apparently, he had been walking down North Lake Way and was hit by a car. It was a hit and run and the driver fled the scene and was never caught. Crawford got all this information from an article in the *Palm Beach Post* about Bobrow's hit-and-run death.

Just as Crawford arrived at the station, his cell phone rang. The name that popped up was Bob Hawes, the ME.

"Yeah, Bob."

"Ten and a half," Hawes said.

"Thanks," Crawford said and hung up.

It was the shortest conversation he'd ever had with Hawes. And because of that, the best.

Crawford walked down to Ott's cubicle. Ott was going through more profiles of Palm Beach felons. Specifically, burglars. Crawford looked over his shoulder at one man who looked particularly felonious. He had tats on every square inch of his bald, shaved head, right down to where the photo was cut off at his neck.

"That's a mighty *baaad* lookin' dude," Crawford said.

Ott started reading. "'Lewd and lascivious behavior, second-degree murder, burglary, video voyeurism, false imprisonment...' and he's one of the nicer ones."

"So, I've been looking into the Palmer sisters and got a little info from Rose. Apparently, their father gave them the money to start up The Max, which, according to Rose, isn't exactly the palace we thought it was."

"What do you mean? Pictures of it look pretty swell."

"Yeah, but she said a lot of the equipment there is broken down. And they're always jacking up the prices with the promise of getting a new ultimate this or ultimate that, which then never shows up."

"Really?"

"Yeah, and the father, whose name was Norman Bobrow, was killed by a hit and run driver back in 2014 on North Lake Way."

Ott nodded. "I remember that. Right after I got down here, I think. A businessman from somewhere up in New York, right?"

"Well, retired, but yeah, must be the same guy."

Ott put his hand on his chin. "Pretty unlucky family, huh?"

"Yeah, that's what I was thinking."

Crawford's cell phone rang. "Crawford," he said, seeing it was the station number.

"Hey, Charlie," Natalie at the reception desk said. "Got a man named Ed Bertoli at the front desk here. Says he was the boyfriend of that woman who was killed."

"Thanks, Nat, be right out," Crawford said, turning to Ott. "Perfect timing. Adriana Palmer's boyfriend is out front. Oh, by the way, for what it's worth, the shoe size for that print at Adriana's house is actually ten and a half."

Bertoli was around forty, rail-thin, and had a droopy mustache flecked with grey. He introduced himself in a monotone, and seemed to be one of those men who felt uncomfortable making eye contact.

Crawford and Ott introduced themselves, shook hands, and Crawford ushered Bertoli over to a far corner of the station's reception area.

"We're sorry about what happened to Adriana Palmer, Mr. Bertoli," Crawford said.

"Thank you," Bertoli said. "She was a special woman. I just thought I'd come in and see if there was anything I could tell you that might help you catch her killer. You know, provide you with information that might be useful."

"We appreciate that," Crawford said. "You were actually on our list to question."

"So, ask away. Ask anything you need to know."

Crawford glanced out the window, then back to Bertoli. "Did Ms. Palmer ever talk to you about the circumstances of her father's death?"

Bertoli thought for a second. "No, not really. She mentioned it every once in a while. I got the idea she and Amanda were very close to him."

"Did Adriana ever...express frustration that the hit and run was never solved? That the driver was never caught?"

"Um, not that I remember. I guess she just thought that the police were doing everything they could." He shrugged. "Tough to catch somebody if there were no eyewitnesses and no evidence."

Crawford and Ott nodded.

"Do you know why Amanda and Adriana changed their last name?" Ott asked.

Bertoli thrummed the side table next to him with his fingers. "That's a good question. And, no, I don't really know. I just know that was a long time ago. But I never talked to Adriana about it."

Crawford nodded. "And I'm assuming, like most identical twins, they were very close, maybe best friends?"

"Definitely best friends, even though sometimes they could fight like cats and dogs."

Crawford glanced at Ott, then back to Bertoli. "What kinds of things did they fight about?"

"Oh, God, I don't know...Amanda second-guessing her on the business, a million money issues she had, the weather, you name it. But usually, it blew over pretty quickly," Bertoli said. "Just curious why you're asking me these kinds of questions. My understanding was that Adriana was shot by a burglar she surprised in her house."

"Yes," Crawford said. "That's maybe all there is to it. We're just trying to cover all the bases. Get as full a profile of her as possible."

Bertoli nodded. "Do you have any idea at all who might have done it?"

"At this point, no," Crawford said.

"But we will," Ott said.

"I hope so," Bertoli said. "I don't want it to end up like her father's death."

"Did Ms. Palmer ever mention having intruders in her house. Was she ever afraid...you know, living all by herself in that big house?"

"No. She had the best security system money could buy."

Crawford pointed out the obvious. "Except last night, when it was turned off."

CRAWFORD AND OTT DECIDED TO SPLIT THINGS UP. OTT WAS

going to track down convicted and suspected burglars in the area and see where that went. Crawford was going to do some of that, but also look into the investigation of Norman Bobrow's hit-and-run death and interview Amanda Palmer again.

The first step for Crawford was finding out who had led the Norman Bobrow investigation. It turned out to be a detective named Willis Seawright, who Crawford had never worked with but knew had a decent reputation. He asked Seawright down to his office to discuss the case.

Seawright sat down in the chair that Ott always used. Crawford wondered whether Seawright would feel Ott's ass-print.

"So, Willy, what can you tell me about Norman Bobrow?"

Seawright thought for a few moments. "Well, first of all, the guy was like an ATM machine to his daughters. I looked at his checkbook and half the checks were written out to them. Then another quarter of 'em to The Max, that's their—"

"Yes, I know," Crawford said. "How much are we talking? The checks?"

"Oh, Christ, I never added them all up. But every one was for at least ten grand or more. I'd say over the course of a year…a hundred thousand? No more, actually. More like two hundred."

"How come their names are Palmer and his is Bobrow?"

"I wondered the same thing. Seems like they were only too happy to take his money, but wanted no part of his name," Seawright said. "I heard they wanted to open The Max in every exclusive zip code in the country, and maybe—no offense, Dad— didn't want to be burdened with some obscure Polish name."

"Seems like the daughters weren't making much money on The Max or else had really extravagant lifestyles."

"Or both."

Crawford nodded. "What did you find out about the actual hit and run?"

"Not much. There were no eyewitnesses, but there was something that was kind of curious."

"What was that?"

"This woman, who lived on Kenlyn and whose house backed up to North Lake Way, was in her backyard, just about to take a dip in her pool—" Seawright shifted in his chair— "and she heard what she described as the 'roar' of an engine, then a 'thump.'"

"A roar, huh? So, what did that mean to you when she told you that?"

"First reaction was a 'roar' might have been the car accelerating right before it hit Bobrow."

Crawford nodded. "When you said it, that was my first reaction, too. Almost like it was intentional."

"Yeah, like instead of hitting the brakes the driver hit the accelerator. Which could have been accidental."

"Do you really believe that?"

"No."

Crawford shook his head and thought for a second. "So, the question is, if someone hit him on purpose, why?"

"Can't help you there."

"Any theories?"

"Sorry, no clue."

"Did you ever go over to the surrogate's court offices and check out his probated will?"

"No. Never did," Seawright said with a shrug.

Crawford nodded. "What about enemies? Did the guy have any? Or owe money to someone? Anything at all like that?"

"Well, yeah, that was one of the main angles I worked. But from what I could tell, he was just this seventy-year-old guy who had a daily tennis game and lived quietly in a house on Pendleton."

"And wrote a lot of checks."

CRAWFORD DECIDED TO LOOK INTO NORMAN BOBROW A LITTLE deeper.

He went down to the surrogate court and read over Bobrow's will and probated estate. What he found was eye-opening.

The first thing that came to light was that several months before Bobrow's death, he took out a first mortgage on his house on Pendleton for seven hundred and fifty thousand dollars. Shortly after that, he wrote checks to his daughters for three hundred thousand dollars each. Willis Seawright had apparently missed that fact because the checks were drawn on a rarely-used account at JP Morgan Private Bank. The second revelation was that, at the time of Bobrow's death, he had only a little more than fifty thousand dollars left to his name. It seemed he'd lived a remarkably frugal lifestyle, which allowed the Palmer sisters to spend like they were the Kardashian sisters.

FOUR

CRAWFORD AND OTT GOT TOGETHER AT THE END OF THE SECOND day after the murder of Adriana Palmer and updated each other on what they'd come up with that day. Ott had spent a half hour interviewing a burglar who had been convicted of breaking into several houses in what Ott called the "Mexican section" of Palm Beach.

"The Mexican section? What are you talking about?" Crawford asked.

"You know...El Brillo, El Bravo, El Vedado."

Crawford laughed and shook his head. "Only some of the most expensive real estate in Palm Beach."

"Yeah, well, they got those Mexican names."

"Ah, I think they're Spanish."

"What's the difference?"

Crawford chuckled. "Oh, I don't know, like the difference between some English guy and us, for starters."

Ott smiled. "Maybe you got a point there."

The three "El" streets did indeed consist of some of the nicest and most valuable houses in Palm Beach, primarily Mediterranean-

and Georgian-style. They were, for the most part, on large lots and had some of the finest banyan specimen trees on the island.

Ott said the convicted burglar repeatedly proclaimed his innocence, and swore that he and a friend were at the dog track in West Palm on the night of the murder. But when Ott asked him for the name of his friend, he said he couldn't remember it. That was pretty fishy. But Ott didn't press it any further, particularly after checking out his shoe size that appeared to be no more than a seven or eight. Ott's gut told him he wasn't their guy, but he knew where to find him if he and Crawford needed to put more heat on him.

Crawford told Ott what he'd learned at the offices of the surrogate court.

Ott scratched his mostly-bald head and tapped the arm of his chair. "If I happened to be suspicious by nature, which I am, I might wonder if the daughters had something to do with what happened to the father."

"Why do you say that?"

"Well, just throwing shit up against the wall, but seems like they kind of bled him dry, so what if he had, say, a million-dollar insurance policy or something."

"Great minds think alike," Crawford said.

Ott leaned forward like a dog on scent. "So, did he?"

Crawford shook his head. "Nah, no such luck."

CRAWFORD GOT THE ADDRESS OF ANOTHER CONVICTED BURGLAR from a West Palm Beach cop who had caught the man in the act, and after his meeting with Ott, dropped in on him unexpectedly. The man's name was Cristobal, and he answered the door wearing dirty cargo shorts, a wife-beater T-shirt, orange sneakers, and an uneasy look on his pock-marked face.

Crawford could smell weed from five feet away.

"Wasn't one of the terms of your parole no marijuana?" Crawford asked, after flashing ID.

"Yes, but it's not me," Cristobal said.

Crawford sniffed again and knew it was coming from inside. "Coming from the neighbor's house, is that your story?"

"Just sayin' I wasn't doing it," Cristobal said.

"Even if you weren't—which you were, 'cause I smell it on you—it's a parole violation if it takes place in your house. What I need to know is where you were on Thursday night." Crawford looked down at Cristobal's sneakers. "And what's your shoe size?"

"My shoe size?"

"Yeah, that was the question."

"Eight."

"And Thursday night?"

"Watching TV with my old lady."

"What?"

"What was I watching?"

Crawford nodded.

"First, *Monster Trucks,* then—"

A woman padded out to the porch in a pink kimono with a cigarette dangling from her lip. She shaded her eyes and looked up at Crawford: "Who are you, studly?"

"Name's Crawford, Detective Crawford. I just asked your husband what you two were doing on Thursday night."

"I told him, *Monster—*"

"Let her answer," Crawford cut Cristobal off.

The woman took a pull on her cigarette, then exhaled. "Yeah, like he was saying, *Monster Trucks,* then this other thing with Kevin Bacon..."

"Yeah, that was good," Cristobal said, nodding.

"What was?"

"*I Love Dick,*" the woman blurted.

"'Scuse me?"

The woman chuckled. "That was the name of the show. *I Love Dick*. Kevin Bacon was Dick."

"Gotcha," Crawford said, turning to Cristobal. "What do you do for a living, Mr. Cristobal?"

"Cristobal's my first name," he said, then with a proud smile, "I'm an artist."

"Oh, are you?"

"Yeah, a painter...houses, that is."

"So, you paint houses?"

"Yup," Cristobal said, as the woman stubbed out her cigarette butt on the porch.

He was getting the vibe that Cristobal wasn't much of a burglar, let alone killer. Just a guy who could slather paint on a wall with one hand while smoking a joint with the other.

"You got a gun?" Crawford asked.

"No," Cristobal said, holding up his hands.

"'Cause my partner's on his way here with a search warrant," Crawford lied. "If we find you got a piece, you're in big trouble."

"You won't."

"Just a bag of weed, huh?"

Cristobal's eyes dropped to the porch.

Crawford couldn't be bothered with a weed bust.

"All right. You could really help your cause if you tell me who's hittin' houses in Palm Beach. Ones on the ocean."

"Would if I could, but I keep my nose clean. Got nothin' to do with guys into that."

"Anymore, you mean?"

"Never did," Cristobal said. "Got wrongfully convicted."

"Of course."

FIVE

THE ABDUCTORS WERE LOOKING DOWN AT THORSEN PAUL.

"Are you sure you have nothing to tell us?" the tall one asked.

"You can't do this to me," Paul pleaded, openly weeping. "You don't think I would've told you everything after what you did to me?"

Paul had dark cigarette burns across his face and one less finger on his right hand. The stump had bled profusely when the shorter man cut it off with a bolt cutter.

"Last chance," the tall one said as the other lit a joint.

"I told you—I fucking told you!" Paul cried with what was left of his voice. "There's nothing left to tell!"

The tall one signaled to his partner with a head flick.

Joint in a corner of his mouth, the short one reached into his pocket and pulled something out. It was a jar. He undid the top, put his index finger in it, then smeared something over and around one of Thorsen Paul's eyes.

"What the hell are you doing?" Paul asked in a wild panic. He considered screaming at the top of his lungs but feared they'd kill him. Once they left, though, he'd scream so loud that they'd hear him in the next county.

The short one stuck his finger in the jar again and smeared the substance on Paul's other eye. Now Paul recognized it by the smell.

"Fucking animal," he moaned.

The tall one laughed while his partner screwed the top back onto the jar, put it in his pocket, then pulled something else out of another pocket. Paul couldn't see what it was. The short one ripped off a piece of duct tape and quickly placed it across Paul's mouth. Paul tried to scream but too late, his cry muffled by the swath of tape. The man laid another piece over Paul's mouth, then stood.

The tall one waved down at Paul. "Well, have a nice swim."

AFTER A QUICK HUDDLE WITH OTT BACK AT THE STATION, Crawford saw it was six-thirty. He called Dominica McCarthy to see if she wanted to have a last-minute dinner. Dominica accepted, but only if Crawford agreed to take her to someplace other than his usual Mexican dive, which she accused him of favoring because of their industrial-strength margaritas that made inhibitions vanish in about three sips.

"For you, Dominica, as I had planned all along, nothing but the best."

"And what would that be?"

"La Sirena," Crawford said referring to an Italian restaurant on South Dixie Highway.

"Wow," Dominica said. "That's pretty upscale, Charlie. Why the big splurge?"

"I just want to take you to a place deserving of your beauty, sophistication, and *je ne sais*...whatever it is."

"*Quoi?*"

"That's it."

"And, let me guess, because you were hoping to maybe get lucky?"

Crawford shook his head. "Unfair accusation. Though I may not like it, I have complete respect for the deal."

"The deal" was something that Rose Clarke and Dominica had cooked up. It was no secret to any of them that Crawford, on occasion, was sleeping with both Rose and Dominica, who, it turned out, were good friends. None of the three even tried to hide it. Finally Rose, after conferring with Dominica, had laid down the law: no more sex without commitment. No more friends with benefits. Starting about a month ago, Crawford had been given an ultimatum: He had to commit to either Dominica or Rose. Until he did, there would be no messing around with either one of them. For Crawford, it had been a good run and fun while it lasted. But— sigh—it was in the rearview mirror now.

"So, pick you up in a half hour?" Crawford said.

"Nope. I know your tricks. If we go in your car, you'll ask yourself up for a drink when you drop me off. Or cajole me into coming over to your place for that stunning view of the Publix parking lot."

Crawford laughed. "It is pretty stunning. But I really mean it, I have no intention of trying to cajole you into the sack." Unless, of course, she was to suddenly change her tune.

Dominica nodded. "I'll meet you at La Sirena in a half hour."

"Okay," Crawford said. "Looking forward to it."

CRAWFORD GOT A CALL ON THE WAY TO LA SIRENA. IT WAS THE dispatcher at the station.

"Crawford," he said.

"Charlie," the dispatcher said, "there was a break-in at 908 North Lake Way. Fernandez in burglary thought you'd want to be in the loop."

"Yeah, I do. Anybody hurt?"

"No, owners came home and noticed a bunch of missing items."

"Okay, thanks. I'm on my way. Hey, give Ott a call, will ya?"

"Next on my list."

The dinner at La Sirena would have to wait for another evening. He dialed Dominica.

"I'm all dolled-up and ready to hit the town," she said, excited.

"Hey, I'm really sorry to have to do this, but something came up and I have to cancel. Well, let's just say postpone."

Dominica sighed. "Damn, I was really looking forward to their Costoletta di Vitello Sirena."

"Next time you can have that along with the most expensive wine in the house."

"Assuming there is a next time."

"I'll beg if I have to."

"I'm looking forward to that too," Dominica said. "Bye, Charlie."

"Bye, Dominica. Sorry."

CAMILO FERNANDEZ, A SHARP, YOUNG COP WHO'D WORKED HIS way up from street patrol to burglary detective, walked up to Crawford as he came through the front door of the house at 908 North Lake Way.

"Hey, Charlie," said the tall, buzz-cut detective. "Welcome to amateur hour."

"What do you mean?"

"Job was either done by a couple of teenagers or incompetent first-timers."

"How'd they do it?" Crawford asked, following Fernandez into the living room.

Crawford immediately saw a shattered bay window and a cinderblock on the living-room floor.

"Tossed that through the window, which set off the alarm," Fernandez said. "Guess they figured they had about five minutes to snatch and grab whatever they could, then get out of here before we showed up."

"Why do you say 'they?'"

"'Cause there're two sets of shoe impressions in the grass out back."

Crawford nodded. "So, what did they take?" he asked, as Ott walked in.

Fernandez nodded at Ott. "Hey, Mort."

"Cam," Ott said, nodding back.

Crawford turned to Ott. "Geniuses threw that block through the window," he said, pointing at it, "then did a five-minute snatch 'n' grab."

"So definitely not pros?" Ott said.

"Not by a long shot," Fernandez said. "So, according to the owners, who are over at a friend's house, they got an Apple MacBook Air, an iPad, some jewelry from the master—" Fernandez pointed —"which is down that hallway. Also, a couple of furs and a small painting done by their kid."

Crawford laughed. "Why the hell would they take that?"

"Got me? Art collectors?" Fernandez said with a shrug. "Plus, I think we got fingerprints up the ying-yang."

"You see any footprints besides those impressions?" Crawford asked.

"Not that I noticed," Fernandez said. "My guess is they exited the same way they came in. And the nice thing is, we got surveillance cameras at the end of the street."

Crawford glanced over at Ott, then Fernandez. "So, you think we got 'em on camera *plus* prints?"

"I think so," Fernandez said.

Crawford looked at his watch, then back to Fernandez. "What else you got?"

"That's about it. Think it's the same ones who did your homicide?"

"I don't know. Our guys weren't real slick either—" turning to Ott — "Guess we're done here."

"So, can I go back to *Bosch*?"

"Yeah," Crawford said. "You watch it enough, and maybe one day you'll turn into a real detective."

THORSEN PAUL FELT THE FIRST LAPPING OF THE TIDE AND heard a distant chittering and clacking sound. Whatever it was, it wasn't good. He couldn't move a muscle below his neck, and the wet sand was seeping cold into his body, causing him to shiver. He tried to scream again, but the duct tape was on too tight. He knew he couldn't be heard more than a few feet away. The clacking noise got closer and then he saw in horror what it was. A phalanx of crabs advancing toward him not three feet from his head.

SIX

It was 8:30 when Crawford got into his car.

He dialed Dominica.

"Hel-lo, Charlie."

"It's not too late for that Costarico di Vitello Sirena you wanted."

"Costoletta."

"Whatever," he said. "I just called, and we have a nine o'clock res there."

"But I just pulled a Lean Cuisine out of the freezer."

"Put it back."

She hesitated for a moment.

"Come on...we'll get a bottle of that rosé that you love. Jean-Louis Columbo whatever."

"Jean-Luc. Your French is as bad as your Italian," she said. "I thought you said you'd beg next time."

"Yes, but this isn't next time. It's a continuation of the same time."

Dominica chuckled. "Okay, you're on. You cancel again, and I'll kill you."

"Not gonna happen," Crawford said. "There could be a

quadruple homicide on Worth Avenue and Ott'll have to work it alone."

THEY HAD JUST FINISHED THE MAIN COURSE. CRAWFORD WAS drinking red and Dominica the Jean-Luc Columbo 2017 rosé.

Dominica had big emerald-green eyes, sharp, high cheekbones, and bouncy dark hair that complemented a walk that was provocative and then some.

"This is officially my new favorite spot," Dominica said.

"Yeah, for me it's a toss-up between here and my Mexican dive."

"You just go there for the margaritas. You don't care what you eat."

"Umm...true."

"So, how's it been, no sex for a month and a half," she asked. "Or maybe you found a new friend."

"No. You and Rose are my only true loves, and I don't stray. And...I don't mind telling you, it sucks."

"No sex?"

He nodded. "See, here's my dilemma. I really don't want to hurt anyone's feelings. Let's say I chose Rose...you obviously would be crushed."

"Obviously. My life in shambles," Dominica said. "You're such a sensitive man, Charlie."

"You joke, but I just bet it would send you into a complete tailspin. And poor Rose, if I chose you, she'd be massively depressed. Not be able to get out of bed. So, you see, that's my dilemma, I don't want to be responsible for all that heartbreak."

Dominica smiled. "You're such a caring man, Charlie."

"Do I detect a little sarcasm?"

"A little?"

"How 'bout you? How is it, not having sex in—" he did some quick math— "seven weeks?"

"Who said I haven't? Rose and I put the freeze on *you*. But we never said we were going to abstain."

"Well, have you?"

"Ah, no comment."

"Come on?"

"No comment."

"You little minx, you."

Dominica nodded, giving him a coquettish-smile. "So, which way are you leaning at this point?"

"Not tellin'."

Dominica chuckled. "Now who's the minx?"

"Guys can't be minxes."

"Says who?"

Crawford shook his head. "Can we not talk about sex anymore? It's such a shallow subject."

Dominica laughed. "Oh, really? Since when."

"Since it got so scarce," Crawford said with a sigh.

"So, what do you want to talk about instead? Football?"

"You don't know anything about football."

"I know that my Dolphins just crushed your pathetic New York Giants."

"Yeah, my boys are going through a bad patch," Crawford said. "Like I am on Palmer."

"What's the problem?"

"We just have one shoe print, for starters."

"That's all Hawes and the techs came up with?"

Crawford nodded.

"So, what was it that came up earlier tonight?" Dominica asked. "The reason you had to bail on me."

"A burglary that took place at a house on the Intracoastal," Crawford answered. "Camilo Fernandez put me in the loop, figured it might be the same guy. Or guys."

"And?"

Crawford thought for a second. "Both jobs were pretty sloppy. My guess, Fernandez's gonna have 'em behind bars within forty-eight hours."

SEVEN

CRAWFORD DIALED THE NUMBER OF THE BEACH & RACQUET Club.

"I'm trying to reach Peter Georgescu, please."

"Yes, sir," said the receptionist. "Hold on a second, please."

A few seconds later. "Tennis shop."

"Peter Georgescu, please."

"Hold, please."

A few more seconds. "This is Peter."

"Mr. Georgescu, my name is Detective Crawford. I'd like to come see you and ask you some questions about Adriana Palmer."

A sigh. "That was so terrible. I'll be done at five-thirty, if you'd like to stop by then. Or I can meet you somewhere."

"I'll be there at five-thirty. Thank you, Mr. Georgescu."

"You're welcome. You know where we are, right?"

"Sure. Across from Mar-a-Lago."

———

HE DROVE INTO THE EXCLUSIVE BEACH & RACQUET CLUB AND

was met by an imperious woman at a reception desk who, he could tell, deemed his chinos and jacket and tie less than sartorially impressive. Something told him that the Men's Wearhouse in West Palm was not where members of the Beach & Racquet shopped, even though he was quite happy with their selection, not to mention prices.

"I'm meeting with Peter Georgescu," he said, showing her ID.

"Not here for a tennis lesson, detective?" she asked with a smile.

"How could you tell?"

The woman let out a nasal laugh. "No whites."

And, sure enough, everyone playing on the eight Har-Tru courts was impeccably dressed all in white. Crawford couldn't even spot a thin blue or red stripe on any of the players' socks, or anywhere else. As for members of any persuasion other than the WASP nation, not one in sight. Except for a Hispanic-looking man sweeping the lines on a far court.

Peter Georgescu was a tall, blond man around thirty-five with a perfect tan and, Crawford guessed, a perfect forehand, backhand, and overhead smash. They sat outside on two wicker chairs that faced the courts. The sun was still strong, so Crawford took off his blue jacket and folded it over another chair. Off to one side, two women were playing singles and, next to them, four men playing doubles.

"Thanks again for seeing me," Crawford said.

"Oh, sure, I just hope you catch whoever did it."

"Me, too. So, tell me about Adriana if you would. I don't know much more than she and her sister ran The Max, and lived in two side-by-side houses on the ocean. You went out with her quite a long time, right?"

"Yes, two years. I thought we were going to get married."

"So, what happened? Why didn't you?" Crawford asked, as he noticed one of the women giving him a sidelong glance.

Georgescu thought for a second. "It was pretty simple: I couldn't afford her. Let's just say that Adriana had a very expensive lifestyle. Clothes, cars, out every night...hey, I make decent money at this job, but between what I made and what she made at The Max, marriage would've been a money-losing proposition."

"Was that something you talked to her about?"

Georgescu chuckled and nodded. "'Til I was blue in the face. She was always on my case to buy her stuff. A new skirt. A new iPad. A new...you-name-it."

"So, what happened?"

"She finally pulled the plug. Said if I couldn't support her, we had no future together."

"So, she was the one who ended it?"

Georgescu nodded.

"And what about her father? I know that he gave both sisters their houses."

"Yeah, poor Norman. Adriana bled him dry, then he was killed."

"What about Amanda?"

Georgescu put his hand over his eyes and turned to Crawford. "In that sense, they were completely different."

"How so?"

"An Acura versus a hundred-fifty-thousand-dollar Mercedes classic. J. Crew versus Hermes. Target versus Saks. Getting the picture?"

Crawford nodded. "So, Amanda didn't live beyond her means, you're saying?"

Georgescu nodded. "Yes, exactly, then there was the whole brother thing."

"Brother thing?"

"Oh, nobody told you about that?"

Crawford shook his head.

"It was something that came out after me and Adriana had been going out for about six months." Georgescu sighed. "One night she told me she'd been molested by her older brother when she was ten years old."

"Oh, God, that's awful. Keep going."

"Just wait 'til you hear the rest," Georgescu said. "She told me all about it that night. In incredible detail. To the point where I wanted to go find the brother and beat the hell out of him."

"I hear you," Crawford said. "How long did she say it went on for?"

"Until he went away to college," Georgescu said. "But what happened was, one night I was scheduled to have drinks with Adriana and Amanda, and Adriana was pretty late. So, I had a few with Amanda, got a little buzzed and, like an idiot, asked her what she knew about Adriana getting molested by their older brother. I was half-thinking that maybe she'd been molested too."

"What did she say?"

"She was taking a sip of her drink and she almost sprayed it all over me. I'll never forget, her eyes got really big and she goes, 'Brother, what brother?'"

"You're kidding." Crawford leaned toward Georgescu. "So, Adriana made it all up."

Georgescu nodded as the two women tennis players, having just finished, approached them. "Yup, totally invented the brother."

"Hello, Peter," one of the women said, looking straight at Crawford. "And your friend in the blue and red tie."

"Hello, ladies," Peter said, standing. "This is Charlie Crawford —" then, gesturing—"meet Gillian and Jan."

Gillian hadn't taken her eye off Crawford. "You play?" she asked.

"Badly," Crawford said. "I'm more a golfer."

"I play that, too," Gillian said without blinking an eye. Like maybe she hoped he'd invite her to play eighteen.

A somewhat awkward pause followed as the women, Gillian anyway, didn't seem to be in a hurry to go anywhere. "Well," Crawford said. "Peter and I were just finishing up—"

"Nice to meet you," Gillian said to Crawford. "Maybe you'll give me a buzz about playing golf. You play at the Poinciana?"

That was the fancy club where the initiation fee was three hundred thousand dollars.

Crawford smiled. "I'm more of a public-course guy."

Gillian tried to hide her dismay, then shrugged. "I guess a golf course is a golf course, right?"

Jan grabbed Gillian's arm. "Come on Gill, these guys—"

"I'm coming, I'm coming," Gillian said, then to both of the men. "'Bye."

And the women walked into the pro shop.

"Women always react that way to you, Charlie?" Georgescu said.

"Hell no," Crawford said. "She must just like guys in ties...What else can you tell me about Adriana?"

Georgescu shrugged. "That's pretty much it," then cocking his head. "Wasn't it enough?"

Crawford reached out and shook Georgescu's hand. "Thanks, actually it was more than enough."

EIGHT

Camilo Fernandez, the Palm Beach burglary detective, walked into Crawford's office the next morning. Ott and Crawford were drinking rotgut office coffee, Crawford filling in his partner about his conversation with Peter Georgescu.

They both looked up as Fernandez came in, a smile lighting his face. "Nailed those incompetent fucks who did the smash 'n' grab job," he said, sitting down next to Ott facing Crawford.

Crawford leaned forward and smiled. "No shit. How many were there?"

"Two," Fernandez said. "Got some really good shots of them from that CCTV camera. Seemed like these geniuses were totally oblivious to the camera being there. They got busted for dealing weed last year. Got off with time served."

"So, what's their story?" Ott asked.

"You want to talk to 'em?" Fernandez said. "They're right here. Cell in the basement."

Crawford and Ott stood at the same time.

"Yeah, let's have a little chat with the boys," Ott said.

DWIGHT AND DEWEY WERE A PAIR OF LATE TWENTY- EARLY thirty-somethings who looked like men who'd get caught at whatever transgression they ever undertook. Starting with stealing candy from the corner store in fourth grade.

Dwight had a small head, moss-colored teeth, and the eyes of a doe facing a sixteen-wheel truck bearing down on it. Scared and stupid, in two words. Dewey was trying hard to act tough, but Crawford thought he might just have an accident in his pants at any moment. He had a thin coat of peach fuzz on his sunburned face, and spindly arms that clearly had never been within twenty miles of a ten-pound dumbbell.

Crawford put his hands on two bars of the pair's jail cell. "I'm Detective Crawford and he's Detective Ott. Why'd you do the break-in, boys?"

"The what?" asked Dwight.

"The fuck you think?" Ott said. "That break-in on the Intracoastal, numb nuts."

Dewey looked at Dwight. Dwight looked up at the ceiling. Finally, Dewey sighed and said: "Heard there was a lot of cash there."

"Who told you that?" Crawford asked.

"Jimbo."

"Who's Jimbo?" Ott asked, his eyes boring into Dwight's.

"Dude down at the car wash," Dwight said.

Ott glanced at Crawford and shook his head. "B'lieve this shit?" Then to Dwight. "Okay, fuckhead, you're gonna have to get way more specific here. Jimbo the 'dude down at the car wash' doesn't really help us."

Dwight shrugged. "Got no idea what his last name is," he said. "Car wash on South Olive and Southern."

Ott smiled. "Oh, you mean Rubber Ducky?"

"Yeah, that's it."

Ott glanced over at Crawford again, who seemed content to let Ott run the show.

"So, how's a towel jockey down at Rubber Ducky know there's a bunch of cash at a house up in Palm Beach?" Ott asked.

"Said his girlfriend is the maid there."

Ott nodded. "Okay, now we're getting somewhere."

"And what's her name?" Camilo Fernandez jumped in.

"Don't know."

"So, to make sure we got this straight," Ott said. "You and Jimbo were just sitting around and Jimbo told you there was a lot of cash at 908 North Lake Way. So, you and hotshot here decided to go throw a cement block through the window and score the cash."

Dwight scratched his face, nervously. "Pretty much. Jimbo said he wanted twenty percent of the take if we did it."

Ott paused for a second. "Why didn't *he* do it? Take a hundred percent of it. Not like heaving a cement block through a window is a special skill."

Crawford suppressed a laugh.

"Couldn't tell ya," Dwight said.

Crawford took one hand off the jail bars. "So, Jimbo told you where the cash was...in the house?"

"Yeah," Dwight said. "But it wasn't there."

"Where's there?" Crawford asked.

"Under some socks in a drawer in the guy's walk-in closet."

"Hm," Ott said with a quizzical look. "That must have been a disappointment. You say anything to Jimbo about his bum steer."

"Couldn't find him."

"He wasn't down at the Rubber Ducky?'

Dwight shook his head.

Ott glanced at Crawford. "Got anything else?"

Crawford took a look down at Dwight's and Dewey's shoes. "What are your shoe sizes?"

"Eight," said Dewey.

"Ten and a half," said Dwight.

Ott nodded, then glanced over at Crawford. "Anything else?"

Crawford shook his head.

Ott glanced at Fernandez.

Fernandez shook his head.

"Okay, boys, we thank you for your time," Ott said, walking away. "You been real cooperative—" then dropping his voice so Dewey and Dwight couldn't hear—"for a coupla dumb fuckin' rednecks."

Ott, Crawford, and Fernandez walked back up to the first floor. Crawford turned to Ott. "Something funny about that."

"Yeah, I know. You mean, Jimbo's role in the whole thing, right?"

Crawford nodded. "Among other things. I think the Crown Vic *could* use a wash."

"Rubber Ducky?"

Crawford nodded. "Let's go."

NINE

"I LOVE THIS," OTT SAID, SPREADING HIS ARMS IN THE CAR.

He, Crawford, and Camilo Fernandez were in the Crown Vic, which was in the process of being transformed from a dirty gray to a gleaming, sparkling, white car at the Rubber Ducky car wash.

"This is my favorite part," Ott said as the long strips of blue cloth splayed out over their soap-covered windshield. "I love the way those things slap all over the place. And the noise they make. There's something almost sexual about it."

"You're fucked up, Mort," Fernandez said, pointing. "And, just for the record, that thing that 'slaps all over the place' is called a mitter."

Ott, in the driver's seat, turned around to face Fernandez. "No shit, and what about that thing that shoots out the foam?"

"The foamer," Fernandez said.

"Makes sense. You know more than just burglary shit, Cam."

"My uncle had a car wash in Texas."

"Gotcha. And did he have a blue mitter like this?"

"I think it was red. It's been a while."

It turned out that Jimbo was not working there so Crawford, Ott, and Fernandez went inside looking for the manager. They found him. The man named Oscar was overweight, had long scraggly grey hair, and a distinct odor. He was sitting at what looked like a card table in a little room that had car-wash supplies piled high around him. It was pretty tight with all four of them in the office.

"He comes and goes," Oscar said, when they asked him about Jimbo. "He's a good worker so I let him get away with it. What do you want him for?"

"Just need to ask him a question or two," Crawford said. "And what's his last name?"

"Smith."

"Easy enough."

"He in some kind of trouble?" Oscar asked, scratching his chest.

"Nah," Crawford said, not wanting Oscar to call and tell Jimbo the cops were looking for him. "Just need some info."

"Do you have his cell number?" Fernandez asked. "Home address would be helpful, too."

Oscar gave him both. "Sometimes he goes on these benders," Oscar said. "Just wanted to warn you."

"Thanks," Crawford said, turning toward the door. "Appreciate your help."

"No problem," Oscar said, nodding at Ott and Fernandez as they walked out.

When they were outside, Ott turned to Crawford. "Think he's gonna call him?"

"Nah, I doubt it," Crawford said. "Let's get in our shiny new car and go find ol' Jimbo."

JIMBO WAS NOT AT HOME. CRAWFORD CALLED UP DENNY KRAL, a Palm Beach plainclothes cop who occasionally helped on cases.

"Hey, Denny, got a job for you."

"What's that?"

"Need you to check on a house every couple hours," Crawford said. "See if a guy comes back there. If you see him, call me, okay? If he goes somewhere, follow him."

"You got it."

Crawford gave him the address for Jimbo Smith as Ott drove away from his house.

Just as he clicked off, his cell rang.

"Crawford," he said.

"Charlie, it's Nico Burke—" a new uniform cop with the Palm Beach Police Department whose voice sounded amped up— "I got a dead body on the beach up on the north end."

"Where, exactly? And what happened?"

"Right opposite Dolphin," Burke said, then took a deep breath. "Guy's buried up to his neck in the sand. Pretty sure he drowned."

"Jesus, you're kidding," Crawford said, as Ott's head swung toward him

"Nope. Tide went out and two boys found him."

"Wow," was all Crawford could muster.

"Yeah, and it ain't pretty," Burke said.

"We'll be there in twenty minutes."

"See ya then."

Ott turned to Crawford, intense curiosity in his wide, round face. "What?"

"Got a guy buried up to his neck in the beach off Dolphin. Drowned, s'posedly."

"Christ," Ott said, shaking his head, "that's a first."

TEN

As reflected on all six faces at the scene, it was a truly bizarre and grisly spectacle. In addition to Crawford and Ott, and the uniform Nico Burke, two crime scene-techs had arrived. One of them was Dominica McCarthy, along with Medical Examiner Bob Hawes. Hawes was famous for milking a crime scene for all it was worth and acting like he was Einstein, even though he was just staring down at another stiff. Except the decedent was not just another stiff: he was a stiff with no eyes. Around the empty sockets were traces of what appeared to be peanut butter.

"This is really fuckin' sick," Hawes said, pointing.

Crawford couldn't argue with that.

"Whoever did it," Hawes went on, "smeared peanut butter on his eyes so the sea creatures could have a feast."

"We got it, Bob." If Ott and he couldn't size up a scene faster than Hawes, they were really slipping.

Crawford looked away from the dead man to Dominica, who had on vinyl gloves and was crouching on the beach near the body.

"Probably not gonna find much, Mac." Crawford called her Mac when they were on the job together, though everyone knew about their relationship. Keeping secrets in a police station was no easy trick.

"Yeah, I know," Dominica said. "I'm gonna go up to the road and look around."

"I saw some tire tracks on the shoulder," Crawford said.

Dominica took a step closer to Crawford and Ott. "Somebody who does something like this, I'm guessing, probably doesn't leave a lot of clues around. You know?"

Ott nodded. "So, you don't think you're gonna find a Skippy jar with a nice, clean set of prints."

Dominica smiled. "Somehow, I doubt it."

IT TURNED OUT THAT SOMEONE HAD DISCOVERED THE BODY ON the beach before the two boys did, because later in the day, a photo of the corpse went viral on Instagram. Based on that photo, the man was soon identified, even without his eyes. His name was Thorsen Paul and— if the name sounded familiar—it was because he had been in the news a lot lately. He was the twenty-eight-year-old wunderkind and MIT drop-out who'd started the Silicon Valley company Next-Red, a technology outfit that claimed to require only a tiny speck of blood for blood tests, which heretofore had required much more than that. Paul also owned a grab-bag of patents that were judged to be worth a fortune before he sold them. Long story short, his company, at one point, had a ten-billion-dollar valuation, and had raised more than seven hundred million dollars from venture capitalists and private investors.

Paul's paper net worth had peaked at $4.5 billion before it all turned out to be a massive fraud. Somehow, Paul had managed to hoodwink an all-star line-up of tech-savvy savants, not to mention a board that had some of the biggest names in business, who'd clawed and fought to become allied with the company. In the end, all Paul had was a concept. A good concept, perhaps, but one that didn't work. When a newspaper reporter exposed it for what it wasn't, the whole house of cards came tumbling down.

Crawford remembered hearing about it from Rose Clarke, who'd said that rich people in Palm Beach were falling all over themselves to invest in it. The way he remembered it was that Thorsen Paul's parents had a house in Palm Beach, even though their son lived in—according to Rose, who would know—the second-most expensive house in San Francisco. That was before he lost everything and, as one Forbes article said, was practically homeless. Crawford remembered Rose thinking about investing, but ultimately deciding she was better off putting her money in what she knew, i.e. real estate. Good move.

Crawford's boss, Norm Rutledge, hastily called for a meeting late that afternoon, knowing that Paul's murder and the barbaric way it was executed would not only be local news, but also national and world. Chief Rutledge's plan, he confided to Crawford ahead of time, was to get out in front of it and do everything possible to put the killer in the Palm Beach jail in the first forty-eight hours. Crawford conceded that was a worthy objective, but he and Ott had yet to solve a murder *that* fast. Not that they wouldn't welcome the opportunity for a quickie, but their stellar crime-solving record owed much to their being turtles instead of hares.

Crawford had two hours before the four o'clock meeting with Rutledge, and decided to spend that time learning everything he could about Thorsen Paul and his company. He went to Google first, as usual, then planned to pick Rose Clarke's brain about the famous victim.

He never got around to the call to Rose because there were twenty-three pages in Google about Thorsen Paul and NextRed. Paul had grown up in Greenwich, Connecticut, and his grandfather, a surgeon, apparently had a profound influence on his life. Paul had decided at an early age he wanted to do something in the medical field, and by age seventeen had enrolled at MIT. At twenty he started NextRed and later that year dropped out of MIT.

Five years later, Paul had investors and venture-capital firms throwing money at him, along with investors like the owner of the largest media company in the world, a former Secretary of Commerce, and an actress who had five Oscars to her name. Until, two years later, when the enterprising newspaper reporter dug deep and discovered what seemed to be such a good idea just didn't work in real life.

Crawford and Ott shuffled into Rutledge's office a few minutes past four. Rutledge was wearing his favorite brown suit and a scowl that always seemed to come with it. Rutledge was tall and stick-like, had dyed mahogany-colored hair, and any number of tics. Today, his upper lip jerked up every few seconds like it had a fishhook in it. Crawford and Ott sat down facing Rutledge and his gunmetal grey desk.

"You don't need to tell us the mayor's put your feet to the fire to solve this yesterday," Crawford said. "And how it's not good to have a photo of a drowned guy with his head sticking out of the sand going viral."

"Yeah, we got that," Ott added.

"You think this shit is funny? Not just the damned mayor, but the head of the Chamber of Commerce, Kiwanis, the—"

Ott held up a hand and said again. "We got it, Norm."

"Loud and clear. And we don't think it's funny."

Rutledge nodded woodenly. "So, what do you have so far?"

"We know a lot about the guy. No idea what the motive was, though," Crawford said.

"Except there must be a hell of a lot of pissed-off investors out there," Ott added.

"Why? What's the backstory?" Rutledge asked.

"Long story short, his company NextRed went from over a hundred and fifty on the NASDAQ to zero."

"Wow," Rutledge said. "I'd be pissed off, too. So, what's the guy's connection to Palm Beach? He have a house here?"

"No, but his parents do. Apparently, they were very well-connected, and a lot of their friends invested in Paul's company," Crawford said. "Also, turns out Paul's fiancée lives here, too."

"Really? What's her name?"

"Ah," Crawford checked his notes. "Carter Pearson. My sense is she's a socialite."

"What's with all these women with men's names these days?" Rutledge veered off-track frequently. "Carter. Whitney. Sam…"

Ott cocked his head. "You do a study of this, Norm?"

"Bailey. Taylor—"

"Guess so," Crawford said.

"So, have you spoken to her yet? This Carter woman." Rutledge asked.

"We have calls in to her as well as both the parents," Crawford said. "Left two messages with each. Can't come on too strong since they're in mourning."

Rutledge nodded. "What else?"

"We're gonna try to interview some of the bigger local investors," Crawford said. "See where that goes."

"What about the guy who posted the shot on Facebook. Of Paul's head?"

"Instagram and already done," Ott said. "We tracked him down. He was just a guy out on an early walk on the beach."

Rutledge shook his head. "It kills me."

"What does?" Ott asked.

"Why would you think to put that on your damn Instagram? I mean…" He let out a long sigh, and his fishhook lip-tic returned.

Crawford and Ott nodded. "We're with you on that," Ott said. "Why call the cops when you can share a murder with your closest thousand friends?"

"Sick," Rutledge said, turning to Crawford. "What's your gut tell you about this?"

"Damned if I know," Crawford said with a shrug.

"I'm gonna take a wild guess here," said Ott, "how 'bout somebody really, really didn't like the guy?"

ELEVEN

CARTER PEARSON WAS NOT PARTICULARLY ATTRACTIVE, NOR DID she appear to be rich. Crawford figured that the vast majority of women in Palm Beach were either one or the other, or both. It was actually kind of refreshing to meet a woman who was plain and, judging by her house, lived a fairly modest lifestyle. It got a little old, believe it or not, one rich woman after another. He and Ott were sitting on a couch in her unpretentious living room on Seaview Avenue, facing her. She wore big, round glasses, had somewhat dull-colored hair, and could've stood to lose a few.

Crawford and Ott had already done the 'sorry about your loss' bit and were hunkering down for as many questions as she'd allow them to ask.

"We assume you knew Mr. Paul as well as anyone, being his fiancée," Crawford started out. "Was there anyone who he told you he feared, or who might possibly have threatened him?"

Carter glanced out the window, locked in a faraway stare for a few moments, then came back to Crawford. "Well, you probably know most of the story. There were a ton of disgruntled investors. I mean, a ton, but I just can't picture businesspeople as killers."

Oh, you'd be surprised, Crawford thought as he flashed back to his first murder case in Palm Beach and a man named Ward Jaynes, a billionaire hedge-fund operator and about the most ruthless man he had ever come across. A quick glance at Ott confirmed that his partner was thinking the same thing.

"But did Mr. Paul ever mention anyone he was afraid of?" Ott asked. "Even if that person never threatened him?"

This time Carter looked down at the floor. Crawford noticed a few flakes of dandruff in the part of her hair.

She looked up at them. "I'm just going to throw out a few names, okay? Please understand that I have no idea whether they could have had anything to do with it or not."

Crawford nodded. "We understand."

Carter nodded back. "Okay, the first is a man named Lionel Marra. He's a lawyer from Philadelphia and also has a house here. Have you heard of him?"

Crawford and Ott shook their heads.

"Well, I've always heard these whispers that he's somehow involved in the Mafia. Even though I didn't think the Mafia was still around."

"Oh, it is. Trust me," Ott said, nodding.

"Anyway, I know he was an investor in NextRed, and recently heard he was arrested for murder in Charleston, South Carolina."

"What was he doing there?" Crawford asked.

"I think he's got a house there, too. Anyway, I don't know any more than that. Man's got kind of a scary reputation, but for all I know he was in jail when Thorsen was killed."

Saying her fiancée's name and what had happened to him triggered a flow of tears, and she buried her head in her hands. "I'm so sorry."

"Don't be," Crawford said, and he handed her a Kleenex box from an end table.

"Thank you," she said, dabbing her eyes, then started to cry harder, "I—I just can't believe he's dead. We were so happy together."

"If you'd like us to leave..." Crawford said, glancing at Ott.

Carter reached for a few more tissues. "No, no, I want you to catch whoever did this. Thorsen was such a fine man and would have been an incredible husband and father"—she took a deep breath, then another, and resumed in a near-whisper— "there was another man who was a...a venture capitalist, who had been trying to get the board to fire Thorsen for quite a long time. Jeremy Birch. I know he and Thorsen had a rancorous relationship, to the point where Birch would call and scream at him on the phone."

"But *threaten* him?" Crawford asked, as Ott wrote the name down in his old leather notebook.

"I don't know for sure, I just know it was this constant battle between the two."

"B-i-r-c-h or B-u?" Ott asked.

"B-i," she said, "like the tree."

"And he lives here, too?" Crawford asked.

"Yes, back and forth between here and New York," Carter said. "And there's a third man Gonzalo Gaetano. Do you know who he is?'

Ott looked up. "A race-car driver. Formula One. Races a lot in Europe."

Carter nodded. "Thorsen told me he had invested fifty million dollars of his own and friends' money."

"Really?" Ott said. "Didn't know he did that well."

Carter shrugged. "I just know that he called Thorsen in a panic on numerous occasions, saying he couldn't afford to lose that money. That it was a matter of life and death."

"But Thorsen did lose it, right?" Crawford asked.

Carter nodded. "Have you spoken to Rod and Mary Paul yet?" She put a crumpled tissue on the table beside her.

"Thorsen's parents? No, we haven't. If you speak to them, if you'd ask one of them to call, please," Crawford said.

Carter nodded. "Well, I think I'd like to be alone now. It's really hitting me hard again."

Crawford stood. "We completely understand and, again, are very sorry for your loss," he said. "Thank you so much for your help. That information gives us somewhere to start."

Ott, on his feet, shook her hand. "Thanks, again."

They walked through the small house on Seaview and out to their Crown Vic. Ott, the designated driver, started the engine and looked over at Crawford. "That guy, Gonzalo Gaetano. I can drive better than him."

"Is that true?"

"No, but the guy's notorious for crashing. Got fired from the Ferrari team, I think it was. Pretty sure he doesn't race much anymore. His nickname was something like Spin-Out."

"So, what's he doing with fifty million dollars?"

"Exactly what I was wondering."

TWELVE

Rod and Mary Paul, Thorsen Paul's grieving parents, added three new names to the list on Ott's well-worn notebook. The first was named Innes O'Rourke.

He was a MIT classmate of Thorsen's who had gotten his rich grandfather to invest ten million dollars in the company immediately after its start-up. Apparently, while NextRed's stock price was dropping like a proverbial stone, Thorsen's classmate constantly called to threaten him with lawsuits, and anything he could think of to keep from losing "my goddamn shrinking inheritance," as he referred to it

Then there was the wife of one of the three heirs to a famous pharmaceutical company. In her first life, she was a *Penthouse* pet-of-the-month, who married the heir when she was thirty-five and he was seventy-five. Word was, she licked her chops when she found out he was childless and had a bad ticker. She only had to wait six years until the ticker stopped ticking. She moved to Palm Beach, had a succession of young lovers and, for the most part, invested wisely. The exception was NextRed, into which she'd sunk forty-five million dollars.

Rod Paul had heard from his son that the heir's widow had sent a retired cop to Thorsen's house, who'd told Paul that he'd "better make her whole or else." When Thorsen said all the money was gone, the retired cop's answer had been, "So, guess that means you want the *or else.*"

The woman's name was Jocelyn Picard.

The third to go on Ott's list came from Mary Paul. A man named Herb Wallace, a fund manager in New York, who had a small place in West Palm and had recommended that some of his high-net-worth customers invest in NextRed. They did, it crashed, he lost his job, his wife, and his co-op in New York. According to Mary Paul, he'd called Thorsen to rant drunkenly that, "you'll get yours, you son of a bitch." He was now down in West Palm, licking his wounds and shotgunning his resume all over New York and southern Florida.

As they drove down the long Chattahoochee-pebble driveway of Rod and Mary Paul's house, Ott glanced over at Crawford. "With the exception of that guy Lionel Marra, I'm kind of agreeing with Carter Pearson, none of these sound like stone-cold killers who'd slather peanut butter on a guy's eyeballs."

"I don't know," Crawford said. "Did Ward Jaynes fit your stone-cold-killer profile when his name first came up?"

"No, but after we met the guy, he jumped right to the top of my list."

Denny Kral, the uniform Crawford had watching car-washer Jimbo Smith's house, called as Ott was pulling into the station.

"Jimbo's home," Kral said, giving the address.

Crawford thought for a moment, not sure he had time for Jimbo. "Thanks, man, appreciate it."

"No problem."

Crawford walked to Ott's cubicle and looked down at his three-quarters-bald head.

"Denny just called. That guy Jimbo's home. I'm gonna take a quick run down there; you don't need to come."

Ott leaned back in his chair. "I'll be looking into our new Thorsen Paul suspects."

Crawford tapped the top of Ott's cubicle. "Talk later," he said, walking away.

"Oh, hey," Ott said. "Guess our vacations are gonna have to wait a while."

"Guess so."

Neither of them had taken a real vacation in more than a year and a half.

"I had a charter boat down in the Keys all lined up, too."

"You gonna go deep-sea fishing?"

"Yeah, Chuck, that's what you do on charter boats."

Crawford smiled. "Not me. I just drink beer."

GREENACRES WAS A LITTLE CITY WEST OF LAKE WORTH THAT nobody's heard of but where you could buy a decent house for only a hundred fifty thousand dollars, an amount that would buy you half a room in a modest section of Palm Beach.

Crawford knocked on the door of a neglected townhouse on Bisbee Street. A blubbery man in his thirties, rubbing his eyes, opened the front door. "Help ya?"

"You Jimbo?" Crawford asked, taking out his ID and flashing it.

"Yeah."

"I'm Detective Crawford, Palm Beach Police."

Jimbo's shoulders pulled back and his eyes got big, like he was thinking of doing something, just not sure what.

"Need to ask you a few questions about a break-in in Palm Beach."

"Din't have nothin' to do with that," Jimbo said, raking one hand across his face nervously.

Crawford was worried Jimbo might suddenly slam the door in his face. "Step out here, would you, please."

Jimbo hesitated, then stepped out onto the stoop.

"So, your friends Dwight and Dewey said you told 'em about a house that had a bunch of cash in a drawer."

"They're not my friends."

"Okay, well, how 'bout this? Two guys named Dwight and Dewey, who aren't your friends, said you told 'em about that cash. They broke in, didn't find any, but told me you wanted twenty percent of whatever they got. Any of this sounding familiar?"

Jimbo started shaking his head. "No. Never happened. They're lying."

Crawford didn't have time to debate the man. "Well, they're in jail right now, you want to join 'em?"

"No, I—"

"Okay, then tell me what happened."

Jimbo pitched a long, theatrical sigh.

"Hurry up or I'm cuffing you and taking you in."

Jimbo held up his hands. "The woman set me up."

"What woman?"

"I don't know her name. She was just someone at the car wash."

Crawford took a step closer to Jimbo. "Okay, Jimbo, break it all down for me. No bits and pieces. And I ain't got all day."

"If I tell ya, what happens to me?"

"You don't tell me and you're in the joint."

Jimbo held up his hands again. "Okay, this woman came to the car wash and when I was drying her car asked me if I wanted to make a lot of money. I told her I was listening. She said there was ten thousand dollars at this house on the ocean in Palm Beach. Said if I went and took it, all she wanted was a grand."

"So, you got Dwight and Dewey to do it, a thousand for you, a thousand for her," Crawford said. "How were you s'posed to get in touch with the woman at the car wash?"

"She gave me a number."

"I want it."

Jimbo nodded. "It's inside."

"What did she look like?"

Jimbo didn't hesitate. "A dime."

"That doesn't help. Hair color? Height? Distinguishing features?"

"Hair I don't know about, she was wearing a hat. Shades, too. But like medium height and good-lookin'. What was the rest?"

"Distinguishing features. You know, a scar or a mole on her face."

"I don't remember."

"Okay, go get that number," Crawford said. "Then I'm gonna give you a number to call."

Jimbo turned to go inside.

Crawford wanted to avoid the possibility of Jimbo coming back with something other than the phone number. Like a gun. "Hold on, I'm coming with you."

Crawford walked in behind Jimbo. It was squalid inside, and smelled like a fat man's armpit. Jimbo walked over to a kitchen drawer, opened it, and pulled out a crumpled piece of paper. On it were seven digits.

"Back outside," Crawford said, then began holding his breath again so he didn't have to smell Jimbo's pigsty.

They went outside. Crawford took out his wallet, pulled out a card and a pen from his inside jacket pocket. He wrote down the main Palm Beach Police Department number and handed the card to Jimbo.

Crawford couldn't afford the time to take Jimbo in and book him. "You wanna ask for Fernandez in burglary. Tell him the whole thing and maybe you get off light."

"Like a little...community service?'

"Not that light," Crawford said, dialing the number Jimbo had given him.

It went straight to a recorded message: *Sorry, this number has been disconnected.*

Crawford had half-expected that. "Your dime gave you a bogus phone number, Jimbo," he said. "How well do you remember her face?'

"Pretty well. Chicks like that don't come by the Rubber Ducky real often."

Crawford put his hand on Jimbo's shoulder. "I want you to call another guy; gimme that card back." Jimbo handed him the card and Crawford scribbled another number. "Name's Harrison Knight, he's a sketch artist. Tell him I told you to call and wanted you to describe a person of interest."

Jimbo's face twisted into something resembling a smile. "Wow, a sketch artist, huh?"

"Yeah. Describe your dime friend the best you can for him, okay?"

"You got it."

THIRTEEN

OTT AND DOMINICA WERE SITTING OPPOSITE CRAWFORD IN HIS office, talking forensics.

"So, the official verdict is Thorsen Paul drowned?" Crawford asked Dominica.

"Yes, saltwater in his lungs."

"I guess sea creatures nibbling on your eyeballs can't kill you?" Ott said. "Bet they can mess up your vision pretty good, though."

Dominica looked at Crawford and shook her head. "Where'd you find this guy?"

Ott chuckled. "So, the residue actually was peanut butter?"

Dominica nodded. "Sure was. We also found traces of chloroform and diazepam in his system, so whoever did it probably rendered him unconscious before they buried him."

Ott shook his head. "Poor bastard."

"And you confirmed that those marks on Paul's face were burns, probably from cigarettes, right?" Crawford asked.

Dominica nodded. "We're not positive they were from cigarettes, but that's our best guess."

"But there's no question about his finger being cut off?" Ott asked.

Dominica sighed deeply. "No question," Then, after a pause: "What did Hawes tell you about Adriana Palmer?"

"A lot less gruesome than yours," Crawford said.

"What exactly?"

"Well, the slugs were semi-jacketed hollow points, nine millimeter."

"Your garden-variety murder weapon," Ott put in.

Dominica nodded. "Any sign of sexual assault?"

"Good question," Crawford said. "But, no."

Dominica tapped the arm of her chair. "Doesn't sound as though any of this is gonna lead to your killers."

"Afraid you're right," Crawford said.

Ott smiled at Dominica. "Always fun talking shop with you, though."

Dominica left for the lab, leaving Crawford and Ott alone.

"That guy, Lionel Marra," Ott said, "the suspected Mafia lawyer Carter Pearson told us about."

"Yeah, what about him?"

"Major-league bad actor, but not our guy."

"How do you know?"

"He's up in Dannemora for life. For ordering the hit of a guy in Charleston and capping someone else. No contact with anyone in the outside world."

"There's always bribing a prison guard."

"Yeah, I guess. Just don't think he's our guy."

Crawford told Ott all about Jimbo Smith, and how he was going to describe the mystery woman to their sketch artist.

"It's a long shot," Ott said.

"What is?"

"Harry Knight's sketch not looking like a thousand other women in Palm Beach County."

"Yeah, but he's come through a couple of times."

Ott nodded.

"All right, so let's split up those other five we got from the Pauls and Carter Pearson."

"Okay, but you gotta give me Gonzalo Gaetano," Ott said. "Me being a fellow driver and all."

Ott had actually attended race-car-driving school once. Got one of the cars there up to 130 mph. Any excuse to drive fast, Ott jumped on it.

"You mean Wipe-Out?"

Ott laughed. "Spin-Out."

"Whatever. So, you take Spin-Out and that guy who was the venture capitalist..."

Ott looked down at his pad. "Jeremy Birch, like the tree."

Crawford nodded. "Yeah, and I'll take the other three.'

"Wait, so you get the former *Penthouse* Pet?"

Crawford chuckled and shrugged. "What can I say? I gotta meet some new women."

Ott smiled and shook his head. "You rascal, you."

"Better than a lot of other things you've called me."

CRAWFORD PUT IN CALLS TO INNES O'ROURKE, HERB WALLACE, and Jocelyn Picard. The only one he reached was Wallace; for the others, he left voicemails. He stressed the urgency of meeting with Wallace, and got an appointment for two that afternoon. In the meantime, he went on Google to see what he could find out about the trio. There wasn't much on Herb Wallace, but O'Rourke and Picard made for eye-opening reading.

At quarter of two, he made the drive over to Wallace's house in an area of West Palm called El Cid. Wallace's house was a small beige stucco with a large for-sale sign in the front yard. Another clear sign that Wallace was short on money. Crawford parked, walked up to the front door, and hit the buzzer. A few moments later a man opened the door. He was wearing a ratty blue bathrobe over bare feet. Everything about him, including his scraggly, three-day facial growth, screamed depression.

"Come in," he said to Crawford, who wasn't sure he wanted to. Between Jimbo's dump and this one, his own small, clean one-bedroom overlooking the Publix parking lot was the Taj Mahal.

They went into the living room, which was a step up from Jimbo's—but not a big one—and sat.

Crawford, not wanting to hang around any longer than absolutely necessary, got right to business. "Mr. Wallace, the reason I'm here is to talk to you about the murder of Thorsen Paul. And specifically, to ask you about what a source told me regarding you calling Mr. Paul and saying, *you're gonna get yours someday.*" He decided to excise the phrase, *you son of a bitch* and not refer to the calls as "drunken rants."

Wallace sighed, as if it all were such a tremendous hassle. "Look, Thorsen Paul turned out to be nothing more than a low-life crook, and I was pissed. Guy ruined my life. I mean, look at me." He raised his hands to his forlorn-looking face.

Crawford didn't feel it was his job to point out that maybe Wallace should suck it up, move on, and try to put that whole bad chapter behind him.

"So, those threats you made, that was as far as it went?" Crawford asked as he saw something long and slimy crawl across the carpet.

Wallace shook his head in disgust. "You mean, did I drag the son of a bitch out on the beach, dig a hole, and bury him in it? Is that what you're asking?"

"Someone did."

"I can't believe you're even sugg—"

"Where were you two nights ago from ten 'til six in the morning?"

"Where I always am at that time. Beddy-bye."

"Alone."

Wallace chuckled derisively. "I wouldn't have been if it weren't for Thorsen."

"What do you mean?"

"I mean my wife left me when I got fired and lost all our money. Thanks to good ol' you-know-who."

Crawford wondered if Wallace was going to blame Thorsen Paul for the bugs crawling around his house, too. He tapped his fingers on a side table, then abruptly stopped, wondering what might have squirmed there. "Who do you think might have done it, then?"

Wallace rubbed one of the bathrobe's lapels. "I'm thinking there must be fifty people who might have."

"Okay, but give me your short list."

Now Wallace was scratching his chin. "My short list? Hm. Well, I'll give you two right off the top of my head. Allen Metzger and David Balfour."

Crawford kept a poker face, but David Balfour was a man he knew well and could officially count as a friend. "I know both those names. Why'd you pick them?"

Now Wallace was scratching his neck. "Because Metzger shorted the stock like crazy when it was going up and went long on it when it was dropping. Basically, got double-fucked—" Crawford was unfamiliar with that term and wondered if it was Wall Street jargon— "and David Balfour had to sell his house in East Hampton to cover his losses."

Crawford knew Balfour had a house up there but didn't think he used it much. Also, he was pretty sure it was Southampton, not East Hampton. Still, it was at least worth having a conversation with Balfour. Allen Metzger, too. Metzger, he knew, was a stock trader who had an office at 777 South Flagler and had been accused of insider trading, but, as best he could recall, not convicted.

"So, I told you why I picked them. Why the hell'd you pick me?"

"Because when someone says, *you're gonna get yours someday,* that strikes me as a threat."

Wallace was scratching his elbow now. Crawford wondered if the man had fleas.

"Wait a minute, first of all, I don't even remember saying that, and if I did, *you're gonna get yours* doesn't necessarily mean that I would be the one doing it."

"I think you're quibbling now, Mr. Wallace." Crawford had to get out of the house.

"I already told you, I was sound asleep at the time it happened."

Crawford stood. "Thanks for your time," he said and headed for the door. He felt like putting on a vinyl glove before opening the front door, but took his chances.

Just as he got to his Crown Vic, his cell phone rang. He looked down at it.

Jocelyn Picard.

"Detective Crawford?"

"Yes."

"It's Jocelyn Picard, returning your call." Businesslike.

"Oh, yes, thank you. Ms. Picard, I'm one of the detectives on the Thorsen Paul case, and I'd like to come and ask you some questions as soon as possible."

"Come on over." Mildly seductive.

"Now?"

"No time like the present." Matter-of-fact.

"Thank you," he said. He got her address, told her he'd be there in ten minutes, and clicked off.

He smiled at the thought of meeting a centerfold, but what he really looked forward to was doing it in a clean house for a change.

FOURTEEN

HE WAS RIGHT. JOCELYN PICARD'S HOUSE AT 601 ISLAND DRIVE on Everglades Island was many, many steps up from the fleabags of Jimbo Smith and Herb Wallace. Crawford was sitting in a large, high-ceilinged living room that looked out on the Intracoastal and had Lily Pulitzer's fingerprints everywhere. The room was awash in pastels—every color of the rainbow—and he wondered if being in it for ten minutes might prove effective treatment for Herb Wallace's depressed funk.

Jocelyn wore teal-colored slacks and a tight, white, silk buttoned top, went a tad heavy on the make-up and, Crawford guessed, was somewhere around forty-five.

He sat on a canary-yellow love seat across from Jocelyn on a pink sofa.

"I know what you're going to ask me about," she said, winding a strand of bleached-blonde hair around her ear.

"I actually have quite a few questions," Crawford said.

"Yes, but you heard that bullshit story going around that I sent some goombah to threaten that fuckhead Thorsen, right?"

Whoa, clearly a charter member of the Potty-Mouth Society.

"That was one of my questions. Is it true?" He couldn't help but think how she must have looked back in her Pet days. The mouth was a tad jarring, though.

"That thing about, *better make her whole or else,*" Jocelyn said, "he never fuckin' said that. He said, 'Mrs. Picard would appreciate the keys to your San Francisco condo.'"

"Really? And how much was that worth?" Crawford asked, thinking that was a pretty bold ask.

"'Bout forty mil, close to how much I lost on Thorsen's suck-ass company," Jocelyn said, tapping her toe on the hardwood floor. "But turned out he had already lost it to the goddamn bank in foreclosure."

"So, that was the end of it?" Crawford asked as he watched a boat speed past on the Intracoastal.

"Yeah, I mean, what could I do?" A smile lit up her face. "Hey, how would you like to come for dinner tonight, Charlie? You don't mind if I call you Charlie, do you?"

There was the faint trace of either a Brooklyn or Bronx accent. Charlie was *Chaw-lee.*

"I appreciate the invitation, but I'm afraid I'm busy." He wasn't, but as hot as Jocelyn Picard was, she wasn't his type. "So, do you have any idea who might have killed Thorsen Paul?" he asked. "I'm sure you hear things. What have you heard?"

"Are you always so 'all-business,' Charlie?" There it was again, the *Chaw-lee.*

"Yeah, pretty dull guy. Married to the job," he said. "Any theories you've heard about Thorsen?"

"Jesus, give it a fuckin' rest, will ya," she said, apparently bored with the whole subject. "I haven't heard a goddamn thing and neither me, nor anybody who works for me, had anything to do with it." She smiled her captivating smile again. "That good enough for you?"

GONZALO CAETANO LIVED IN A ONE-STORY RANCH HOUSE ON

Debra Lane, not one of the snappiest addresses in Palm Beach. It had been named, no doubt, like so many subdivision streets, for the developer's wife or daughter or girlfriend. Gaetano's lawn could have used a good mow, and the exterior of the house a paint job. The interior design, if you could call it that, was clearly the work of a bachelor who knew he had to put something on his walls, but didn't much care what. Directly above the couch where Mort Ott was sitting hung a large *Jaws* poster and, facing it, presumably to give the room a little more gravitas, one for *Citizen Kane*, a movie Ott seriously doubted Gaetano had ever seen.

Ott started off by lobbing a few softball questions, like how had he been doing lately on the racing circuit? Ott, wannabe stock car driver that he was, loved both Formula 1 and stock car racing. Gaetano recounted getting a fourth in one race, a seventh in another and, with a sigh, a couple of crash and burns, which he had survived intact, while his cars had not been so lucky. He also mentioned he was entered in the upcoming Belgian Grand Prix, even though his racing schedule had been greatly reduced.

Ott smiled and served up his preliminary hardball question. "I was told, by what I consider to have been a reliable source, that you were extremely...let's say, agitated about the loss of your investment in Thorsen Paul's company NextRed. Is that correct?"

Gaetano looked as if a chicken bone had just gotten lodged in his throat.

"Well, yes. You would be too. It was a helluva a lot of money down the drain."

"Fifty million dollars was the number I heard."

Gaetano nodded and sighed. "Yup."

Ott thought about how he was going to phrase his next question. "No disrespect intended, but it seems to me unlikely that all that money came from your racing earnings, correct? I mean, do you have family money or something?"

Gaetano reacted as if he'd been cruelly dissed. "I've *won* a few, you know. It hasn't been all fourths and sevenths—" then, answering the family-money question— "my father was an out-of-work, manual laborer."

"Well hell, my father was a locker-room attendant, so we're even," Ott said. "And I didn't mean to play down your racing. I remember you won that one in Adelaide a couple of years ago." Something told Ott it was more like ten years ago.

"Yes, and also Baku City."

Ott nodded as he strained his geographical knowledge: Baku City was somewhere in Ukraine, he thought. Or maybe Bulgaria.

"So, it wasn't all racing money and it wasn't family money...where else did it come from?"

The chicken bone was back in Gaetano's throat. He nervously scratched the side of his face. "Let's just call it family *and* friends..."

"Would you mind telling me all their names?"

Gaetano sighed and looked away. "Why do you need this information, detective. Am I a suspect or something?"

Ott shook his head and proceeded not to answer the question. "These are just routine questions which me and my partner are asking certain investors in Paul's company. I'm sure you can appreciate the fact that we have to start somewhere."

Gaetano tried hard to smile. "Yes, I can," he said. "How about if I email you a list?"

"Sure," Ott said, reaching for his wallet and a card, "Here's my card with my email on it." Ott handed him the card. "Are these friends local or...from Mexico, maybe?"

Gaetano tapped the arm of his chair. "Yes. Some are from there."

"Where exactly? Not that I know my Mexican geography."

"Mexico City, Guadalajara, a few other places."

Ott nodded. "You get back there a lot?"

"Not often. Maybe once every couple of years. I fly my parents here every once and a while."

For the time being, Ott had run out of questions. So, he asked the one he always asked: "You hear things I'm sure, Mr. Gaetano. Do you have any idea who might have killed Thorsen Paul?"

"I have no idea. Probably a lot of investors wanted to kill Bernie Madoff, but nobody did. Maybe it had nothing at all to do with what happened to NextRed."

Ott hadn't considered that. "Like...what are you thinking?"

Gaetano didn't hesitate. "You know a man named David Balfour?"

Ott knew Balfour a little, knew he was a friend of Crawford's. "Heard the name, why?"

"'Cause supposedly Paul was having an affair with Balfour's girlfriend."

"Really?" Ott said. "So, this was going on while Paul was engaged?"

"So, I heard," Gaetano said. "Hot and heavy."

"What else did you hear?"

Gaetano cocked his head. "That Balfour went crazy when he found out."

"What does that mean, 'went crazy?'"

"I heard he went to Paul's house and smashed up Paul's Jaguar with a golf club. Took off just before the cops got there."

This had never popped up on Ott's radar screen.

He stood. "Well, thank you, Mr. Gaetano, I appreciate your time, and please send me that list."

"Will do."

Ott shook his hand, turned to walk away, then turned back. "I'll be rooting for you in the Belgium."

FIFTEEN

CRAWFORD WALKED INTO HIS OFFICE AND SAW SOMETHING ON his desk.

It was a sketch with a yellow sticky note on the upper right-hand corner that read: *Charlie, hope this helps—Harrison Knight.*

Just one glance at the sketch and Crawford had a hunch who it might be. He sat at his desk and pondered it for a few minutes. Then he called Jimbo Smith.

"Hello?"

"How come you're not in a jail cell, Jimbo?"

"I told the guy I'd turn myself in later today. He was cool with that."

"Better happen. Or else I'll send a bunch of cops down there. Sirens blaring, lights flashing... the whole thing."

"I'm going."

"Okay. In the meantime, I got a little job for you that might help lighten your sentence a little."

"What do I gotta do?"

"I want you to go somewhere and ID someone."

"Uh, okay. Where?"

Innes O'Rourke, the MIT classmate of Thorsen Paul's, had volunteered to come to the police station in South County. He was a thin man with a washed-out complexion, eyebrows that almost connected, and madras shorts from the 1980s.

"Thanks for coming in, Mr. O'Rourke," Crawford said when they met in the reception area.

"You're welcome," O'Rourke said, decidedly lacking in enthusiasm.

"We can sit over here," Crawford said, ushering O'Rourke toward two chairs in the corner of the reception area.

"As I mentioned, I'm one of the detectives on the Thorsen Paul murder case and just wanted to ask you a few questions."

O'Rourke didn't respond.

"Is that all right with you?"

"Yes, sure. I mean, I'm not going to be able to help you, but go ahead," O'Rourke said, biting his lip.

"According to a source I deem reliable, you persuaded your grandfather to invest ten million dollars in Paul's company. Is that correct?"

"Correct."

"Then, when there were problems with the company, negative news reports were coming out and, as I understand it, the stock was plummeting in value, you got on the phone repeatedly with Mr. Paul, threatening lawsuits against him and his company."

"Correct."

"And, as I understand it, some of those calls were threatening to Mr. Paul himself."

"Incorrect."

"You never threatened Mr. Paul personally? Just lawsuits?"

"Correct."

Crawford was getting sick of the man's one-word answers. "Mr.

O'Rourke, while I appreciate the brevity of your answers, maybe you could tell me where it all ended up."

"Nowhere."

"What do you mean, 'nowhere'?"

O'Rourke sighed like he was exceedingly bored and rubbed one of the eyebrows. "I mean it went nowhere because the lawsuits I threatened weren't going to get blood out of a stone. So, we never went through with them."

"Meaning, there was never going to be any money to recover?"

"Correct."

Christ, thought Crawford, *this is how they taught you to speak at MIT? One-word sentences? Really?*

"And I assume you know nothing about the death of your classmate. And give me a little more than a 'correct' or 'incorrect,' will you, please?"

"I don't know a damn thing about Thorsen's death and, in fact, I am very sorry about it. For one thing, Thorsen and I had a reconciliation about a month ago and, for another, no one deserves to die like that."

Crawford nodded. *That's for damn sure.*

"Okay, Mr. O'Rourke, last question: where were you two nights ago from approximately ten 'til six in the morning?"

"Sound asleep."

Crawford eyed him closely. "Okay then, I appreciate your help and thank you for coming in," he said, getting to his feet.

O'Rourke simply nodded. Not even one word this time.

Shortly after Innes O'Rourke left, Ott stuck his head in. "Wanna do a recap?"

"Sure," Crawford said. "You did yours, right?"

"Yeah, just finished up Birch," Ott said.

Crawford took the sketch that Harrison Knight had drawn out of his drawer. "Before you tell me about yours," he handed the sketch to Ott, "who's this?"

Ott's eyes got big. "Holy shit," was all he said.

"I got Jimbo going to ID her in person. Should be hearing back from him any minute now."

"Wow, then what do we do if he IDs her?"

"Go pay her a visit and have a nice, long talk. Arrest her if we got enough," Crawford said, leaning back in his chair. "So, tell me about Birch."

"Okay. He struck me as one of those guys who's never satisfied with anything. A natural-born complainer. I believe what Carter said about him calling Thorsen Paul and screaming at him all the time. But a killer? No way in hell. He said the NextRed loss was just a blip in his portfolio. He's moved on and has already forgotten it. I believe him."

Crawford, his hands together, nodded. "Okay, so he's out. What about your race-car-driver friend?"

"Hm. He's not such a quick rule-out, even though he doesn't strike me as the violent type."

Crawford leaned forward. "So, tell me what you're thinking."

"Well, I don't really have a complete handle on him yet. I'm guessing that he personally didn't kick in much of the fifty million, but that it came mainly from rich friends. It would be really helpful to know exactly who those friends are. I'm thinking you should have a little sit-down with him. See what your take is. What about your people?"

"So, of my three, I don't think any of them had anything to do with it. Just disgruntled investors who bet on the wrong horse."

"Like Birch, you mean, they've put the whole thing behind them?"

"Yeah, well, with the exception of Herb Wallace. His whole life got turned upside down and he blames Paul for everything. But a killer who'd dream up a way like that to kill a guy? Not him. No way in hell."

"Plus, there's no way this was a one-man job, right?"

"Exactly. Take at least two to sedate him, transport him, and bury him."

Ott nodded. "My guy Gaetano said something about there being a million people who probably wanted to kill Bernie Madoff, but nobody did."

Crawford nodded. "Good point."

Ott smiled. "What about the Pet?"

"I was wondering how long it would take you to get around to her," Crawford said. "She's still looking good, but what a smut-mouth."

"Really?"

"Yeah, bigger f-bomber than you," Crawford said. "P.S. She didn't do it and I strongly doubt anyone who worked for her did either."

Ott nodded and swallowed. "So, I gotta tell you what I heard about your friend David Balfour."

"Yeah, I know," Crawford said. "Wallace told me he lost his whole investment. Said he had to sell his summer house, which I think is bullshit."

"No, not that," Ott said. "Something totally different."

"What?"

Ott told him about Thorsen Paul's alleged affair with David Balfour's girlfriend.

"What a dirtball Paul was," Crawford said after Ott told him the whole story. All Crawford knew was that Balfour wasn't seeing his long-time girlfriend Bree Ackerman anymore and that it seemed to have ended abruptly. "Screwing around when he was engaged."

"That's what I thought, too."

"Guess I better talk to David. See what his story is."

"Smashing the car with a golf club kinda got my attention."

Crawford nodded. "I'll talk to him."

His cell phone rang. He looked down at the display. "My buddy Jimbo," he said to Ott.

"Yeah, Jimbo. Did you see her?" Crawford hit the speaker button.

"That's her," Jimbo said.

"No question about it?"

"Nope."

"Okay, thanks. Good work." He clicked off and looked up at Ott. "You ready to go check out the hard bodies at The Max?"

Ott was already on his feet.

SIXTEEN

CRAWFORD AND OTT WERE SITTING IN AMANDA PALMER'S office, having just shown her the sketch that bore a resemblance to her, bolstered by the fact that Jimbo Smith claimed she looked a lot like the woman at the Rubber Ducky who'd put him up to the burglary in Palm Beach.

"I don't care what that fat slob had to say," Amanda said, shaking her head. "And I resent the fact that you had him come here under false pretenses. Joining the club, ha! It'd take twenty years to get that lard-ass in shape."

She didn't seem nearly so sweet and cooperative as she had the night of her sister's murder.

"So, it wasn't you at that car wash?"

"Never been there in my life. And in case you haven't noticed, there are lots of women in Florida who are five-six and have green eyes," Amanda said. "And besides, why in God's name would I be trying to recruit someone to burglarize a house? Craziest thing I ever heard."

Crawford had a theory, but it wasn't fully fleshed-out yet. Still, what more could they do?

Ott asked her one last time if the woman in the sketch was her, and again she denied it vociferously. Then she looked at her watch and said she had to go, she was late for an appointment away from the Max.

Crawford had another question, but not for her. "Do you mind if we just look around the gym a little?"

"Have at it," she said, putting a scarf around her neck. "I gotta be honest with you two, if this is how you conduct your investigation, I'm not real optimistic about how the case is going to turn out."

Crawford saw Ott open his mouth to shoot back at her, but he bit his tongue.

"Sorry you feel that way," Crawford said, as Ott and he walked out of Amanda's office ahead of her.

Ott looked around the large open space of The Max and gave his quick assessment. "Nothin' but a bunch of stuck-up rich chicks."

"You sound like a junior-high douche."

Ott shrugged but didn't disagree. They walked around, and Crawford did indeed see a few machines with 'Out of Order' signs on them.

"Well, it's official," Ott said.

"What is?"

"I don't want to join."

Crawford snickered and pointed. "I want to go ask that woman in the cubicle next to Amanda's office something."

Ott nodded. "You mean her assistant?"

Crawford nodded and walked toward the cubicle. He peeked his head in. "Knock, knock."

The woman looked up, startled. "Oh, you scared me."

"Sorry," Crawford said. "Can we ask you a question or two? We're the detectives on the Adriana—"

"Yes, I know. I'm Kit. How can I help?"

"Were you here the night Adriana was killed?"

The woman nodded. "Sure was. I actually was in Adriana's office, paying a bunch of bills."

"And Amanda was in her office?"

"Well, what happened was, Amanda came into Adriana's office at about six, said she'd been here since early in the morning and was going to head home. Adriana asked her if she'd do her a favor."

"What was that?"

"She asked if she'd drop some of her dry cleaning at her house—" *Bingo*, Crawford thought; that was the missing link—"because she was going to do a big shop at Publix and would have her hands full."

"Where was the dry cleaning?"

"Right here in Adriana's closet."

"So, Amanda took it? The dry cleaning."

Kit nodded. "Yes, I remember her telling Adriana, 'Yeah, sure, easy-peasy.'"

"Thank you," Crawford said. "That's all we need to know."

Kit shrugged. "That's it?"

Crawford nodded. "Thanks for your time."

He and Ott walked out of her cubicle, toward the double doors of The Max, then outside.

Ott patted Crawford on the arm. "I had no idea where you were going at first."

Crawford stopped and turned to his partner. "*That's* what Amanda was doing at Adriana's house."

WHAT WAS MADDENING WAS THEY STILL DIDN'T HAVE ENOUGH on Amanda to take her in.

Crawford even called up the chief assistant prosecutor for Palm Beach County, who he had worked with in the past, and laid out everything he had. The prosecutor said it wasn't enough, told him he needed a smoking gun. *Thanks a lot*, he thought, *easy for you to say*.

Crawford was beginning to feel as though he were going in ten directions at once. He and Ott were putting in fifteen-hour days, then going home to sleep and change their clothes. Crawford had called

David Balfour on their way to The Max, said he needed to talk to him, but didn't say about what. Balfour asked him over for a drink at seven. Crawford looked at his watch. It was 6:45 now.

He dropped Ott at the station, drove to Balfour's house, and parked.

He knocked on Balfour's door at a few minutes past seven.

Balfour opened it. David Balfour reminded him of a doctor he used to see on old TV reruns when he was a kid. Dr. Kildare was his name: a handsome, indefatigable physician who was always in good shape and never had a hair out of place. He had always been tan, too, which was curious, because on the show he seemed to log long days and nights in the operating room.

"Come on in, Charlie," Balfour said. "Long time no see. You got a murder you want me to suss out for you?"

Crawford smiled as he followed Balfour in. "Ah, not exactly."

CRAWFORD WAS DRINKING A BEER AND BALFOUR A SCOTCH AS they sat in Balfour's well-appointed living room.

"So, what's up?" Balfour asked. "I can see from your expression you've got something weighty on that brilliant, crime-solving mind of yours."

Crawford just blurted it out. "Thorsen Paul. Tell me all you know about him."

Balfour took a quick but long pull of his drink. "I see you already know."

"What do you mean?"

"About his affair with Bree. And, knowing how thorough you are, probably about me losing my shirt on NextRed."

Crawford nodded and leaned closer to Balfour. "I know about both. And I want you to tell me you know nothing about his murder."

"I know absolutely nothing about his murder," Balfour said.

"Nothing at all?"

"What did I just say, Charlie?" Balfour sounded defensive. "Look, I didn't like the guy, I admit it. But who the hell would like a guy who had an affair with his girlfriend while cheating on his fiancée? I mean, what a scumbag."

"I hear you," Crawford said. "Was it true that you went and did a number on his Jaguar with your driver?"

"Four iron," Balfour said. "Not one of my better moments. I paid to get the car fixed the next day."

"And what about your NextRed investment?"

"What about it?" Balfour said, downing the rest of his drink. "I lost five million bucks. Was I pissed off about it? Damn straight I was. But I'm a big boy, I've had big losses on investments before."

Crawford set his beer bottle down. "The way I heard it, the loss forced you to sell your Southampton house."

Balfour frowned. "That's complete bullshit. Fact is, I never used that place. All I did was pay a fortune in real-estate taxes and upkeep on it. It was time to sell it." Balfour looked at Crawford's empty beer. "Another?"

"Sure. Why not?"

Balfour went to the bar, got another beer from the refrigerator, and poured another scotch for himself. He came back in and handed Crawford the beer.

"Thanks."

"You're welcome," Balfour said, sitting back down. "What's this I heard about peanut butter on Paul's eyes?"

Crawford nodded.

"Jesus, that's a helluva way to go," Balfour said in a tone that didn't sound nearly as sympathetic as it could have been.

SEVENTEEN

CRAWFORD AND OTT GOT TO THEIR RESPECTIVE OFFICES EARLY the next morning, after both deciding they needed to research their remaining Thorsen Paul suspects further. Ott had a nagging suspicion that Gonzalo Gaetano might be hiding something, or at least leaving something out. Gaetano had yet to email Ott the promised list of investors who'd collectively put fifty million into NextRed. And, as Ott told Crawford, Gaetano had been jumpy, and his eyes flitted around a lot more when they were talking about NextRed as opposed to Formula One racing. Ott decided to look into where Gaetano had grown up— Mexico City. While he was probably no Mexican national hero, he certainly would be a name people knew, as he had won the Mexican Grand Prix a decade or so ago.

Ott walked down to Camilo Fernandez's cubicle. Camilo, donut in hand, looked up at Ott.

"Hey, Mort."

"Hey, Cam. Got a question for you...you speak Spanish, right?"

Fernandez chuckled. "What do you think this accent is...Russian?"

"So, that's a yes?"

"*Sí.*"

Ott waved his arm. "Come on, I got a job for you."

Ott wrote out six questions for Fernandez and appointed him his official translator. Then Fernandez looked up the number of the main Mexico City Police Department and dialed it. It seemed a logical starting point. Someone answered, and Fernandez began chatting away in Spanish.

After *como estas,* Ott was lost.

Fifteen minutes later, Fernandez hung up: "Okay, they put me on with a high-ranking guy who was a fountain of knowledge."

"What did he say?" Ott asked,

"Said Gaetano was a poor kid who made good. Grew up in the slums, started hot-wiring and boosting cars when he was like twelve, and the rest is history. Developed a love of fast cars and by the time he was nineteen had a few sponsors."

"So, like he told me, his parents were poor?"

"Oh yeah, big-time poor. Lived in the barrio, the guy said."

Which confirmed the fact that his parents had nothing to do with the fifty-million-dollar investment in NextRed.

"When you asked whether he knew if Gaetano was hooked up with any rich or influential Mexican business people, politicians, or people like that, what did he say?"

"Said he didn't know the answer, but his sense was Gaetano hadn't spent much time in Mexico in the last ten or fifteen years."

So, the question remained: Where'd the fifty million come from? And would any of the people who put it up be willing to torture and kill a man over the loss?

"That's *muy* helpful, Cam, I appreciate it."

"No problem," Fernandez said. "You need me to call anyone else, just let me know."

"What was the name of the guy you spoke to? You said it so fast I didn't get it."

"Ignacio Puig. I told him we might be getting back to him."

Shortly afterward, Crawford had come up with a shocker on

another front. He didn't have enough on Amanda Palmer to arrest her for her sister's murder, so he'd gone to Wikipedia, not expecting much, and typed in 'Amanda and Adriana Palmer Palm Beach, Florida.' The first result that popped up on the Fox News website was the headline, "Twins Car Crash in Hawaii—Was it Intentional?" Below it was a photo of a badly smashed car that looked to be at the bottom of a cliff. Crawford read the article, which had been originally published a little more than a year ago:

Twin sisters Amanda and Adriana Palmer of Palm Beach, Florida, were driving on a cliff-top road in Pahoa, when their car suddenly careened off the road and plummeted into ocean-side rocks more than fifty feet below. Miraculously, neither one of the sisters were seriously injured. Investigating officer Honi Kahele said that the sisters were reportedly observed by a pedestrian fighting in the front seat of their late-model car, just before they plunged off the cliff. Officer Kahele went on to say that there was no sign of braking having occurred before the car hurtled off the cliff to the rocks below.

Directly below that search result was an article dated a week after the first. It was from the *Daily Mail*. Crawford knew the *Daily Mail* was a half-notch above the *National Enquirer* in credibility and that most articles in it should be treated with a grain of salt—his favorite *National Enquirer* headline was "Snake with Human Head Found in Arkansas."

This headline shrieked: "Bombshell Twins: Attempted Murder-Suicide?" Crawford also knew enough to realize that a headline that ended in a question mark was as likely to be as untrue as true. But he read on eagerly anyway.

Ten days ago, twin sisters Amanda and Adriana Palmer were in a car that nosedived off a cliff and crashed to the seaside rocks below in Hawaii. Speculation now centers on eyewitness accounts that the two were locked in a furious, physical struggle immediately before the horrendous "accident." The two had also been observed at a restaurant not far from the crash site, engaged in a "heated shouting match." One unnamed police detective even suggested that one sister had forced the car off the cliff, possibly as part of a spontaneous murder-suicide attempt. Both sisters have been unwilling to respond to numerous requests for interviews from the Daily Mail. Together, they are proprietors of an ultra-chic fitness center in West Palm Beach, Florida.

Wow, Crawford thought, *a lot of bad vehicular history in the Palmer/Bobrow family.* He figured out what time it was in Hawaii at the moment, thinking a call to Officer Honi Kahele might be in order. Six hours...which would make it 9:30 a.m. there. He looked up the main number for the Hawaii Police Department and was about to dial it when his cell phone rang.

"What's up, Mort?"

"So, in doing my usual incredibly thorough research job, I came across something about David Balfour."

Not who Crawford had hoped Ott would be reporting on.

"Tell me."

"Took place at some shindig at the Poinciana," Ott said, referring to the exclusive, blue-blood, country club. "Long story short, Balfour threatened to kill Thorsen Paul."

Crawford groaned. "Jesus, really?"

"Yeah, a call came in that there was a disturbance there, so Phil Wall, who was on duty, went there. According to his report, a bunch of bystanders had to separate Balfour and Paul 'cause they were yelling at each other and about to really get into it."

"Must have been about Bree Ackerman," Crawford said.

"I guess."

Crawford thought for a moment. "I'm surprised we never heard about that. Sounds like there might have been a bunch of eyewitnesses."

"I hear you. So, what do we do?"

"Guess I gotta talk to David again."

"All right, man, just figured you'd want to know."

"Yeah, thanks, talk later," Crawford said and clicked off.

He thought for a second. David Balfour: Temper? Yes. Killer? Hard to believe.

He dialed the number of the police department in Hawaii, and five minutes later was on the phone with Honi Kahele. Crawford explained why he had called: to get Kahele's insights and whatever particulars he could offer about the Palmer sisters' car crash the year before.

"It was pretty weird," Kahele said. "This guy who had car trouble saw the whole thing."

"You mean, them go off the cliff?"

"Yeah, he was waiting for a tow truck and the two came along in a black Honda. Not going very fast, but the guy said one of the sisters was pulling the other's hair and he could hear them yelling at each other. Screaming like bloody murder, he said. Then the car suddenly took a sharp right, like one of them had yanked the wheel, and over the edge it went."

"Then what happened?"

"He called us. A chopper went there, dropped a guy down a rope and found 'em both alive. A lot of bruises and cuts, one had a broken arm, but both alive."

Crawford was taking notes on a yellow pad. "I read this one article about there being a suspicion that it was a—"

"I know," Kahele cut in. "A murder-suicide attempt."

"Exactly, but kinda spur-of-the-moment. In your opinion, was there any evidence pointing to that?"

"That strikes me as a reach, but maybe."

"So, in that scenario, which one would have been the attempted murderer?"

"In that scenario, if it was true, it would have been Adriana. She was the passenger, so she would have been the one who yanked the wheel, but—"

"I know, it's a reach."

They talked for another few minutes, then Crawford thanked Kahele and hung up. He had a lot to process, a bushel barrel of theories and conjectures pinballing around in his head.

He decided he wanted to talk to Adriana's past two boyfriends again—Ed Bertoli and Peter Georgescu. He also needed to buttonhole Gonzalo Gaetano. Ott was grousing about Gaetano not sending him a list of his investor friends, having now requested it three times. That definitely qualified as suspicious.

He phoned all three but only reached Bertoli. He set up a meeting with him at his restaurant an hour later and left messages for the other two.

BERTOLI'S WAS A COZY LITTLE PLACE WITH RED-CHECKERED table clothes, candles in Chianti bottles, and two short waiters scurrying around, one with a mustache, one with a neatly-trimmed beard. It was the tail-end of the lunch hour and Crawford was sitting with Ed Bertoli at a table in the back of the restaurant. Having already had an early lunch at Green's, Crawford simply nursed a club soda.

"Thanks for seeing me on short notice," Crawford said.

"No problem. How's your investigation going?"

Crawford gave him the standard answer. "We're making progress. If you would, can you describe any identifying marks— tattoos, moles, scars— on Adriana Palmer's face or body."

Bertoli cocked his head. "But you *have* her body. Can't you just go see for yourself? Funeral's not 'til tomorrow."

"Just need confirmation. A standard thing we do." Which was not exactly true.

"O-kay. Well, she had a little scar on her neck, from a car accident."

"The one in Hawaii?"

"Yeah, how'd you know about that?"

"Read about it," Crawford said. "What else?"

Bertoli blinked a few times. "Well, she had a mole on her—" Bertoli coughed uneasily— "well, on her left breast, actually."

"The scar on her neck, where exactly was it? And was it vertical or horizontal, and how long was it, would you estimate?"

Bertoli held up his thumb and forefinger. "I'd say just shy of an inch. Front of her neck, and horizontal, on the left...no, her right side."

"Anything else?

Bertoli thought for a few moments. "Not that I can think of. Pretty much blemish-free for the most part."

Crawford nodded. "The other thing I wanted to ask you about were debts Adriana may have had."

Bertoli was nodding vigorously. "Now that's a subject I know a lot about," he said. "Because it was something she talked about constantly."

"Can you be as specific as possible?"

"Sure can. Where do I start? First of all, there was the huge debt on The Max. Adriana was frustrated about how it kept getting bigger and bigger. Even with all their members and as much as they charged, it just kept growing."

"I can understand how that would be frustrating."

"Yeah, but it was more than just that. She had a lot of college debt, a mortgage, and always seemed to get further and further behind on her credit cards."

"Was that true with Amanda, too?"

"Oh, God, no. Amanda was a miser compared to Adriana. I don't think she had any money problems at all, beyond the overall debt of The Max. Actually, this was a sore point between me and Adriana, her always talking about how rich Amanda's boyfriend was."

"You're talking about Ted Bartow, right?"

"Yeah, supposed to be worth a hundred million or so," Bertoli said. "Adriana was always rubbing it in my face about how I couldn't buy her things. It got old after a while."

Crawford nodded. "I can imagine."

A waiter came up to them. "Anything else, Ed?"

Bertoli glanced at Crawford, who shook his head. "Thanks, I'm good."

"We're fine," Bertoli said.

Crawford took a sip of his club soda. "Well, thanks a lot. I really appreciate your time. What do I owe—"

Bertoli held up his hand. "For Palm Beach's finest, it's on the house."

On his way out to the Crown Vic, Crawford pulled his iPhone out of his jacket pocket. He had gotten a message from Gonzalo Gaetano saying, "I am up at Sebring Raceway for a couple of days practicing for the Belgian Grand Prix. As soon as I'm back, I'll be more than happy to meet with you."

Well, isn't that inconvenient?

Crawford's first instinct was for Ott and him to drive up there. Wherever Sebring was. He only knew it was somewhere in Florida. Actually, it would probably be fun for Mort to check out. Not that they had time.

Back at his desk, he looked up Sebring on the map. Right smack in the middle of the state. A part of Florida he had no reason, and no desire, ever to visit.

Five minutes later, he got a call-back from Peter Georgescu. Georgescu confirmed the scar on Adriana's neck but didn't volunteer any knowledge of the mole on her breast. Then Crawford walked down to Ott's cubicle to catch him up on the most recent developments.

"Sebring, huh?" Ott said. "Used to be a helluva track. But from what I've heard, it's kind of fallen on hard times."

"What do you mean?"

"Well, like one night of the week any kid with a license can show up and drag race his car," Ott punched a few keys on his iPad. "It seems Sebring's glory days are long gone. Also heard guys with drones sneak in there and fly 'em around. Track makes for a good runway. Landing pad, too, I guess."

"Yeah, but can a driver like Gaetano go up there and practice?"

"I guess, but before we drive all the way up there, we should make damn sure that's where he really is. Something a little dodgy about this guy."

"Maybe take a drive by his house."

Ott nodded. "Might save a four-hour round trip."

"Before we go to his house, I want to have another conversation with that guy in Mexico City."

Ott reached for his desk phone, then paused. "I'll get Fernandez for you. What do you want to ask?"

"I just have a hunch where the money might have come from. Kind of a longshot, but worth looking into."

"The fifty mil?"

Crawford nodded. "Yeah, I'm thinking maybe it wasn't the cleanest money around."

EIGHTEEN

A HALF HOUR LATER, THEY DROVE UP TO GONZALO GAETANO'S unassuming ranch house on Debra Lane and found a black Audi in the driveway.

"Sebring, huh? Then what's his car doing here?"

"You'd think if he was going to give me a cock-and-bull story about going up there," Crawford said, "he'd at least hide his car around back or garage it."

"You'd think," Ott said, getting out of the Crown Vic. "Why don't I go around to the back door, just in case?"

"Good idea."

Crawford stepped up onto the front porch, noticed a peephole, and pressed the buzzer. He thought he heard steps inside but couldn't be sure. A minute later, he hit the buzzer again.

"Palm Beach Police, Mr. Gaetano, open up."

He waited another half a minute. Nothing.

He pounded on the door. "Open up!"

Still nothing. Then, finally, the door opened. It was Ott, standing with a man about his height.

"Look who I found tryin' to make a run for it," Ott said. "Charlie, meet Gonzalo Gaetano. Not as fast on his feet as driving an F1."

"We need to talk," Crawford said. "Looks like you're trying to avoid us."

"That's not true," Gaetano said.

"Don't give me that," Crawford said, pointing the man back into his house.

The pair followed Gaetano into the living room with the *Jaws* and *Citizen Kane* posters.

Crawford sat in a wing chair and leaned toward Gaetano. "Thought you told me you were up in Sebring practicing for the Belgian Grand Prix."

Gaetano shook his head. "I said I was going up there. And I am."

"No, you said you *were* there, and you're not," Crawford said. "We want to know who your investors in NextRed were."

Gaetano looked around the room as if it were a jail cell and sighed. "See, here's the thing: the investors are in an LLC and I don't know the names."

Crawford glanced at Ott and shook his head. "All right, start from the beginning. Who did you first approach to raise the money for the investment in NextRed?"

Gaetano leaned back in his sofa. "No, that's not how it happened. A man called me—"

"What man? From where?"

"A man named Alejandro Castillo, from Guadalajara. He's an accountant."

"Keep going."

"He told me he represented a group of investors who wanted to invest in NextRed. He said he knew that I knew Thorsen Paul, and he'd pay me a finder's fee for the introduction."

"Wait a minute," Crawford said. "Why couldn't they just buy stock? It was listed on the NASDAQ."

"No, no, this was about a year before it was on the NASDAQ."

"Okay, so what happened next?"

"I talked to Thorsen and he was interested in talking to the investors, so I gave him Alejandro Castillo's number and they took it from there."

"Wait, how did you know Thorsen Paul?"

"I know his fiancée Carter Pearson. Met him through her. He and I ended up playing golf a few times together."

"Okay, first of all, we need Alejandro Castillo's number," Crawford said. "And, also, how many people are in this LLC?"

"I don't know. You'll have to ask Castillo that."

"So, they put their fifty mil into NextRed. And did you get your finder's fee?"

Gaetano glanced down. "Ah, yes, I did."

Crawford shot Ott a look. "I've heard more convincing yeses before. You sure you got it?"

"Yes."

"Then you won't have a problem showing us a bank statement showing the deposit?"

Gaetano squirmed in his chair. "Well, see, they actually deposited it in my parents' account...for tax reasons."

Crawford shot a glance at Ott, who was shaking his head.

Crawford went on. "So, the fifty mil goes into NextRed and, what, two or three years later, NextRed crashes and burns?"

Gaetano nodded slowly.

"So, these Mexican guys in the LLC just go, 'Oh, well, bad investment, too bad?'"

"No, not exactly."

"So...*what* exactly?"

Gaetano exhaled deeply. "One of them came here."

"And what?" Crawford said impatiently. "Don't make us pull teeth here, Gonzalo."

"Had a meeting with Thorsen."

"And how'd that meeting go."

"Ah, not so well, I heard."

"Come on, Gonzalo, specifics."

"I don't know, I wasn't in it."

"But you heard," Crawford said. "What was his name?"

"I never heard a name."

"But you saw him?"

Gaetano shook his head.

"You sure?"

Gaetano nodded.

"What kind of guy do you think he was?" Ott asked. "Would you say a friendly, good-natured kinda guy or maybe...a mean, nasty kinda guy."

Gaetano didn't answer right away, his eyes glued to the tops of his black Nikes. "I wouldn't know."

Crawford tapped the arm of his chair. "This whole thing's a little sketchy. I mean, how'd these guys know about NextRed in the first place?"

"I can't answer that," Gaetano said. "My guess would be that the accountant finds investments for them."

"This guy Castillo?"

Gaetano nodded.

Crawford glanced at Ott, then Gaetano. It was showtime. "Well, I just had a conversation with a man in Mexico City who's with the Unidad de Policia Embajada," he started. "He told me about a gang called Zamora Cinco"— Gaetano flinched almost imperceptibly— "I can tell by your reaction you know exactly who they are."

Gaetano shrugged and shook his head, but it was not a convincing denial.

"So, the man I spoke to told me that in their extensive investigation of this gang—he called them Z5—they found phone records of calls not only to you, but to your parents from someone in the gang."

"You know anything about that, Gonzalo?" Ott asked.

No reaction.

"Of course, you do," said Ott. "We're told Z5 are hombres you're not likely to forget."

"That's for damned sure," Crawford said. "They're like the Sinaloa Cartel—they run drugs and kill people—but their specialty is kidnapping. Evidently, their MO is to kidnap some rich person, or politician, or his kid and demand a big ransom. They also specialize in just about every kind of extortion you can think of."

"Yeah," Ott piled on, "like call you up, and tell you they're gonna kill your son or daughter unless you come up with a million bucks by Sunday. Shakedowns, shit like that."

Several beads of sweat had appeared on Gaetano's forehead below his short-cropped hair.

"Are you hot, Gonzalo?" Ott asked.

"No, why?"

"You look a little stressed. Like you don't want to talk about this."

"Your parents were paid a visit by someone from Z5, right?" Crawford asked.

Gaetano shook his head. "No, I don't know anything about this. And I've never heard of that gang. I've lived in the States a long time and almost never go back to Mexico."

"I don't blame you," Ott said. "Pretty dangerous part of the world. Guys with chainsaws cutting peoples' heads off, giving their victims acid baths, or shoving 'em into a drum filled with oil and lighting a match...where do they come up with that stuff?"

The sweat began to run down the side of Gaetano's face. His shoulders had slumped forward.

"Oh, I forget one," said Ott. "They take a razor blade and peel your face back—"

"I think he gets the idea, Mort," Crawford said, holding up a hand. "So, I had a nice long talk with this inspector down there, and he has phone records of five conversations that you had with a woman named Rafaela Arroyo. Name ring a bell?"

Gaetano wiped his face with his shirt sleeve. "She was just someone who wanted to know about NextRed."

Ott looked at Crawford and chuckled. "Oh, I think there's more than that."

"Think real hard, Gonzalo," Crawford said. "What did she talk to you about?"

Gaetano exhaled deeply again. "I can't remember every detail of those calls. It was a long time ago."

"That's bullshit," Crawford said. "The last one was three weeks ago."

"So, put on your thinking cap and tell us about that conversation," Ott said. "NextRed was as dead as a cartel vic, so it had to be about getting their money back."

"Wait a second, please," Gaetano said, standing and walking to a thermostat on the far wall. He turned the dial and walked back. "Now...what did you say?"

"My partner asked what exactly you and this woman, Rafaela Arroyo, talked about in your last conversation," Ott said.

Gaetano exhaled. "She wanted to know if I thought Thorsen Paul had any assets left."

"And if he did?"

Gaetano didn't answer.

"We all know the answer to that," Crawford said.

Ott nodded. "Yeah, she and her compadres were going to help themselves to whatever was left."

"What did you tell her?" Crawford asked.

"I told her I didn't know."

"I bet she wasn't very satisfied with that answer," Ott said.

"What do you mean?"

"Well, my guess would be she told you to get him to come up with some fucking money."

Gaetano's silence confirmed Ott's guess was right.

"So, then, maybe Arroyo came to Palm Beach?" Crawford asked.

"I wouldn't know. I never saw her."

"That's because she didn't need you," Ott said. "And if she did need something from you, all she had to do was go to your parents' house and call from there. Tell you she was going to—"

Crawford held up his hand. "No need to go there, Gonzalo is well aware what she could do." Crawford paused a few moments. "Know what this inspector told me about Rafaela Arroyo?"

Gaetano was silent.

"Well, I'm gonna tell you. He said she was right up there with that guy El Chapo. Every bit as brutal. Got a reputation for being sadistic and ruthless. Kind of makes sense, don't you think?"

"What do you mean?"

"I mean, 'cause she's a woman. You know how it is down there. Hell, you know better than we do. It's a macho society. How many gangs have you heard of where a woman is top dog? Bet you can't come up with any others. So, to get where she is, she had to out-macho the macho men." He glanced over at Ott, who seemed to be enjoying his monologue. "Which means she had to be really good at torture and murder. Probably pretty smart, too."

Ott nodded. "Yup. Smart and violent. But when I looked into Z5, I didn't see anything about peanut butter on the eyeballs. Is that a new wrinkle they came up with? Maybe Rafaela Arroyo's brainchild?"

Gaetano's whole face was glistening with sweat, and he had big wet patches at the armpits of his shirt.

"Okay, Gonzalo, maybe we'll leave it there for today," Crawford said. "I wish I could thank you for being forthcoming and candid, but I can't, because you weren't."

"Yeah, you're gonna need to try a little harder next time," Ott said, "or you might end up watching the Belgian Grand Prix from the big house."

NINETEEN

WHEN CRAWFORD AND OTT GOT BACK TO THE OFFICE, THEY rehashed their conversation with Gaetano and decided that, although there was undoubtedly more to get out of him, they'd made a pretty good start. The man was clearly not a murderer, but a guy trying to escape with his and his family members' lives. They also concluded that Gaetano probably never got his finder's fee, despite his claim. Why bother, when all Z5 had to do was threaten to chop off his mother's head?

They talked about jumping on an Aeroméxico flight down to Mexico City, or Guadalajara, or wherever it was Rafaela Arroyo hung her hat. But they quickly ruled that out. Ott said it would be like Davey Crockett and Jim Bowie hunkering down in the Alamo and trying to fight off a couple thousand Mexican soldiers. Bound to end badly.

Next, they debated whether to talk to Norm Rutledge about the conversation they'd just had with Gaetano. The purpose would be to keep the chief in the loop because they felt they had to. As far as Rutledge coming up with any brilliant solution, that wasn't going to happen: Rutledge was a master at poking holes in things, not coming up with inspired plans. Crawford had once told Ott that if they'd followed Rutledge's by-the-books procedures, they wouldn't have solved a single one of their cases. An exaggeration, but not by much.

———

CRAWFORD DIALED THE CELL PHONE NUMBER OF THE detective in Mexico City while Camilo Fernandez stood by to serve as translator.

Cam ended up speaking to the detective for another fifteen minutes. It was long enough to be told, several times, that Rafaela Arroyo was not someone you wanted as an enemy. But then, that had already come across loud and clear.

The Mexican detective confirmed that Rafaela had a reputation for being even more vicious than her male counterparts in gangs like the Sinaloa cartel, Los Zetas, the Tijuana cartel, and Los Negros. He said he'd send their complete file on Rafaela and Zamora Cinco, adding that it was voluminous. Crawford thanked him via Fernandez and clicked off.

Ott, who had been listening and Googling at the same time, handed Crawford his tablet. "Here's one I didn't see before." It was an article about Rafaela that included a photo of her. "Not a chick I'd be in a big hurry to bring home to Mom."

She had a dark complexion with bleached blonde hair the color of Cheetos, and the biceps of a weightlifter. She towered over a dark-haired man next to her, who wore a tattooed number five in the center of his forehead.

"Jesus," Crawford said. "Looks like she's six feet tall."

"At least."

Crawford handed the tablet back to Ott. "Reminds me of this women's gang in the Bronx when I was up in New York," Crawford said. "Their nickname was the Bad Barbies. Real name was the Trinitarios, and they'd go at it with this Dominican gang all the time. I think they were hooked up with MS-13 or maybe it was another one called Barrio 18. Anyway, their specialty was luring male gang members into a house. You know, promise 'em sex and weed, then guys hiding inside would hack 'em up with machetes."

"Christ, that's a tough way to go," Ott said.

Crawford nodded.

A full thirty seconds went by.

"So, what are you thinking?" Ott asked.

"About how to lure Rafaela Arroyo here," Crawford said.

"Send her a picture of you in your Dartmouth football uniform."

"Don't be a douche."

Ott rapped his knuckles on Crawford's desk. "Hey, how 'bout this? Make her think there's still a pile of money in a Thorsen Paul bank account here."

Crawford perked up. "I like it. Maybe when Paul saw where things were headed, he siphoned off a bunch of money and put it in an account of his father's or something."

"Yeah, but you know what Rutledge would say about luring her up here, right?"

"What?"

"Something like, 'No way we're having a shoot-out on in my town with a buncha cartel Banditos.'."

"Sounds about right," Crawford said. "So, I guess we just don't tell him."

St. Edward's Catholic Church was distinctive for three reasons.

First, it was the church that JFK and Jackie attended when he was president and staying at the "Winter White House" up on North Ocean for a little R&R. Today, Palm Beach had become the Winter White House of another president.

Second, it stood directly across the street from Green's Pharmacy, where Crawford and Ott had lunch and/or breakfast on a regular basis.

Third, it was the one church that lapsed-Catholic Charlie Crawford infrequently attended. He had been a good Catholic boy, Charlie had, until the priest scandals some seventeen years back left him disillusioned with the church. He still went to mass several times a year, and squeezed into the little box on the occasional Saturday to confess his sins, which were nothing too egregious.

Today, it was the location for the funeral of Adriana Palmer. The ceremony was short and orderly, and in attendance were fifty to sixty people, young for the most part. From their spot in the back, Crawford spotted Ed Bertoli in the left front pew and Peter Georgescu right behind him. In the right front pew, Amanda Palmer sat next to Ted Bartow, both looking suitably somber.

"Looks like a lot of hard bodies from the gym," Ott said, scanning the crowd.

"You're in the house of the Lord," Crawford whispered back. "Can't be lustful."

"Oh, sorry."

The funeral had ended, and people were filing out.

Crawford and Ott studied the men and woman as they passed. Peter Georgescu smiled and nodded at Crawford, Ed Bertoli only nodded. Then came the woman named Gillian, whom Crawford had met briefly at the Beach & Racquet Club. She smiled, nodded, and popped her lips at Crawford.

Finally, Ted Bartow and Amanda came down the aisle. She was looking straight ahead, almost trance-like, and didn't notice them. But the scar on the right side of her neck was almost as noticeable as the hickey on the other side.

TWENTY

AFTER THE FUNERAL, CRAWFORD DROVE STRAIGHT TO JIMBO Smith's ramshackle house in Lake Worth. Ott and he had decided that Ott would work on the Paul case, which they'd caught Norm Rutledge up on. At least enough so he wouldn't badger them with questions three times a day

Before setting out, Crawford had first checked with Camilo Fernandez, who'd not yet heard from Jimbo, leading Crawford to chide himself again for not being on top of Jimbo turning himself in. But, fact was, he had bigger fish to fry.

Jimbo Smith was at home, if you could call it that. The scent of his house came wafting out, and hit Crawford's nostrils like a landfill piled high with decomposing fish and dead skunks. Jimbo was avoiding eye contact. "I'm getting a little sick of you not doing what you tell me you're gonna," Crawford said. "Come out to my car, we need to talk."

Jimbo shrugged. "What's wrong with right here?"

Lots, thought Crawford, but he wasn't about to tick off the laundry list of smells. "Come on," he said gesturing toward his car, "won't take long."

They got in the car and Crawford lowered all four windows. "You forgot to tell me about the first job your guys Dumb and Dumber did."

"Huh?"

"Dwight and Dewey. The first job for your lady friend from the carwash. They broke into her house at 897 North Beach Boulevard. Ring a bell?"

He dropped his head and sighed. "Hey, man, is there a law against breaking into the house of the person who hired you to break into it?"

Crawford had to chuckle. "That's a damn good question, Jimbo, and—tell you the truth—I don't know the answer. I just want details. What exactly did the woman you met at Rubber Ducky tell you to do?"

Jimbo glanced out the window, then back to Crawford. "Told me there was five thousand dollars in a jewelry drawer at that location. Told me there'd be a window left open in the back."

"So, you got Dwight and Dewey on it?"

"Yup. The lady told me it had to be done at a specific time. Between six and six-thirty last Monday. No one would be there then, but someone would be later on."

Crawford nodded. "So, your cut was twenty percent?"

Jimbo nodded. "Only problem was, there was only a grand in the drawer."

Crawford nodded. Sounded plausible since Adriana always seemed to be in a cash bind.

"So, what happened, Dwight and Dewey made up for it by grabbing a string of pearls and some other jewelry?"

"I guess. They didn't tell me about that. Just gave me a measly two hundred bucks."

A pretty slick plan, Crawford thought: *a cold-blooded, premeditated murder meant to look like a spur-of-the-moment slaying by burglars.* Adriana had a lot to gain by killing her sister: sliding into Amanda's bank accounts, leaving her own mountain of debt behind, inheriting her sister's rich boyfriend Ted Bartow. Okay, Ted did seem like a bit of a twit and probably not the sharpest tool in the shed, but she'd put up with that in exchange for a man whose net worth was a hundred million dollars. Plus, she wouldn't be second-guessed by her sister about how to run The Max.

The interior of the Crown Vic was starting to smell a little gamey. "Okay, Jimbo, thanks for filling me in."

Jimbo smiled at Crawford and didn't move. "I was thinking... maybe you need a good CI? You know, a confidential informant."

"Yeah, I know what CI stands for. You really think you're up to the job?"

"Damn straight. I can uncover all kinds of crimes for you. Nip 'em in the bud, so to speak."

Crawford smiled and tapped the Vic's wheel. "You think there're lots more nefarious schemes being hatched down at the Rubber Ducky?"

"Well, that's just where I work. See, I spend a lot of time hanging out in other places. Bars, pool halls, strip clubs, and shit."

Crawford patted him on the shoulder. "I bet you do. Tell you what, Jimbo, I hereby appoint you my unofficial CI. Which means any time you see a crime being cooked up or committed, you give me a call. If it's any good, I'll find a way to take care of you. How's that?"

Jimbo beamed. "You got yourself a deal, man."

"Okay, now, put your hands out."

Jimbo hesitated for a second but did as he was told.

Crawford snapped his set of cuffs on Jimbo's wrists. "But first you get to visit your buddies Dewey and Dwight."

DWIGHT AND DEWEY, THE BUNGLING BURGLARS, HAD BEEN unable to raise bail and thus remained in the basement jail of the Palm Beach police station on County Road. Crawford told Ott about his conversation with Jimbo and, though they didn't really need to talk to the two burglars, figured maybe they'd have information that Jimbo couldn't provide.

Ott, walking ahead of Crawford, approached their jail cell. "Hey, boys. So, what's new and exciting in your lives?"

"Funny," Dewey grunted.

"Treatin' you well, I hope?" Ott said. "Food good?"

No answer.

"Okay, well, we know you hit that house at 897 North Ocean Boulevard along with the one up on North Lake Way," Crawford said. "And we know you went in through an open window out back. And we also know—" he looked at Dwight— "you left a nice size ten and a half shoeprint right below the window. What we don't know is exactly when you did the job."

Dwight and Dewey looked at each other. Dewey shrugged.

"A little before seven," Dwight said.

"How do you know that?"

"Because we were late. Jimbo said we had a window between six and six-thirty."

"We know," Crawford said, "That's what he told us. So, the question is, did you see her there?"

Dwight flicked his eyes at Dewey, then looked down.

Crawford and Ott both knew that was a yes.

TWENTY-ONE

"I THOUGHT MAYBE SHE WAS GOING TO POP ME, TOO," DWIGHT said. "She aimed her pistol at me, but I hightailed it."

"Describe her," Crawford said.

Dwight did, then explained how he had wandered through the dining room into the far end of the foyer the night of the murder, and had seen the shooter from afar. Dewey had not seen her at all.

Dwight described her pretty generally since, as he said, he had been scared out of his mind. Crawford doubted he had great powers of observation to begin with. He took out his iPhone, scrolled to The Max site, and showed a photo of Amanda and Adriana Palmer posing together.

"Yeah," Dwight said. "It's definitely one of 'em."

"You're absolutely sure?" Crawford asked.

"Hey, man, she was only like twenty feet away."

"And what was she wearing?" Crawford asked, remembering Amanda's skin-tight blue jeans and blue St. Barth's T-shirt.

"Ah..." Dwight thought, "blue jeans and a T-shirt with writing on it."

"What color? The T-shirt."

"Black, I think."

Dark blue. Close enough.

Crawford turned to Ott. "That about locks it up."

Ott smiled and nodded.

Crawford turned back to Dwight and Dewey. "That intel might have just earned you boys a lighter sentence. We'll put in a good word with the DA."

Dwight managed a crooked smile, while the dumb-as-dirt look remained on Dewey's face.

THEY WERE IN NORM RUTLEDGE'S OFFICE CATCHING HIM UP ON the Adriana Palmer—now officially, Amanda Palmer—murder. Rutledge was wearing his second favorite suit, a pea green one. It had wide lapels that had gone out of style at the turn of the century.

Rutledge leaned back in his faux-leather chair and gazed out the window. "So, you got the broad dead to rights. I mean you know she's actually Adriana, not—" he turned to Crawford— "what's the other one's name again?"

"Amanda."

"Yeah, Amanda, and you know she was the shooter 'cause that weasel down in the basement can ID her. So, what's to think about? Bring her in and book her."

"That's where we're going," Ott said.

"Where?"

"The Max. Home of the hard bodies."

Rutledge, notorious lecher he was, perked up. "You fellas need a little backup?"

OTT PARKED THE CROWN VIC IN FRONT OF THE MAX AND A young valet came running up.

Ott greeted him with a smile as he got out of the Vic. "We're not going to be long. If you can just get the exterior."

"Yes, sir, you got it," the valet said.

They walked inside and up to the receptionist's desk.

"Gentlemen," said the perky receptionist, "what can I do for you?"

"We're here to see Amanda Palmer," Crawford said.

"Oh, sorry, Amanda went out of town on business," she said.

A frown tightened Crawford's face. "When?"

"Just this morning."

"Where was she going?" he asked.

"I'm not sure," the receptionist said. "Her executive assistant would know."

"We'd like to see her right away," Crawford said.

"Sure, and your names?"

"Detectives Crawford and Ott. We've met her before."

A few minutes later, they stood by the glassed-in cubicle of the twenty-something woman named Kit, who they'd spoken to last time they were there.

"She told me she's been negotiating since last week to buy a club up in New York," she told Crawford and Ott. "And last night they apparently reached a deal."

"So, she flew up there this morning?" Crawford asked.

"Yes."

"What airline?" Ott asked.

"Air Bartow," Kit said, with a smile. "Her boyfriend Ted's jet."

Someone had once told Crawford that one out of every sixty-eight people in Palm Beach had a private jet, so why not Ted Bartow?

"Flying into JFK or LaGuardia?" Crawford asked.

Kit shrugged. "I'm not sure about that."

Time to bear down. "Ms. Williams, this is an urgent matter.

Would there be paperwork or something in Ms. Palmer's office?" Then to Ott. "Give Signature a call, see what you can find out." Signature was the airport for private jets, located adjacent to PBI, the airport in West Palm Beach.

"Sure," Kit, standing up. "We can go have a look there if you want."

"Yes, please," Crawford said, following Kit out of her cubicle. Ott was already on the line with someone.

They walked into Amanda Palmer's office, which looked like a messy lawyer's office. There were piles of paperwork everywhere, particularly on Amanda's stand-up desk.

"Sorry, kind of a mess," Kit said, walking behind the stand-up desk.

The first thing Crawford saw was a brochure titled *The Beaches of Croatia*. Then another that said *The Dalmatian Coast*.

Ott said thank you and clicked off the call. "Ted Bartow's Citation Ten was going to Newark, not JFK or LaGuardia."

"Why would—"

Ott shrugged. "It was scheduled to land about a half hour ago."

Crawford looked back down at Amanda Palmer's stand-up desk and spotted another brochure: *Zagreb, Dubrovnik, and Split*.

He turned to Kit. "Do you know if Ms. Palmer has a travel agent?"

"Yes, a woman at Sienna Charles on Worth Avenue."

Crawford wasn't familiar with it. Ott was already looking up the number.

"Had Ms. Palmer mentioned anything to you about taking a trip? Specifically, to Croatia?"

"She told me a couple of times recently that she was feeling kind of burned out. Then came her sister's murder..." She shrugged.

Crawford nodded and looked over at Ott, who was talking on the phone again. "Anything?"

Ott held up his hand as he listened. "Great, thank you very

much," he clicked off. "She's on a flight to Zagreb tonight. Newark to Zagreb."

"What time?"

"Nine-thirty."

Crawford looked at his watch. It was 1:05 p.m. "Call 'em back and book me on the next flight to Newark."

TWENTY-TWO

I<small>T WAS TWO HOURS AND FORTY MINUTES FROM</small> PBI <small>TO</small> N<small>EWARK</small>, and the earliest flight that the travel agent at Sienna Charles could get Crawford on left at 4:30. Which meant he'd get in at 7:10. That gave him two hours and twenty minutes to track down Amanda Palmer at EWR/Newark.

Piece of cake.

Except, as Crawford found out, the New York weather was sketchy. He read on his phone: *Torrential downpours. One- to two-inch accumulation over a six-hour period.*

Maybe not such a piece of cake.

Crawford thought about Ott coming with him, but figured that Ott's time was better spent on Thorsen Paul, which they had temporarily detoured away from with the recent developments on the Amanda Palmer murder.

On Crawford and Ott's ride back from The Max, Crawford had called Ted Bartow and left a voicemail asking him to call as soon as possible. On the way to the airport, Crawford got two calls. The first was from Bob Hawes, the Medical Examiner.

"Hey, Charlie, you're never gonna believe it?" Hawes was amped up.

"What?"

"When I autopsied Adriana Palmer, turns out her fingerprints—"

"Let me guess, weren't hers?"

"How the hell—"

"Tell you later." Crawford hung up. Good old better-late-than-never Hawes.

His phone rang again. Caller ID said Ted Bartow.

"Hello."

"Hi, Detective, Ted Bartow, you called me?"

"Yes, thanks for getting back to me. Ad—" he almost said Adriana — "Amanda Palmer took your plane up to Newark. What can you tell me about what she's doing up there?"

"She and I are buying a health club."

"Oh, really, and what's the name of it?"

Pause. "Ah, I'm sure she must have told me but...I don't remember."

"You said 'we,' meaning your money and hers?"

"Why do you need to know the financial details, Detective?"

"It's all part of my investigation of Adriana's murder."

"Okay, well, I gave her a cashier's check for a million dollars and she was going to make one out for the same amount."

"So, the health club cost two million dollars?"

"Yes."

"So, you'd, what, own it fifty-fifty?"

"Exactly."

"And, I'm just guessing, but your cashier's check was made out in her name?"

"Yes, she then endorses it and hands it over to the owner of the health club."

"But you don't remember the name of the club or its owner?"

"No, she just told me it's on Madison Avenue somewhere."

Crawford wondered if, while Ted Bartow had his checkbook out, he might also be interested in buying the bridge that connects Manhattan to Brooklyn.

He hung up, called Ott, and filled him in.

He could almost see Ott shaking his head in disbelief.

"I always had the sense there's a shitload of 'stupid money' in Palm Beach," Ott said. "Especially among the members of the lucky-sperm club."

"Maybe just gullible people."

"No," Ott said emphatically, "stupid people."

"I need you to check out a few things," Crawford said. "Call Kit the assistant at The Max and find out where Adriana's bank accounts are. Then, you might need to get a judge to okay it, but find out if she cleaned them all out last night or this morning."

"Okay, I'm on it. What else?"

"See if you can find out if Adriana had a nice, fat insurance policy with her sister as beneficiary. It's been eight days since her 'alleged' death. Some insurance companies, if you really stay on top of 'em, can get a check out pretty fast."

"That fast? You sure about that?"

"Yeah, I remember my aunt got one in just over a week."

"Okay, anything else?"

"Yeah, I seem to remember that there's no reciprocity between the U.S. and Croatia. Can you check that out?"

"Oh, shit, meaning we can't haul her ass back here if you miss her in Newark?"

"Afraid not."

"Fuck."

CRAWFORD HAD A CHATTERBOX NEXT TO HIM ON THE FLIGHT UP to Newark. The flight left late—5:05 to be precise. He decided it was probably better to have someone talk his ear off rather than be checking his watch every two minutes and worrying about not arriving in time to arrest Adriana Palmer.

The woman in the seat next to him told him in excruciating detail about the lives of her four children, from basically the womb to the present day. The only one who seemed vaguely interesting was her forty-year-old son who was a roadie for either Iron Maiden or Iron Butterfly. She wasn't sure which, only that they were on a tour at the moment and flew to each venue in their own "private metal."

Crawford looked at his watch at 7:25 and got the distinct sense that the JetBlue flight was circling. Ten minutes later he was sure of it. He even thought he was beginning to recognize the clouds as the plane went around and around. He looked at his watch again—7:45. What he had thought earlier was going to be a cake-walk was now clearly going to be a tight squeeze.

***

MORT OTT SPENT THE LATTER PART OF THE AFTERNOON convincing a judge to let him gain access to Adriana Palmer's bank accounts, then going to Wells Fargo on South County Road, followed by several conversations with a life insurance company. He put in a call at 7:50 to Crawford. The call went to voicemail, which told Ott that Crawford was still in the air; otherwise, he was certain, his partner would have picked up. Ott left a message to call him. The information he'd collected was too much to leave in a voicemail.

Next, Ott took a drive up to Gonzalo Gaetano's house on Debra Lane. This time, though, Gaetano's black Audi was nowhere in sight. Ott checked behind the hedge, but it wasn't there. He walked up to the garage. The door had a long, narrow glass window at eye level. He looked through and saw the Audi and its interlocking-G hood ornament. At first, he couldn't place where he had seen the G's before, then he remembered the belt a girlfriend in Cleveland had once given him.

He hit the buzzer again. "Come on, Gonzalo, I know you're in there."

After a few more moments, the door opened.

"Detective," Gaetano said.

"Gonzalo," Ott said. "Hey, I like those Gucci G's on your car."

"I came up with it first."

"Really? I had the impression Gucci's been around a while."

Gaetano shrugged. "So, why did you want to see me, Detective?"

Ott shook his head. "You know damn well. You're holding out on us. You're not telling us everything you know about Rafaela Arroyo and Thorsen Paul's murder. Let me be more specific: My partner and I think your Mexican friends killed Paul."

Gaetano frowned. "They're not my friends and you have no proof of that."

"No, but there's a hell of a lot of circumstantial evidence."

"What's that?"

"It means a prosecutor would take on the case based on certain known facts," Ott bluffed. "And you know what, Gonzalo? You'd likely be named an accessory."

"I don't even know what that means."

"Meaning you would be implicated in the death of Thorsen Paul."

"That's crazy, I never—"

"On the other hand, if you cooperated with us, you might never be charged. You understand what I'm saying now, right?"

Gaetano nodded as Ott's phone rang. Ott took the phone out of his pocket and looked at the display.

Crawford.

He glanced at Gaetano. "Hold on, gotta take this."

Ott punched the green button and walked into the foyer. "Hey, man, do I have some intel for you. For starters, Adriana cleaned out her checking and savings account at Wells Fargo at nine o'clock this morning."

"How much?"

"Two-point-seven million. It included a CD, which she took an early-withdrawal penalty on. But here's the big news: she got a big life insurance check just before five today. Guess where from?"

"You tell me."

"Prudential. Their headquarters is in Newark," Ott said, looking at his watch. It was 8:25. "Where are you now?"

"Getting ready to get off the plane," Crawford said. "It's gonna be tight. I never had a chance to call Newark police or the TSA. Do that for me, will you? Tell 'em I'm going to be making an arrest. Tell 'em to try to hold the plane if I'm not there in time. Plane to Croatia takes off at gate sixty-two."

"You got it," Ott said, lowering his voice. "I'm at Gaetano's house. Trying to turn up the heat."

"How's it going?"

"He's looking hot again."

"Good. Scare the shit out of him."

"I'm on it. I'll call the airport cops and TSA now. Alert 'em to what's goin' on. Good luck, man. Looks like you're gonna have to run through the airport like O.J."

TWENTY-THREE

CRAWFORD HAD ASKED THE FLIGHT ATTENDANT IF SHE COULD seat him as far forward in the plane as possible, explaining that he was a detective on a homicide case and needed to exit the plane quickly. That's why he'd ended up in the second row of first class, right next to the blabbermouth, who'd finally run out of family members to blather about.

When they opened the plane door, Crawford got ready to bolt.

"So nice talking to you," said the woman next to him. "Hope we run across each other again."

"Yeah, me, too," Crawford said, thinking, *Highly unlikely, thank God, since I'm probably never flying first class again.*

He glanced down at his watch for the seventeenth time.

9:15.

Once out of the jet, he hurried down the gangway to the terminal, where he ducked past the couple in front of him and started running.

A quick glance in the terminal around him showed that his JetBlue flight had taxied to Gate 2. The good news was, Adriana's flight was departing from the same terminal. The bad news was,

Flight 605 to Dubrovnik left from gate 62. He really was going to have to do an O.J.

So, he did. Fortunately, he wasn't wearing clunky shoes; although his new Sperry Billfish slip-ons weren't exactly Nikes, they got the job done. After two minutes of dodging people and suitcases, he saw gate 62 ahead. He also saw two cops at the gate and what looked like the last of a line leading into the jetway to board the Lufthansa plane.

"Charlie Crawford, Palm Beach homicide!" he shouted, out of breath, to the cops. "You guys waiting for me?"

They turned to him. "Yeah, hey, you made it," said one with short hair and bushy eyebrows walking toward him.

Crawford stuck out his hand. "Thanks for showing up," he said, shaking their hands, then turning to the woman at the desk and flashing his ID. "We need to get on the plane. I have a warrant for the arrest of one of your passengers."

The woman frowned. "Really?"

"Yes, her name's Amanda Palmer," Crawford said.

The desk agent looked down at her manifest. "First class. 3A."

"Thank you," Crawford said, heading toward the jetway.

The desk agent and two cops walked in with him. "I hope this won't be too disruptive," the desk agent said to Crawford.

Like a shoot-out, you mean? "Me, too," he said.

The desk agent stopped and let Crawford and the two cops go ahead without her.

"What did she do?" the other cop asked.

"Killed her twin sister," Crawford said.

"That's pretty hardcore," the cop said.

At the jet's hatch, two flight attendants greeting passengers looked surprised to see two men in blue. Crawford took out his ID and showed it to them. "Detective Crawford. I have an arrest warrant for your passenger in first class seat 3A."

He and the two airport cops brushed past the flight attendants and began scanning passengers and seats. Sure enough, there the suspect was, calmly taking a sip of white wine. She looked up and—spite in her eyes—recognized Crawford. "What the—"

"Adriana Palmer, I have an arrest warrant for you. Charge is the murder of your sister Amanda Palmer. Please stand up. We need to escort you off the plane."

Adriana put the wine glass down. "First of all, *I am* Amanda Palmer. Very much alive, as you can see. Second of all—"

"No, you're not." Crawford had pulled two sheets of paper out of his jacket pocket. "These are blow-ups of your driver's license and your sister's, both renewed earlier this year. You have a scar on your neck, your sister does not."

Adriana started shaking her head. "How dare you come crashing onto—"

"Miss Palmer, please stand up. We're escorting you off the plane."

She stared at the airport cops. "Are you in on this too?'

One of the cops nodded. "He's got a warrant for your arrest. Do what he says and—"

"Wait," Adriana muttered under her breath. "I'll give each of you fifty thousand dollars to leave. I have it on me. In cash." She reached for a black leather bag at her feet.

Crawford eyed the cops in disbelief. He pulled out his handcuffs. "You're giving me no other choice but to lift you out of that seat and put these on you."

Adriana leaned closer. "A hundred thousand?"

Crawford reached down with one of the cuffs, slipped it around her wrist and snapped it. "Get up."

She stood, finally, then spat in his face. "Bastard."

TWENTY-FOUR

THERE WERE NO FLIGHTS TO PALM BEACH UNTIL 7:04 THE NEXT
morning. Protocol was that Crawford should take Adriana Palmer to
a Newark jail and get her to spend the night behind bars, but that
was too complicated. So, Crawford simply booked a room at the
airport Holiday Inn. The desk clerk did a double take when she saw
the couple approaching bound by handcuffs, like maybe they were
dipping their toes into early-stage bondage and discipline.

Her suspicions seemed to be confirmed when Crawford asked
her if the beds had metal bed frames. "Ah, yes, the singles do,"
she said.

"Perfect," Crawford said. "We need one bedroom with two single
beds."

"SHE'S RIGHT HERE IN THE NEXT BED," CRAWFORD SAID INTO
his iPhone to Ott. He'd made the call from the bathroom. "If I don't
make it back to Palm Beach, it's because she offered me two hundred
grand and told me how great the beaches are on the Dalmatian Coast.

Showed me pix on her phone, I gotta tell you, man, they look pretty cool."

"Get another two-hundred K out of her and I'll meet you there," Ott said.

"Beats workin'."

Ott laughed. "So, what time's your plane get in?"

"Nine fifty-eight a.m. So, I'll be at the station around ten-thirty."

"She'll have a cell right next to Dumb and Dumber."

"Her partners in crime."

"Yeah, they can hatch new plots together."

"You mean, for when she gets out in fifty years."

"Exactly," Ott said. "Okay, man, mañana."

Crawford clicked off and walked out into the bedroom.

He did a double-take when he saw Adriana. She had one arm handcuffed to the metal headboard and was lying on the bed completely naked, a suggestive smile on her face. "Three hundred thousand, the beaches of Croatia and...me."

Crawford was impressed she could strip naked with one hand. "Please, get under the covers, will you?"

She didn't move. "I'm really good."

He went over to the closet and found a blue blanket on the shelf. He took it down and covered her with it.

She reached down with her spare hand and pulled it off. "Really good," she said again.

"I'm sure," Crawford said. "But spitting in my face wasn't the greatest foreplay."

TWENTY-FIVE

CRAWFORD GOT A WAKE-UP CALL AT 5:45. HE WAS UNDER THE covers, fully dressed. He glanced over at Adriana, who hadn't woken up yet.

Four hours later they were on their descent into PBI.

And an hour after that, she was in a cell in the basement of the police station at South County Road, and Ott was in Crawford's office, briefing him on his conversation with Gonzalo Gaetano the day before. "I basically said that either he cooperates with us, or gets named as an accessory in Thorsen Paul's murder."

"And he bought it?"

"Yeah, I think he did," Ott said. "I could see the cogs turning in his head. But I'm sure he was also thinking about not getting on the wrong side of Z5."

Crawford nodded and thought for a few seconds. "Been thinking about what you said a while back."

"What was that?"

"About luring Rafaela Arroyo up here. Making her think there's a pile of money in a Thorsen Paul bank account here. Then trying to sell it to Rutledge."

"Yeah, and what did you come up with?"

"That instead of it being in a Thorsen Paul account, he squirreled it away in someone else's."

"You still thinking his father's? Or what about the girlfriend, Carter?"

"They're both logical. But it would put 'em in Arroyo's crosshairs."

Ott nodded, and they fell silent once more.

"What about Thorsen's brother?" Crawford asked.

"Didn't know he had one."

Crawford smiled. "You're lookin' at him."

ANOTHER ISSUE WAS HOW *NOT* TO PUT GONZALO GAETANO'S life in jeopardy. Because it definitely would be, if Gaetano contacted Alejandro Castillo and told him he'd learned that Thorsen Paul secretly gave his brother a large amount of money for safekeeping—then it turned out to be a lie. Because whether Crawford and Ott busted Rafaela Arroyo or any cartel members in the operation, Z5 would ultimately be looking for revenge. And even if their leader ended up dead or behind bars in the most secure jail in the world, it wouldn't be long before a Z5 member with a gun or a machete showed up on Gaetano's doorstep. To say nothing of his family's in Mexico.

Crawford and Ott debated it a long time and ultimately concluded their concerns were legit: a successful trap would also be a death sentence for Gaetano, at least if he were thought to be the source of the bogus story.

Finally, Ott thought he had a workable idea. "What if we call up this guy Alejandro Castillo. Tell him we were NextRed investors and we know there's a lot of Paul's money in an account somewhere."

"Good concept but flawed."

"How so?"

"So, you're saying we call Castillo and tell him we heard Paul had 'clients' who might be able to track down this NextRed money? First of all, how did we hear about him in the first place? And, second, how'd we know how to get to Castillo?"

"Details."

Crawford thought for a moment. "Let me try this out on you. You're the ex-CFO of NextRed—"

"What's that stand for?"

"Chief Financial Officer."

"Okay."

"And you know about Castillo because one of your jobs as CFO at NextRed was to know who all the investors were. You tell Castillo you have reason to believe Thorsen Paul's brother has, pick a number...fifty million squirreled away."

Ott beamed. "I like it."

"Inspired by your idea," Crawford said, pointing at himself. "Then Z5 comes after me. The fictitious brother."

"That's the part I don't like so much."

"Yeah, well, if we control it, I'll be all right."

"But how are we gonna do that?"

"Details," Crawford said. "I also have a strong feeling they'd only send out one or two hitters."

"Why?"

"They show up in big numbers, they'd be easier to spot. Too visible."

"I buy that," Ott said. "So, Mr. Fictitious Brother, what's your name gonna be? John, Bob, Bill—"

"Nah, parents who name a son Thorsen aren't gonna name another one John, Bob, or Bill."

"I see what you mean...Seymour?"

"No, that's lame."

"Archibald?"

"Too old-fashioned."

"Barnaby?"

Crawford shook his head. "I'm thinking...Weston."

Ott nodded. "Yeah, that's got a nice ring to it."

"Plus, it goes with Thorsen."

"Okay, we got your name. What's mine? The CFO?"

"We have to use the real name of the NextRed CFO. Otherwise, they'll already know. Should be easy enough to find out what his name is."

Ott shook his head slowly.

"What?"

He sighed. "I still got a big concern: the guys with chainsaws who'll come after you."

Crawford smiled. "Thank you, Mort, I appreciate your concern. I just need to go to Home Depot, get my own. Make it a fair fight."

TWENTY-SIX

IN CRAWFORD'S FIRST PALM BEACH CASE A FEW YEARS BACK, HE had enlisted the help of Dominica McCarthy, crime-scene tech extraordinaire, to bring down a nasty piece of work named Ward Jaynes. It had turned out to be seriously dangerous, and put Dominica in a vulnerable position in which her life was almost, but not quite, at stake. Turned out, though, she liked it. Liked the risk and danger, so much so that she'd made Crawford promise to include her if he ever needed help again.

And, as it turned out, he did need her again. It turned out the CFO of Thorsen Paul's company had been a woman named Valerie Rosen. They tried to locate her and spoke to her ex-husband, a few of her friends and several colleagues from NextRed, but nobody knew where she was. One friend said she took the blow-up of NextRed really hard and had moved to Hawaii. Another one said Australia. Someone else said she joined a cult God-knows-where.

This time, though, Crawford didn't plan to spring it on Dominica the way he had before. Back then, he'd taken her out to an elaborate dinner, plied her with three glasses of wine, then sprung it. This time, he'd simply say he had a possible job for her that he'd like to discuss at dinner, and was she interested? He was pretty sure he knew what the answer would be.

So, he called her, said he had a police-business proposition, and was she free to discuss it at dinner? Clearly intrigued, Dominica said sure, so he picked her up at her apartment in West Palm and drove her to a place famous for soft-shell crab. Their plates had just arrived, and the waiter had poured them another glass of pinot grigio.

Crawford looked down at his plate approvingly. "Perfect," he said. "Crisp and golden."

"My father used to take us to Joe's in Miami to get these." Dominica had grown up in Miami. "When I was young, I liked 'em even better than stuff at Dairy Queen or Steak 'n' Shake, which is saying something."

Crawford shook his head. "I dunno, a steak shooter 'n' fries? Pretty hard to beat that." He prepared to dig into a crab. "Do you know the lifecycle of one of these bad boys?"

"No, do tell."

"Okay, so they're basically blue crabs that have gotten too big for their shells. And in order to keep on growing, they shed their shell and make way for bigger ones. I saw this video once on the whole process."

"What a thrilling life you lead," Dominica said. "Keep going, I'm on the edge of my seat."

"Wiseass," Crawford laughed. "Well, basically, they molt."

"Molt? What's that again?"

"You never heard of molting?"

"I've heard but I forget."

"Okay, let me educate you, my child."

Crawford had his iPhone out and was googling *molt*. "Okay, here you go. 'Of or pertaining to an animal shedding old feathers, hair, or skin, or an old shell, to make way for a new growth.'"

"Oh, so like what birds do?'

Crawford nodded. "Exactly. Cats, snakes, birds, chickens, you name it."

"Cats molt?"

Crawford scrunched up his eyes. "Sure they do, but back to crabs: So, in order to shed its shell, the crab forms a soft shell underneath, swells its body with water to break the old shell, then crawls out. That takes about ten minutes, then it goes through the process of forming a new shell. Which can take a couple of days."

Dominica clapped her hands. "Wow, I'm impressed."

Crawford held up a hand. "Wait, there's more. One thing you never want to do is boil a soft-shell crab."

"Why?"

"'Cause it'll just kind of fall apart."

"Okay, good to know," Dominica said. "Is it okay if we eat now before these molted crabs get cold?"

FINALLY, CRAWFORD DECLARED HIMSELF OFFICIALLY STUFFED. He had finished spelling out the role he had for Dominica. Her quick answer?

"In a heartbeat. But I've never been a CFO before," she said. "What's the job description?"

"Not totally sure," Crawford said. "Just know it stands for Chief Financial Officer. So, I'm assuming it has to do with money."

"Makes sense."

"And NextRed was a company that turned into a Ponzi scheme."

"But it started out legit, right?"

"Yeah, apparently. But the company couldn't deliver on its promises. The product didn't do what it was supposed to do. So, they had to start making things up. Then along came a zealous investigative journalist, blew the whole thing out of the water."

"Zealous, huh?"

"Yeah, hang around me long enough and you'll have a big vocabulary."

"I'd like to...hang around you."

"But we digress. So, you think you can handle the role?"

"Sure," Dominica said. "All I have to do is call up that guy Castillo, tell him I know where Thorsen Paul stowed away fifty million, and say I want a hundred K to tell him where it is."

"Exactly. Then what?"

"Then, assuming he agrees to it, which we know he will, I tell him I want the money up front. Then when I get it, I tell him all about Weston Paul a.k.a. Charlie Crawford."

"You're a quick study."

"It's not that complicated."

"Just one little tweak," Crawford said. "Let's make it fifty-three million instead of fifty. Fifty's too round a number; fifty-three sounds better."

Dominica shrugged. "Hey, what's another three million among friends?"

A SONG CAME ON THE RADIO AS CRAWFORD DROVE DOMINICA home. It was that one about loving the one you're with, which had always struck Crawford as being good, solid, practical advice. The problem was the "deal" he had with Dominica and Rose. It was making the whole 'love the one you're with' concept unworkable.

He wanted to void the unsigned deal and turn the clock back two months.

He pulled up to her building but, instead of driving up to the porte-cochere to drop her off, Crawford drove to a dimly-lit parking space.

"What are you doing?" Like she didn't know.

He leaned into her and gave her the best kiss he could muster. A world-class performance, in his humble opinion.

Dominica came up for air, looked him in the eyes, and smiled. "That was very nice, Charlie, but I gotta go."

"But—"

"You know the deal," she said putting a finger up to his lips. "It was that song, wasn't it?"

"What song?"

"You know damn well."

Crawford played dumb. "I don't know what you're—"

Dominica shook her head and smiled. "Who do you think you're dealing with here? You don't think I know you cold by now?"

Busted.

He smiled sheepishly. "Well, you gotta admit, it is a pretty good song."

TWENTY-SEVEN

After getting Dominica on board, the next step was to get a house for "Weston Paul." So, who else to talk to but Palm Beach's premier real estate agent Rose Clarke? When Crawford called the next morning and asked if he could stop by, Rose said she was showing but would be free at two o'clock. So, Crawford dropped by at a little past two.

Rose had her own office at the real estate firm, unlike the vast majority of her colleagues, who inhabited cubicles in the office's central open space. She met Crawford at the reception area.

"Welcome to my world," she said, and gave Crawford a peck on the lips. An honor, he knew, as most of her other customers and friends only got cheek smacks. "So, what exactly are you looking for? I've got a house on the ocean whose owners just reduced the price by a million dollars. Or maybe a nice fixer-upper on Barton for a mere three point five. Whatever your little heart desires, Charlie."

"How 'bout something on the ocean for three hundred thousand?"

Rose laughed. "Fifty years ago, maybe."

They sat in Rose's office and she closed her door.

"I've got kind of an odd request," Crawford said.

"Okay. Request away."

Crawford rubbed his forehead. "Do you know anyone who wants to rent their house for a week...for free?"

Rose chuckled. "Oh, yeah, they're lined up around the block."

"I know, not something people are gonna jump at, but what if you told them it was a public service? For the good of Palm Beach and all its citizens? And, trust me, it really would be."

"I do trust you, but can you give me a few details? I mean, this is going to be a tough sell."

"Yeah, I'm sure," Crawford said, glancing at a diploma on the wall. "What if you told them that it's to assist the Palm Beach Police in a high-level sting operation?"

Rose smiled. "Hmm, I might be able to work with that."

"You could tell the owner they might end up getting a special commendation from the mayor, or something. Hell, maybe even a key to the city."

Rose was nodding. "You know, I have a friend, lives in California, who's hoping to get a variance to add a second-story deck to the back of his house. He could probably use a friend or two in high places. When do you need it?"

"Um, tomorrow."

"Jesus, Charlie, how about a little notice?"

"Okay, I guess the day after would be okay."

"How accommodating of you."

Crawford smiled but didn't say anything.

"What?"

"Would you mind giving him a call now?"

"I THINK I MIGHT HAVE GOTTEN A LITTLE AHEAD OF MYSELF," Crawford said.

Ott sat across from Crawford in Crawford's office. "What do you mean?"

"Well, we got Dominica, stepping into the shoes of Valerie Rosen, all lined up. And there's a good chance we got a house for our guy Weston Paul to live in. Problem is, we haven't run any of this by Norm."

"So? We've gone down the rogue highway before."

"Yeah, but not to lure a bunch of Mexican killers into our fair city."

"You thinkin' Norm might have a problem with that?"

Crawford laughed. "Ah, yeah. If I was in his shoes, I sure as hell would. It's all about how we sell it."

They agreed they had to get Rutledge in the loop. Their fear was that if they did go rogue—and, in fact, they had already started the process—and the whole thing either blew up or the case was never solved, Rutledge would have grounds for some kind of disciplinary action. Not that he'd necessarily take action, but he could. And, the truth was, Ott and Crawford liked what they did. What would they do if they lost their jobs? It was a little late in life to become brain surgeons.

They didn't discuss it, but they also wanted to preserve their perfect records of solving Palm Beach murders. Crawford had had a 77 percent clearance in New York, and while that was considerably higher than the average detective in the Big Apple, it was a long way from perfect. He looked at his vocation in terms of a grade. 77 percent was a C, not even a C+. He'd been a B student at Dartmouth, which was fine, but he had every intention of maintaining his A+ in Palm Beach.

Crawford called Rutledge and said they needed to see him.

"When?" asked Rutledge.

As the former *Penthouse* pet Jocelyn Picard had said, "No time like the present."

They walked into Rutledge's office to find him wearing his favorite brown Dacron suit again. He picked his nose with impunity while listening to Crawford explain how he planned to play "Weston Paul" in a house that "a real estate agent friend" would make available.

"Jesus, Crawford, do you have any idea what you're talking about here? Any fuckin' idea at all? I mean, I looked into these guys, Zamora Chinko—"

"Cinco," Ott corrected him.

"Whatever, they're a brutal outfit. They got about twenty different ways to kill people, one worse than the next."

"We'd be doing this with tight controls," Ott said.

"What the hell's that s'posed to mean?"

Ott looked at Crawford for backup. "We got a whole game plan, which we'd like to lay out for you," Crawford said. "If you can make it better, have at it."

Get him vested in the plan, Crawford figured, like they needed him to flesh it out.

"I'll listen, but I'm tellin' you, you got an uphill battle."

Crawford spent the next twenty minutes walking Rutledge through the plan. Complete with the fifty-three million dollars stashed in a fictitious account of the fictitious Weston Paul. Then he stopped and waited for the Rutledge's response.

"So, you're gonna be holed up in some house, posing as this guy Chilton whoever—"

"You're not so hot with names," Ott said. "It's Weston."

"Okay, Weston. So, how you gonna get the house, again? It's not like we have five million in the budget to buy one."

"Like I said, I spoke to a friend who's a real estate agent," Crawford said. "She might have one for us to borrow. Won't have to spend a dime on it."

"The owner okay with having a bunch of bullet holes in it?"

Crawford rolled his eyes. "Owner lives in California, never uses it, and is a good friend of the agent."

"Let me guess. The agent wouldn't happen to be Rose Clarke, would it?"

"It would be," Crawford said.

Rutledge shook his head and smiled. "Must be nice to have so many girlfriends, Crawford."

Crawford ignored him. "She told the owner he'd be performing a public service that'd be good for the community."

"Well, that's true," Rutledge said, cocking his head. "And the guy didn't ask any questions?"

"He did, actually. But Rose said it was top secret and she couldn't go into it in detail, only that it was a 'sting operation.'"

"Well, that's true, too," Rutledge said, pointing at Crawford. "So, you get to live your lifelong dream, huh?"

"And what would that be, Norm?"

"Living in Palm Beach."

Crawford laughed. "Nah, I'm pretty happy with my little hovel."

Rutledge leaned back in his Naugahyde chair, put his hands together behind his head, and seemed to be weighing it.

Crawford glanced at Ott, thinking he'd actually sold Rutledge the plan.

Finally, "I'm not likin' one fuckin' thing about this whole plan," Rutledge said, spittle in one corner of his mouth. "A posse of desperados come riding into town, strapped and ready to torture and maim the locals. Have you read about these mutts, Crawford? Seen any photos of what they do to their vics?"

Crawford had, and Rutledge was right, it wasn't pretty. He glanced over at Ott, who seemed uncharacteristically speechless.

"Look, here's the main thing," Crawford said. "It'd be a whole lot better operating on our turf than theirs. And that's the only other alternative. Going down there and wandering around in the desert trying to track down this...'posse of desperados'."

Rutledge shook his head and threw up his hands. "No way in hell we're giving them any reason to come here."

It was Ott's turn. "First of all, Norm, they've already been here. You remember the guy they buried on the beach? Peanut butter on his eyes? Fish bait?"

"Okay, Ott, I know what happened," Rutledge said.

"I'm just—"

Rutledge put up his hands again. "Got it."

Crawford wasn't giving up yet. "So you're saying—"

"Let me say it loud and clear: No more fuckin' Mexican murderers in my town. End of discussion."

Crawford shrugged and glanced at Ott. "Okay, I guess that means the case is dead?"

Rutledge tapped his desk and smiled his wise-old-lawman smile. "No, it doesn't. What it means is, it's time for another away game. You had to go up to Charleston to wrap up that case last year. Hell, man, you just got back from nailing Amanda Palmer in New York."

"Adriana."

"Okay, Adriana. So, I'd say you boys do some of your best work on the road."

Crawford eyed Ott again. "What do you think, Mort?"

"For starters, I think Mexico is a hell of a lot bigger place than Charleston, South Carolina."

"More dangerous, too," Crawford said.

"No shit," Ott chuckled. "I think I'll stay home."

Something started rattling around in Crawford's brain. It needed fleshing out but had promise. He turned to Rutledge. "Actually, I wouldn't mind giving it a shot."

Ott swung around. "You outta your fuckin' mind? You want to end up like Thorsen Paul? I mean, how do you think we're gonna find this Amazon killer when the whole Mexican army can't?"

"Ever think they might be paid *not* to find her."

Rutledge's eyes were going back and forth from Crawford to Ott like he was watching a tennis match.

"I don't know, Charlie, I think you're crazy," Ott said, "but 'cause your instincts are normally good, I'll think about it."

Crawford smiled. "I'm not going without you."

Ott smiled and glanced over at Rutledge. "How 'bout we make a deal, Norm?"

"What the hell you talkin' about?"

"If we go after Thorsen Paul's killer in Mexico, the town of Palm Beach springs for a one-week fishing trip to Cabo San Lucas for me and Chuck. We haven't had a vacation in a year and a half."

"Twenty months, but who's counting?" said Crawford.

Rutledge shook his head. "I can't authorize that."

Ott shrugged. "Why not? Who's gonna stop you? I can see the headline now: "Chief Rutledge Authorizes Major Cartel Bust.""

Rutledge thought for a moment. "Gonna need to run it by the mayor."

"The mayor?" Crawford frowned. "What the hell's she got to do with this?"

"To authorize the fishing trip."

"Come on, Norm," Ott said. "You can authorize it. We'd be right around the corner from Cabo already."

"Yeah, stone's throw away," Crawford chimed in.

Rutledge had his computer out and was scrolling down. He looked up. "You're so full of shit. It's over eleven hundred miles from Mexico City to Cabo San Lucas."

Ott looked hurt. "You don't need to say we're full of shit. Maybe just...geography-challenged."

"It's just a two-hour flight," Crawford said. "Like West Palm to New York."

"Speaking of the mayor," Ott said, "how many times a day do you hear from her, bugging you to get this case wrapped up? Three, four times?"

"More," Rutledge said.

"And Bowen?" Ken Bowen was the town manager.

"Couple times."

"And that woman at the Chamber of Commerce?"

"All right, all right, you made your point."

"Point is, a little fishing trip is a small price to pay to get those people off your back and the—" Ott did the finger quote—"*desperados* dead or in jail."

Rutledge shook his head, looked out his window, then turned back to them. "All right, you got your fishing trip, after you go reel in the Mexicans."

"Nice play on words," Ott said.

"Okay, get out of here," Rutledge said. "I'll have Vera take care of the tickets and hotel. Better go get packing."

"Don't cheap out on us, Norm," Crawford said. "We want nice hotel rooms."

Ott smiled. "Yeah, no *cucarachas*."

TWENTY-EIGHT

CRAWFORD AND OTT WALKED INTO CRAWFORD'S OFFICE. OTT plunked himself down in his chair as his partner closed the door, something he rarely did.

"Are you losing it, man?" Ott said. "It's tough to go fishing if you're dead."

Crawford leaned across his desk. "I had a brainstorm in there."

"Trying to catch a cartel boss in Mexico?" Ott rolled his eyes. "Seemed more like a brain fart."

"No, no, listen," Crawford said. "You're right, no way in hell could we ever take down Rafaela Arroyo in her own country. No way. I doubt we'd be authorized to make an arrest there. We got no jurisdiction and we'd never be able to act independently of the Mexican cops. With them, yeah, maybe a tiny chance; on our own, never gonna happen"

Ott threw up his hands in surprise. "Okay, so why are we going?"

"Breadcrumbs, my friend, Hansel and Gretel."

"What the hell?"

Crawford pushed back in his chair. "Tell you on the flight down. We gotta get packed."

CRAWFORD AND OTT HAD A RESERVATION THE NEXT DAY TO Mexico City. It made one stop—in Detroit—which struck Crawford as anything but a direct route. But, surprise, surprise, Vera had put them in first class. "Nothing but the best for my detectives," she said when Crawford thanked her.

"I was going to book you guys into the Four Seasons but thought Norm might have a problem with how much it cost," Vera said. "So, I got you into the Presidente InterContinental. Obama stayed there, so I guess it's pretty good."

"So, it's just for *presidentes*?" Ott asked.

"Yeah, apparently they're making an exception."

Before they left, Crawford had to break the news to Dominica McCarthy that she wasn't going to get the chance to play CFO of NextRed. She was surprisingly disappointed, and made him promise that she'd get to play a supporting role in some future op.

In the hours before they caught their plane, they did as much prep work as they could squeeze in. Thus far, they had set up two meetings in Mexico City. The first was with two detectives in the Mexico City Police Department, who were part of an elite anti-drug, anti-gang taskforce. The second meeting was with two DEA agents who had extensive dealings with Zamora Cinco, and were intimately familiar with its leader Rafaela Arroyo. Crawford also hoped to squeeze in some face-time with an FBI agent stationed in Mexico City. And most importantly, he wanted to meet with Mexican police in Rafaela Arroyo's backyard, to subtly leak the story about Weston Paul ending up with fifty-three million dollars from his brother's company.

They had read reams and reams of newspaper articles and watched innumerable YouTube videos. While drug trafficking and murder had been part of Mexican people's lives for many years, its impact was no less toxic in many parts of America. Chicago, known to some as Murder City, was a leading center for drug distribution and a place where gangs were deeply entrenched. Its scourge had also been felt in Miami and many other American cities for decades.

The numbers Crawford read were staggering—since Mexico's militarized war on drugs was launched in December of 2006, more than two-hundred-thousand Mexicans had been killed and thirty thousand had gone missing and were presumed dead. Violence reached record levels in 2017 with 29,168 homicides. Despite the war on drugs and gangs, the numbers were going up, not down.

"You know what I read," Ott said, sipping a scotch in seat 4A next to Crawford. "How private planes would fly into Tijuana from Guatemala, and right there at the airport was this tunnel that went underground across the border to this place called Otay Mesa—"

"Yeah, south of San Diego."

"Oh, you read about it, too. Yeah, almost a half-mile long, complete with lights, a ventilation system, railway, and an elevator."

"Belonged to the Sinaloa cartel, supposedly."

Ott nodded. "Pretty slick," he said. "Go underground from Tijuana Airport in Mexico and end up in some industrial park in California."

"Yeah, these guys sure know how to dig tunnels, I'll give 'em that," Crawford said. "That's how they sprung El Chapo from prison."

Ott took another sip of scotch then put his glass down. "So, you haven't told me about Hansel and Gretel yet."

"Okay," Crawford said, tapping the tray in front of him. "We both agree there's a snowball's chance in hell of us taking down Rafalea Arroyo in Mexico, right?"

"Right."

"And we both agree that it's way too dangerous to even try, right?"

"Right."

"And we both agree that we're better off if she comes to Palm Beach?"

Ott nodded. "Yeah, as long as she doesn't come with half her gang."

"Agreed," Crawford said. "And, according to everything you read and everyone you talk to, there're more than a few corrupt cops in Mexico."

"So they say."

"So, what we do is talk to as many cops as we can. Tell 'em we're looking for Rafaela Arroyo 'cause we suspect she killed a guy back home. Reason she killed him was she invested millions in his company and lost it all when it went belly-up. Then we let it drop that we have evidence that, in fact, the guy actually siphoned off fifty-three million to his brother before the company went bankrupt."

"I get it. So, the breadcrumb trail goes from a crooked cop to Rafaela's doorstep."

"Exactly. So, then she hears about the money and hotfoots it back to Palm Beach."

"Looking for Weston Paul."

Crawford nodded.

Ott thought a second, looking for holes, then raised his glass. "Gotta hand it to you, Charlie, that was kind of a brainstorm."

"Thank you, Mort, they don't come along often," Crawford said. "By the way, I don't think Norm had any expectation we were going to be coming back with Rafaela either."

"Then why'd he push for the 'away game?'"

"So he could tell the mayor and everyone else he was doing every-thing he possibly could to catch Paul's killer. You know, pro-active Norm, sending his guys on a two-thousand-mile trek to bring back the killer."

Ott thought for a second. "I didn't give him that much credit, but now that I think about it, I think you're right." Ott shook his head. "That conniving son of a bitch. Never had any intention of us going to Cabo either."

Crawford nodded. "I think it's really important we go to Zamora."

"I hear you," Ott said. "'Cause it's more likely that cops there are gonna be on her payroll?"

"You catch on quick."

A few minutes went by.

"Hey, you ever see that movie *Sicario*?"

Crawford nodded. "Yup. All those bodies stacked up in the walls of that house. That was pretty hardcore."

"Yeah, and my man Benicio del Toro blowing away the drug kingpin and his whole family at the nice family dinner. Talk about taking no prisoners."

"No kidding," Crawford said. "I just hope we don't get anywhere near a desert. Never been a big fan of deserts. Nothin' but a bunch of sand, cactus, and—" Crawford shuddered— "snakes."

Ott reached into his coat pocket and pulled out a piece of paper. "Oh, that reminds me," he said. "Knowing how you feel about snakes, I printed this out."

Crawford looked down at the piece of paper and saw a huge, nasty-looking snake, then farther down the page what looked like a Gila monster. He pushed the page away. "Okay, Mort, I don't need to see that."

Ott ignored him. "It's called a Crotalus Basillicus, Basillskos being the Greek word for king, and are most frequently found in western Mexico. They can get as long as seven feet and produce large amounts of highly toxic venom—"

"Okay, I get the idea. Let's just make sure we stay away from western Mexico."

Ott read down to the end of the page. "Then there's this sucker —" he pointed. "It's called the Mexican bearded lizard, 'a species of lizard in the Hel—the Helodermatidae family, one of the two species of venomous bearded lizards found principally in Mexico and northern Guatemala—'"

"Let's stay away from northern Guatemala, too."

Ott read on. "'It and its congener, the Gila monster, are the only lizards known to have evolved an overt venom-delivery system.'"

A flight attendant bent down and smiled at them. "You gentlemen ready for dinner?"

Crawford smiled back at her. "Thank God you came along."

"Well, thank you," she said. "What can I get you?"

"My friend here will take the chicken," Ott said, "and I'll have the steak."

"Coming right up," she said and walked away.

"We're like an old married couple," Crawford said. "You ordering stuff for me without even asking."

Ott raised his glass. "That's what you wanted, right?"

Crawford nodded and clinked glasses with his partner.

AN HOUR FROM LANDING, OTT ASKED, "YOU THINK WE COULD track her down if we wanted to? Rafaela?"

Crawford shook his head. "I doubt it."

"Yeah, I was thinking a one in five chance."

"Try one in ten."

"Yeah, we'd have to get pretty lucky."

"From what I've heard, nobody's gotten close to her, even with that million-and-a-half-dollar reward." The DEA agent had told him that there was a thirty-million-peso bounty on Rafaela Arroyo's head.

"Which could have something to do with her knowing who to pay off," Ott said.

Crawford nodded. "Only that guy El Mencho has a bigger award," Crawford said, referring to a man named Nemesio Oseguera Cervantes, a former cop turned hitman and most recently head of a criminal enterprise known as the Jalisco New Generation cartel.

Ott shook his head. "I'm gonna miss going to Cabo and hooking a marlin."

"I'm not. I suck at fishing."

"Now you tell me. Why didn't you mention that when I first came up with the idea?"

"I don't know, you were on a roll with Rutledge," Crawford said. "I didn't want to slow you down."

Ott shook his head. "How can you suck at fishing? You just sit around, drink beer and when you get a bite, reel it in."

"I get bored and sunburned."

"Jesus, Charlie, I wish I'd known, I could have asked for a...I don't know, a bullfight or something."

Crawford shook his head. "Nah, not real keen on seeing a guy with funny slippers and a red cape sticking a sword into one of God's creatures."

"Christ, man." Ott shook his head. "Talk about no fun at all."

TWENTY-NINE

THEY CHECKED IN TO THE INTERCONTINENTAL PRESIDENTE IN Mexico City at eight o'clock that night. The young woman at the desk, whose name tag read Evita, became the instant brunt of Ott's lame humor. He greeted her with the comment, "Don't cry for me," then proceeded to tell her that they were staying in the Obama suite.

She glanced at Crawford, clearly hoping he wasn't a jokester, too.

Crawford pointed to his head. *"Hombre's* a little *loco—"* pulling two of the ten Spanish words he knew out of thin air.

"GUTEN MORGEN, SEÑOR." THE HOTEL EMPLOYEE MAKING THE wake-up call apparently thought Crawford was German.

Crawford crawled out of bed wearing only black boxers, got down on the floor, and did forty push-ups. He normally did fifty, but this morning found himself running out of breath in the mid-thirties. Then he realized why: the elevation of Mexico City was close to 7,500 feet, a hair shy of Aspen, Colorado.

He dialed Ott's number in the room next door.

"Guten Morgen," Ott said.

"You got the same guy, huh?"

"Jawohl, herr commandant."

Crawford laughed. "Meet you in the lobby in fifteen minutes."

CRAWFORD HAD SPOKEN TO ONE OF THE MEXICAN DETECTIVES the night before and agreed to meet that morning at 8:00 at a Starbucks not far from the hotel. Crawford would have preferred something with a little local color, but the detective seemed set on Starbucks. Crawford was surprised when he spotted one of his beloved Dunkin' Donuts shops smack in the middle of Benito Juarez Airport the night before.

Two men sitting at a table waved at Ott and him as they walked into the Starbucks.

"Guess we don't look German to them," Ott said.

Crawford indicated that Ott and he would order their coffees, then join them at the table.

Ott got a grande and a bacon, gouda, and egg sandwich, and Crawford chose an espresso and a steak, egg, and tomatillo wrap. Then they walked over to the men, who stood and introduced themselves.

One had a trim mustache and spiky dark hair, and introduced himself as Juan Miguel Alvarez. The other cop wore wraparounds over a weathered face. He introduced himself as Elias Marquez.

"Welcome to Mexico City," Marquez said, in mildly accented English.

"Thank you," Crawford said, and Ott nodded.

"So, you used to be up in New York?" Marquez said to Crawford.

Crawford nodded. "Fourteen long years."

"I read about some of your cases," Marquez said.

"This one's right up there with any of them," Crawford said, sitting. "So, what can you guys tell us about Rafaela Arroyo?"

"The baddest of the bad," Marquez said, without hesitation.

"Obvious question is, how does a woman get to be so high up?" Ott asked.

"Just what you'd think," Alvarez said, also a proficient English-speaker. "She's smarter and more violent than any man."

Ott nodded. "And that's saying something."

Alvarez chuckled. "Yeah, but you haven't met her."

"Have you?"

"No, but I've seen what she's done."

"And it's pretty fuckin' scary," Marquez chimed in.

Ott turned to Crawford and smiled. "Maybe we should go home."

"You laugh," Marquez said. "But, trust me, she really is bad news."

"I trust you," Ott said, taking a sip of coffee.

"You want to sit around and listen to war stories about Rafaela Arroyo and Z5?" Marquez said. "'Cause we got 'em, if you do."

"No," Crawford said. "Just want to hear your thoughts about how to track her down."

"I gotta be honest with you...good fucking luck," Marquez said. "She's had a big price tag on her head for three years and she's still out there."

"Where's 'out there?'" Ott asked.

"Zamora. Somewhere up in that area."

"Zamora's between here and Guadalajara, right?" Crawford asked.

"I'm impressed. You know your Mexican geography."

Crawford put down his half-eaten breakfast wrap. "And I'm impressed," he said to Marquez, "at how good your English is."

"Thanks," Marquez said. "Got a good ol' American education."

"Oh, yeah. Where?"

"Athletic scholarship to Arizona State," said Marquez, raising his fist. "Go, Sun Devils."

Ott laughed. "Whatever the hell a sun devil is. You get a bull-fighting scholarship or what?"

Crawford rolled his eyes for the benefit of the officers and leaned toward Ott. "Lose the bullfighting jokes, okay," he said. "Sorry about him."

Alvarez slapped Marquez on the shoulder. "My man here was a soccer star. Could have gone pro."

"If it weren't for a fucked-up knee."

"Charlie played football at—"

"Back to Rafaela Arroyo," Crawford said. "That's all you know? She's in or near Zamora?"

Marquez and Alvarez nodded in unison.

"And if I recall," Crawford said, "Zamora's got a population of around a hundred fifty thousand?"

Alvarez nodded. "Yeah, that's about right."

Crawford finished his espresso and put it down. "So, what would you guys do if you were going after her?"

Alvarez looked at Marquez, who answered: "I'd get Seal Team Six, the Mossad, and as many Delta Force guys as I could round up and feel pretty good about my chances."

Crawford chuckled. "And if they weren't available?"

"Then I'd go small. A handpicked tactical force," Marquez said.

"What about the High Command GAFE?" Ott asked. He'd told Crawford about them on the flight down. GAFE stood for Grupo Aeromovil de Fuerzas Especiales, an elite force of no more than a hundred members specially trained in counter-terror tactics.

Marquez glanced at Alvarez knowingly. "A couple years ago, I might have been good with that," he said. "But that was before a bunch of them defected to Los Zetas."

"You're kidding," Crawford said.

Marquez smiled. "Us Latinos seem to have a harder time resisting the temptation of drug payoffs than you Yanquis"

"Don't kid yourself," Crawford said. "You offer just about anybody enough and they'll sell out."

"That's pretty cynical," Marquez said. "But not you, right?"

"Maybe I've never been offered enough," Crawford said.

"Something tells me you might be one of the incorruptibles."

Crawford glanced over at Ott. "Only 'cause my partner keeps me on the straight and narrow."

Ott smiled and caught the segue opportunity. "Speaking of money, when you talked yesterday—" he was addressing Marquez— "did Charlie tell you why Rafaela Arroyo ended up in our peaceful little town?"

"No, actually I was just about to ask," Marquez said.

Ott glanced over at Crawford. "Why don't you tell 'em?"

Crawford gave the cops a condensed version, complete with where the hidden fifty-three million dollars had ended up, but halfway through it, he realized there was a flaw in the story. If he said Thorsen Paul had siphoned off the money to his brother, it would beg the question why didn't Thorsen Paul, while being brutally tortured, give up his brother and tell his torturers Weston had the money? So, in mid-stream, he decided he needed to tweak the script.

"See, our theory is that after Arroyo stuck a few cigarettes in Thorsen Paul's face and cut off one of his fingers," Crawford said, "she figured he'd tell her everything she wanted to know after that. But what Thorsen Paul didn't know was that a trusted employee of his company—his CFO named Valerie Rosen—was having an affair with his brother, Weston. And the two of them figured out how to loot what was left of the failing company."

"The fifty-three million?" Marquez said.

"Exactly. See, everything was chaos at the company, and Thorsen Paul was so busy trying to avoid corporate and personal bankruptcy that he wasn't watching where the money went. Wasn't his job anyway; that's what the CFO did."

"That's unbelievable," Alvarez said, "so the two of them—"

"Walked off with the money," Crawford finished his sentence. "And Thorsen never knew."

Alvarez shook his head. "Wow."

"So, Arroyo could have stuck a pack of burning cigarettes in Paul's face and cut off all his fingers and he'd never give up his brother," Crawford went on.

"'Cause he had no idea," Alvarez said.

"Exactly."

"Tell ya what I've heard about Arroyo, she always did the dirty work herself," Marquez said.

"The torture, you mean?"

"Yeah, word on the street was that was her favorite part of the job," Marquez said. "Plus, I don't think she trusted anybody like herself."

"One question," Alvarez said. "Did this Weston guy let his brother get tortured and killed?"

"No," Crawford said. "'Cause Weston never knew about it."

Ott wanted in. "'Til he saw it on the news."

THIRTY

CRAWFORD AND OTT LEFT STARBUCKS A FEW MINUTES LATER with containers to go. Crawford could see that Ott was chomping at the bit.

"Jesus, Charlie, that was pretty slick improvising. I loved the whole bit about Weston and Valerie Rosen having the affair and swiping the fifty-three mil. Very smooth, my brother."

"Thank you, Mort. Thing is, it probably was lost on those two."

"What do you mean?"

"They hardly struck me as crooked cops on Rafaela's payroll."

"Yeah, but you never know. Cops talk to cops who talk to other cops...You know the drill. Before you know it, the story gets where you want it to get."

"Long shot. We just gotta keep dropping crumbs."

Ott nodded as they crossed the street.

"That guy Marquez seemed more American than us," Ott said.

"What did you expect? Man was a Sun Devil."

They were on their way back to the Presidente, where they were scheduled to meet the two DEA agents in the lobby at ten o'clock.

Crawford spotted the pair waiting at the end of the reception desk when they walked in.

"Zack Remsen," said the taller of the two, putting out his hand. He had a boyish face and didn't look a day over twenty-five, though Crawford had read his jacket and knew he was thirty.

"Jack Timpson," said the other. Short, big hairy hands, long skinny sideburns.

"You're kidding," Ott said with a smile, as he shook Timpson's hand, "not just Zack and Jack, but Remsen and Timpson."

Timpson shrugged and smiled. "What can I say? They're our names."

"Let's go have a seat over there," Crawford said, pointing to a corner of the ultra-modern lobby.

"How do you like the hotel?" Zack asked as he sat on a leather couch.

"Killer view from my room," Ott said.

"Pretty nice," Crawford agreed as they all sat facing each other.

"You boys are a long way from home," Zack said. "So how can we help you?"

Crawford set down his Starbucks cup. "My first question is, what can you tell us about Mexico's extradition treaty? I got some mixed signals about it."

"If you're talking about someone as high-profile as Rafaela Arroyo," Jack said, "it should be no big deal. 'Cause even with the whole wall thing, Peña Nieto"—the Mexican president— "wants to be on our good side. The problem, obviously, is catching her."

"Here's a deal-killer, though," Zack said. "If you want to go for the death penalty, you can pretty much forget it."

Jack nodded. "Like a lot of countries, Mexico won't extradite a felon unless they're guaranteed he won't face the death penalty in the States. If the maximum penalty is life, they're okay with that."

Crawford glanced over at Ott. "I don't see that as a deal-killer. We just want to make a bust. A life sentence would be fine."

Ott nodded. "Yeah, take our thirty-million-peso reward and call it a day."

"I hear you," Zack said with a smile.

"What do you know about Z5?" Crawford asked.

Remsen eyed his partner, then Crawford. "My opinion, they're worse than Sinaloa and tied with Los Zetas for nasty. What do you think, Jack?"

"Thing is, the government's taken down a lot of Zeta's big honchos in the last couple of years, so they're more fragmented than they used to be," Jack said. "So, if I was gonna pick one to put out of business, it would definitely be Z5."

"What's it like working here?" Ott asked. "No offense, but some days it seems like Afghanistan."

Remsen shook his head emphatically. "Hell, no. For us, it couldn't be safer."

Timpson nodded. "Nobody fucks with the DEA."

"Really. Why's that?"

"'Cause of Kiki Camerena."

"Who's he?"

"You don't know your Mexican history, I see," Zack said. "He was a cop in California, then a Marine, then a very effective DEA agent, 'til he got kidnapped, tortured, and killed."

"Wait, was there a series on Netflix about this guy?" Ott asked.

"Yup, sure was," Zack said. "Supposedly he was killed by the head of one of the smaller gangs, a nasty bastard by the name of Miguel Gallardo. Story is, Camerena got tortured over a thirty-hour period and when they found his body a month later, a hole had been drilled through his head with a power drill. They also found out he had been injected with meth, so he'd stay conscious while they were torturing him."

Crawford glanced over at Ott, whose mouth had dropped open.

Timpson continued. "It was apparently payback for Camerena finding out about a two- thousand-five-hundred-acre marijuana plantation that produced a billion dollars' worth of weed a year. What happened was, four hundred fifty Mexican soldiers showed up in a fleet of helicopters and destroyed it. Gallardo went bullshit."

"And?" Ott asked.

"One of the biggest homicide investigations ever. Heads were rolling everywhere. Including the former director of Interpol in Mexico and high-level police chief in Guadalajara. Gallardo and two of his top guys got arrested. And for the guys we couldn't extradite into the U.S., we sent in a bunch of bounty hunters who brought 'em across the border. Moral of the story is don't fuck with the DEA. It's got a big, bodacious country behind it."

Ott glanced at Crawford. "Makes you kind of proud to be an American, huh, Chuck?"

Crawford was still thinking about the poor bastard getting a hole drilled in his head.

"So, anyway," Jack said, "the drug kingpins have more or less left us alone since then."

"You suppose that'll apply to two detectives from a sleepy little town in Florida?" Ott asked. "Hands off or the wrath of God and America comes crashing down on you?"

Timpson shook his head. "No offense, Mort, but there's a big difference between a federal government agency and your little police department."

Crawford wanted to change the direction of the conversation from general history back to Rafaela Arroyo. "So, what's the latest you've heard about Arroyo?"

"Nothing lately," Jack said. "Tell us more about why you're after her."

So, Crawford did, using the opportunity to mention the fifty-three million dollars that "authorities strongly suspected" was in the hands of one Weston Paul.

Twenty-five minutes later, Remsen and Timpson left. Crawford and Ott compared notes.

"Nice job," Ott said. "I'd say you Hansel-and-Greteled that pretty well."

"Thanks," Crawford said, "but those guys go into the 'extremely unlikely' category of feeding info to Rafaela. We need to get the story out to more Mexican cops. Specifically, Mexican cops up near Zamora. I think we gotta take a little trip up that way under the guise of going after Rafaela."

"One little problem."

"What's that?"

"'Member when you said you never wanted to go to western Mexico?"

"Yeah, I know."

"What?

"It's in western Mexico. Home of the Mexican bearded lizard."

Ott shook his head. "No, worse, home of that bigass whatchamacallit snake."

THIRTY-ONE

After meeting with Remsen and Timpson, they had lunch at the Presidente and talked about everything they'd learned. Ott had his MacBook Air out and was reading an article from the *Los Angeles Times* about the murdered DEA agent, Kiki Camerena.

"Listen to this," Ott said to Crawford. *"'Because of the Camarena case, even the mere allegation of a threat is the tripwire that unleashes DEA's fury,' Jay Bergman, former regional director of the DEA's Andean office, told the* Los Angeles Times *in 2015. 'The message is loud and clear: Just thinking about harming an agent will turn your world upside down.'"*

Ott smiled and raised a fist. "You know, I can be kind of cynical sometimes, but I gotta tell you, when the U.S. of A. wants to, it can really kick ass."

"Amen," Crawford said, looking at his watch. "Now we get to learn what kind of ass kicking the FBI is doing down here."

They'd made a two o'clock appointment with FBI Agent John Syzmanski at the American Embassy. After that, they planned to come up with a full plan of attack.

It was a short walk from the Presidente to the American

Embassy at 305 Paseo de la Reforma. Crawford had spoken briefly to John Syzmanski the day before, mentioning that he had strong reasons—actually, he'd said "indisputable reasons"— to believe that a Mexican cartel boss named Rafaela Arroyo was responsible for the murder of a man in Palm Beach. Syzmanski had expressed doubts that he'd be able to help, but said he'd be happy to discuss and evaluate it.

Syzmanski looked like he could have played linebacker for the University of Alabama.

Close.

He'd played linebacker for Penn State.

"How was it having a coach who was a legend?" Ott asked Syzmanski about iconic Penn State coach Joe Paterno.

"Joe was a great coach," Syzmanski said, leaning back. "Looked the other way a few too many times, though..." A reference to Paterno's failure to follow strict disciplinary and reporting protocols when he learned an assistant had been sexually assaulting boys.

"You're probably sick of the subject," Crawford said, giving Ott a sharp glance. "Anyway, let me tell you about our case."

Syzmanski nodded. "I took the liberty of looking into it," he said. "That NextRed guy was the victim, right?"

Crawford nodded, then Ott and he took turns filling Syzmanski in on the murder and their prime suspect.

"I haven't gotten much into Z5," Syzmanski said. "But I do know that some of their members were trained in commando and urban warfare by Israeli and U.S. Special Forces."

"You mean because they defected from GAFE?" Crawford asked.

"Yeah, exactly," Syzmanski said.

"What do you concentrate on down here?" Crawford asked.

"Something that the public's not much aware of," Syzmanski said. "The presence of Hezbollah in Mexico and other parts of Latin America."

"You're kidding?" said Ott.

"Isn't that the jurisdiction of Homeland Security?" Crawford asked.

"Yeah, we do it together," Syzmanski said. "Also, making sure no ISIS guys cross the border. We first got wind of Hezbollah almost ten years back when a mutt names Jameel Nasar was arrested in Tijuana. He was trying to form a Hezbollah network in Mexico and South America. Never really went anywhere, fortunately."

Crawford tapped the arm of his chair. "I remember something on the news a few years back, where some senator claimed that a band of ISIS terrorists had crossed the border from Mexico."

"ISIS, Al Shabaab, Hezbollah...all kinds of rumors," Syzmanski said. "The congressman you're talking about told a reporter that the Border Patrol had confirmed ten ISIS guys were caught trying to cross over. I looked into it; it was bullshit."

"And yet you're still tasked with watching for that?" asked Crawford.

Syzmanski nodded. "You know, gotta stay vigilant."

Crawford and Ott nodded back. "So, back to Rafaela Arroyo. You think we'd run into an extradition problem?"

"I doubt it," Syzmanski said. "Your biggest problem is taking her in."

"Yeah, we're trying to figure out whether it's even worth the effort," Crawford said.

"That I can't assess, but going up to Zamora and hoping you're going to bump into her on the street? That ain't gonna happen."

They talked to Syzmanski for another half an hour, planted the Weston Paul story, exchanged cards, then left the embassy.

As they walked down the steps, Crawford looked at his watch. It was 3:30.

"Want to go get a *cerveza* somewhere," Ott asked, "figure out what we do next?"

"A little early for me," Crawford said. "I want to go check out this museum near here. Let's hook up after."

Ott stopped and turned to Crawford. "What's the name of your museum?"

"The Frida Kahlo Museum. She was married to a painter named Diego Riviera. I like their stuff."

"You don't get enough art shit in Palm Beach?" Ott said. "Well, just so happens there's a place I wanna see, too."

"What is it?"

Ott took out his iPhone. "Hang on a second," he scrolled down. "It's called—ready for this—Torre Latinoamericana. It's like Mexico City's answer to the Empire State Building. Tallest building in the city— or was anyway. I'm a sucker for that kinda stuff. Apparently, you get these killer sunsets from the top."

"Sounds good. So, you go there, I'll go see my art shit, then we'll meet back at the hotel in two hours. That café in the hotel's supposed to be pretty nice."

———

"IT WAS A VERY COOL BUILDING," OTT SAID, LEANING BACK IN A comfortable barstool in Café Urbano. "Built on what they call 'highly active seismic land.'"

"Meaning lots of earthquakes?"

"Yup. Withstood one in 1985 that was an 8.1 magnitude. No damage."

"That's pretty impressive."

"How was your museum?"

Crawford put down his beer and wiped his lips. "Fantastic. I'm an even bigger Frida Kahlo fan than before. Think she's even better than Diego Rivera."

"Husband-wife team, huh?"

Crawford laughed. "Not sure they've ever been called that, but yeah. She did these incredible self-portraits. I mean beautiful...kind of haunting too."

"Listen to you."

"Nice sunset from your building?"

"Yeah, it was...thing was only six hundred feet tall versus double that for the Empire State Building. But, hey, it's Mexico, right?"

"Let's talk shop." Crawford set his beer down. "What do you think about going to Zamora?"

Ott took a long pull on his Paloma Cartuja, a combination of white tequila, yellow chartreuse, grapefruit juice, cinnamon, and lime juice that was fast becoming Ott's new favorite drink. "Tell ya the truth, I'd rather sit around and drink these than hike up into the mountains."

"You're already in the mountains."

Ott took another sip of his fluorescent drink. "Okay, I'm good with going to Zamora and dropping crumbs. Just as soon avoid Rafaela and the gang, though."

Crawford nodded. "That's an honest answer."

"What do you want to do?"

Crawford's cell phone rang. The caller ID showed more digits than for an American phone number.

"Hello?"

"Detective, it's Elias Marquez." The Sun Devil. "I got a tip for you."

"Whatcha got?" Crawford asked, putting his iPhone on speaker.

"Know what FES is?" Marquez asked.

"Yeah, the Mexican version of our Seals. Special Navy unit. Aren't they the ones who caught El Chapo after he escaped from prison?"

"Yup. Operation Black Swan," Marquez said. "Anyway, they just captured three members of Z5 up in Zamora. High-ranking guys, too. One had an eight-hundred-thousand-dollar reward."

Ott moved closer.

"When did this happen?" Crawford asked.

"This afternoon. One of them's in the hospital, the other two in jail," Marquez said. "I thought you might want to talk to them."

"How far is it from here?" Crawford asked.

"Five and a half hours by car."

Crawford covered the iPhone. "Let's go. Leave first thing tomorrow morning."

Ott nodded.

Crawford took his hand off the phone. "We'll leave here around six tomorrow morning. Get there a little before noon."

"Tell you what I'll do," Marquez said. "I'll send you an email with the name of the jail, directions how to get there, and who you contact. I'll call and tell 'em you're coming."

"That'll be great," Crawford said. "We appreciate it. Thanks."

He clicked off.

"You sure this is a good idea, Charlie?" Ott asked.

Crawford didn't hesitate. "No."

───────

CRAWFORD ASKED FOR ANOTHER WAKE-UP CALL BUT DIDN'T need it, sleeping only fitfully until he finally climbed out of bed at 5:30 the next morning.

The night before, Ott had arranged for an Avis car to be waiting for them outside the Presidente. Sure enough, when they walked out, there it was: a 2018 Chevy Cruz in matador-cape red.

"Seems only right," Ott said, opening the driver's door, "we get a car with a Spanish name."

It was a memorable trip. It took them through the Toluca Valley west of Mexico City, one of the highest valleys in Mexico, surrounded by inconceivably tall mountains, including the impressive Nevada de Toluca volcano. They made good time, because the four-lane motorway was as solid as any in the states but had much lighter traffic. They were surprised at how few trucks they saw, the majority being in a military convoy just outside of Morelia. Also, outside of Morelia was an enormous body of water that reminded Crawford of one of the Great Lakes. The Mexican countryside was varied, colorful, and oftentimes lush, which surprised Crawford, who'd expected nothing but deserts, cacti, and Gila monsters.

"Know where we are?" Ott asked on the outskirts of Zamora.

"Yeah, Zamora," Crawford said. "Time to Hansel-and-Gretel our Weston Paul story."

They had another surprise when they reached Zamora proper: they still had another two hours to go. Apparently, Elias Marquez didn't know his geography so well, as their final destination, where the Z5 gang members were being held, was a town called Mazamitla. On the far outskirts of Zamora, they stopped for gas and struck up a conversation with a young couple from California in the gas station's small restaurant. The couple had visited the area often, and explained that Crawford and Ott were about to enter a part of Mexico nicknamed *La Tierra Caliente*, which translated to the hot country. The man, James, told them that "hot country" had nothing to do with the weather but instead referred to the continual, violent clashes between rival drug cartels in the states of Michoacán and Jalisco.

After a little over six and a half hours on the road, they reached their destination. Mazamitla was a town about the size of Palm Beach, roughly ten thousand people. It had been founded by the Aztecs in 1165. Crawford's first impression of the mountain town was that it seemed like it belonged in the Swiss Alps, not Mexico. Driving in, they saw glass-and-wood chalets perched on the sides of steep hills over an immaculate hamlet: no trash-strewn streets, no stray feral dogs, no rubble in front of houses, all of which were things that they'd observed in other towns along the way. The police station was easy to find. It had two men with machine guns, body armor, and helmets guarding the front door.

Ott parked the Cruz and they walked past the guards, Ott giving them a smile, Crawford nodding.

A woman at the reception desk saw them, dialed three numbers, and said something terse in Spanish. As they approached the desk, a short man with a mustache and Coke-bottle glasses came through a door from behind the reception desk.

"Detectives," he said with a broad smile in heavily accented

English, "welcome to Mazamitla. I'm Colonel Malaga of the Policia Federal Ministerial." He thrust out his hand and Crawford and Ott shook hands with him.

"Thank you," Crawford said. "I'm Detective Crawford."

"And I'm Detective Ott."

Elias Marquez had emailed Crawford Malaga's name the night before, so Crawford had done enough homework to know that Malaga was hardly a small-town cop. The Policia Federal Ministerial, or PFM, was the premier federal investigative agency, answering directly to the Attorney General of Mexico, who was by reputation a tough son of a bitch.

"I'm borrowing the office of the police chief here, so if you'd like to come back, we can talk," Malaga said.

"Sure," Crawford said, and Ott nodded.

They followed Malaga back to a small office that smelled of Mexican take-out. Malaga went around a desk and motioned for Crawford and Ott to sit opposite him.

"So," Malaga said, knotting his hands together, "I understand you want Rafaela Arroyo for a crime you suspect she did in the States."

"Yes. Murder, to be specific," Crawford said.

"That's her specialty," Malaga said. "We haven't found out from her men here where she is yet—" he winked "—but another hour or so and we will."

"So, assuming you do—"

"We will."

"Then what are you thinking we do?" Crawford asked.

"Go after her," Malaga said. "I've got eight men of my own right here. Plus, another four on the way."

"Who are the other four?" Ott asked.

Malaga cocked his head. "What's the word in English..." He paused for a moment. "Bounty hunters. Very good at catching people."

"And that's okay with the Attorney General?" Crawford asked.

"The Attorney General is a very busy man," Malaga said with a smile. "I think the American expression is, 'What he doesn't know won't hurt him.'" Malaga pushed up his glasses. "I want to make one thing very clear to you. Along with the bounty hunters, this is my arrest. You are simply along for the ride. Later, if you and the United States government want to try to extradite her, that is your business. Understand?"

Crawford shot a glance at Ott, who was studying Malaga carefully. "That's fine with us."

Ott nodded. "So, what do you suggest we do right now?"

"Have you had lunch yet?" Malaga asked.

"Not yet."

"Well, there's a very good place just down the street," Malaga said. "I suggest you go have a nice lunch, and by the time you come back we'll know where Rafaela Arroyo is."

CRAWFORD AND OTT WERE HAVING AN EXCEPTIONAL MEAL AT the restaurant Malaga had recommended, the Cava Nostra. Crawford took a bite of something called *buenaza* spinach salad, then put down his fork.

"Damn, that's good," he said, watching Ott consume a plate of empanadas. It was time to trade gut reactions to Vincente Malaga and his operation.

"Something tells me he's not going to politely ask the two in jail where Rafaela is," Ott said.

"Something tells me he didn't want us anywhere near the station."

"Yeah, or we might hear the screams," Ott said, grim-faced.

Crawford nodded. "Waterboarding, maybe?"

"Could be anything," Ott said with a shrug. "I got a feeling the good guys are just as good at torture as the bad guys."

"If, in fact, there are any good guys," Crawford said. "What did you make of him bringing along bounty hunters?"

"I didn't know what to make of it. Aren't there enough guys in that Policia...whatever it's called."

"Policia Federal Ministerial," Crawford said. "Yeah, you'd think so."

"I don't know, man, we can still pull the plug," Ott said, taking a sip of his mineral water. "Nice scenic tour of the countryside, then we go home."

"Yeah, but if we pack it in, we miss out on the opportunity to drop crumbs in Arroyo's backyard."

"True. So, we just keep our heads down. Let Malaga and the boys risk their lives."

Crawford wiped his mouth with his napkin. "Yeah. Anything happens, we hide behind the biggest cactus tree we can find."

THEY WERE BACK IN THE POLICE CHIEF'S BORROWED OFFICE, facing Vincente Malaga.

"Good news," Malaga said with a smirk. "At first our boys couldn't seem to remember where Arroyo was, but then their memories came back, and all of a sudden they remembered."

"Is she far from here?" Crawford asked.

"No, not too far," Malaga said. "Maybe a half-hour."

"And how many are there with her? Do you know?" Crawford asked.

"Just four, including her."

"And you believe this guy?"

"He wouldn't lie to me." The smirk again.

Crawford glanced at Ott. "So, let's go get 'em."

AS MALAGA SAID, HE HAD EIGHT MEN—INCLUDING HIMSELF— from Policia Federal Ministerial and another four men, recently arrived, who looked like characters out of Quentin Tarantino's movie, *Django Unchained*: lots of facial hair, crude tattoos, cigarettes dangling out of the corners of their mouths, and floppy, leather hats.

"This is my son-in-law Duarte," Malaga proudly introduced one of the bounty hunters, a stocky man who appeared to be in command. "He used to be with GAFE."

Crawford nodded at Malaga's son-in-law, who shot him a Clint Eastwood, squinty-eyed stare.

All of Malaga's men, including the bounty hunters, along with Crawford and Ott proceeded outside, and prepared to load into two Toyota Land Cruisers, a Land Rover Defender, and a Hummer H2.

Malaga called something out to the group in Spanish, then turned to Crawford and Ott. "Okay, this is what we know: Arroyo's house is on top of a high hill, maybe a thousand feet up. We want to take the bitch alive, so you can have a souvenir of your trip to Mexico."

Duarte chuckled and said in barely passable English. "Yeah, take the bitch alive."

Twenty minutes later, they were in the middle of nowhere. They had taken a dirt road off of the main road, and were following it as it wound alongside a shallow stream. Duarte and three of his bounty hunters rode in one of the Land Cruisers, three of Malaga's men in the Land Rover Defender, another three in the other Land Cruiser. Malaga drove the Hummer with one of his men, Oscar Cano, riding shotgun. Crawford and Ott shared the back seat.

On both sides rose mountains with jagged rocks leading up to their peaks. It reminded Crawford of a raft trip he'd taken to Colorado with his parents. But instead of a slow-moving stream, they'd navigated the roiling waters of the Rogue River.

"Great place for an ambush," Ott murmured next to him. "Saw a lot of TV shows where the cowboys were riding along and, all of a sudden, there's a thousand Indians firing arrows down at them."

Crawford shook his head. "Nice thought."

"Just sayin'," Ott said. "Think they called it a box canyon."

Crawford turned to Ott and spoke in a whisper. "I was thinking about *Sicario*."

"What about it?"

"That it would be nice to have your guy, Benicio del Toro, and Josh Brolin along for the ride. Or better yet, that guy Javier Bardem with his awesome bolt gun."

"Wrong movie but a helluva gun."

CRAWFORD LEANED FORWARD AND ASKED MALAGA. "WE getting close?"

Malaga turned back to him and laughed. "You're like my kids. 'Are we there yet, *Papa*?' Another mile or so."

Ott turned to Crawford. "Wonder if she's got a lookout?"

"Wouldn't you?"

Crawford nodded as he looked up into the rocky peaks.

Malaga's cell phone rang. "*Sí*, Pedro," he answered.

Then he just listened.

In the rearview mirror, Crawford saw the expression change on Malaga's face. It went from assured and confident to stressed and tense in just a few seconds. Then he clicked off.

"The prisoners escaped," Malaga said to Oscar Cano.

"How?" Cano asked.

"I don't know exactly. I never trusted those Mazamitla police or their chief."

Malaga pulled the Hummer, which was in the lead, over to the side of the dirt road and stopped. The other vehicles followed.

Malaga got out of the truck. So did Cano, Crawford, and Ott. Then the rest of the men climbed out and gathered around Malaga, who spoke to the group, then translated for Ott and Crawford.

"I just found out," Malaga said, "that the prisoners escaped. Which means they probably called Rafaela Arroyo as soon as they got their hands on a phone."

Several of the men nodded.

"Meaning we've lost the element of surprise," Malaga went on. "We're close to her house now, so we need to be very careful. All right, back in your vehicles and get your guns ready."

Duarte did not move. "Why don't we just go on foot from here, *suegro?*" he asked, using the word for father-in-law.

"'Cause we're safer in the SUVs," Malaga said. "They're armored."

"Yeah, but they can't take heavy artillery."

"Come on, Duarte, back in your vehicle."

Duarte didn't look convinced but did as Malaga said.

Crawford and Ott got into the back seat while Malaga climbed in and stepped on the accelerator.

Crawford slid his Sig Sauer P226 9mm pistol out of his shoulder holster. Ott did the same with his Glock.

Crawford had checked out the other men's weapons, which consisted of German G3 and HK33 battle rifles and several Mexican FX-05 Xiuhcoatls, which were similar to the German G36. He saw that the bounty hunters all had AR-15s. Ott and he had their pistols, which would only be effective if they got close.

A few minutes later, a house on top of a hill came in to view. "See it?" Oscar Cano said, pointing up.

Crawford craned his neck to see the two-story stone house that looked as though it had been built into the surrounding rocks.

Suddenly, an ear-splitting explosion came from behind them. Crawford turned to see the Land Rover Defender burst into flames, three of Malaga's men trapped in it.

"*Hijo de puta!*" Malaga cursed, as he swung the wheel of the Hummer hard to the left.

"Fucking RPG," Ott shouted as another rocket-propelled grenade hit one of the Land Cruisers.

Malaga yanked the wheel hard to the left in an attempt to turn back.

Automatic-weapons fire tore into their windshield, hitting both

Malaga and Cana multiple times. The Hummer slowed as Ott, from behind, shoved Malaga to the right, climbed between the captain's seats, and slid behind the wheel.

Crawford reached into the front seat, grabbed Cano's HK33, and started firing it through the open side window in the direction of the incoming fire. Ott, at the wheel, began weaving the truck from side to side down the dirt road to avoid being hit by another RPG from behind.

From the back seat, Crawford kept firing. He went through the whole twenty-shot clip, then reached into Cano's pocket for his spare clip, jacked it in, and started firing again. He saw two men with automatic rifles rise up from behind the rugged landscape above them, and spray the back window with bullets. He leaned over the console beside the blood-spattered cops piled into the passenger side of the vehicle.

"You okay?" Ott shouted.

"Yeah, but these poor bastards are dead."

Ott shook his head. "Fuckin' armor worked well."

As the Hummer roared down the trail, Crawford saw only dust around them, though the hostile gunfire continued. Through the dust, he glimpsed another vehicle roaring up behind them. As it neared them, he realized with relief that it was the remaining Toyota Land Cruiser.

"Talk about ambush," Ott said. "Prisoners sure got revenge."

Crawford looked back. The Land Cruiser was riding their bumper. "This thing go any faster?"

"Got it floored," Ott said. "Get that guy off my ass."

Crawford leaned out the window and motioned to the driver to slow down.

The Land Cruiser dropped back a few feet.

"We're out of range now," Crawford said.

"Right," said Ott, eyes locked on the dirt road. "Unless they got a Tomahawk missile."

THIRTY-TWO

THE AMBUSH SURVIVORS WERE LICKING THEIR WOUNDS BACK IN the Mazamitla police station. No one said much, no doubt counting themselves lucky to be alive. Of the three men in the Land Cruiser, two had escaped injury, but a third was badly wounded. He had been taken to the hospital. All three men in the Land Rover Defender that had been hit first were presumed dead and incinerated.

Ott had a two-inch cut on his forehead from a piece of flying glass, which the local police had bandaged for him. He and Crawford were back in the police chief's office, but instead of Malaga behind the desk, this time it was the chief himself. His name was Pacho Nuñez, and he spoke no English. So a woman who was a middle-school teacher and spoke English well had been recruited to translate. Crawford had recounted the details of the mountain assault, which the translator translated. Now, Nuñez was telling Crawford and Ott about the prison break. He said his jailer told him that he had found one of Rafaela Arroyo's men trying to hang himself with a sheet in one of the cells.

Ott looked at him suspiciously. "With the other guy in the cell with him?"

Nuñez listened to the translator, then nodded. "Actually, the two were in different cells. But it turned out to be a lie anyway."

"Okay, so what really happened?" Crawford said.

"My jailer said the prisoner grabbed his gun when he was cutting him down, but I didn't believe him. One, because I had drilled it into my jailers never to go into a cell with their weapon, and two, because something in my gut told me he was lying," the teacher translated.

"What did you do then?" Ott asked.

The translator translated the question. Nuñez cocked his head, smiled and rattled off a quick answer.

"I have a way of getting people to tell me the truth."

That was becoming a standard answer. Impatiently, Crawford raised his hand. "So, what was the real story?"

Nuñez leaned back in his chair, put his hands together, and spoke softly for a full minute.

The translator turned to Crawford. "The prisoner was wearing a large diamond earring, worth a lot of money. He said he'd give it to the jailer if the jailer let him go. The jailer said no, or at least that's what he told Chief Nuñez. A few minutes later, the prisoner told him it was worth two hundred thousand pesos—"

Nuñez jumped in with something in Spanish.

"What did he say?" Crawford asked the translator.

"He said that was...'bullshit.'" The teacher's faced reddened as she repeated the curse. "It was only worth about fifty thousand."

"I don't care what it was worth," Crawford said. "What really happened?"

"The jailer told the prisoner to take the earring off as he unlocked the cell. The prisoner gave him the earring, and then the jailer unlocked the other prisoner's cell and let them escape out the back. The jailer waited a few minutes, then hit himself in the face with the butt of his gun. Once his nose and lips were bleeding, he started yelling."

The translator paused and Nuñez resumed. When he stopped, the translator turned back to Crawford.

"The chief said he didn't believe a word of the jailer's story. He made the jailer empty his pockets. And there it was, the diamond earring."

Nuñez said something and smiled.

"He said, 'And now the jailer's in jail.'"

Ott leaned forward. "And responsible for the deaths of five people."

Nuñez's face turned grim and he nodded solemnly.

"Thank you," Crawford said to the translator. "I have one other question for Chief Nuñez. Why did Vincente Malaga have his son-in-law along on the capture of Rafaela Arroyo? It seems strange that men from Policia Federal Ministerial would join forces with civilians. In this case, bounty hunters."

Halfway through the question, Crawford sensed that Nuñez knew what he was asking. A tiny smile appeared on his face.

The translator started to translate, but Nuñez put up a hand and spoke.

When Nuñez was done, the teacher translated: "I think you might have guessed what the answer to your question is, Detective. The bounty hunter, Duarte, had made a lot of money catching people who have big rewards on their heads. That's because his father-in-law finds out where they are, then together they capture them. That way both Duarte and Malaga get credit for the capture, but Duarte gets the reward money. Then, and this is only Chief Nuñez's guess," said the teacher, "Duarte gives his father-in-law half the reward money."

Nuñez spoke again and the translator translated. "It was a cozy little relationship."

"Yeah," Crawford said. "*Was* being the operative word."

Nuñez nodded before the translator had time to translate.

Crawford figured this was probably his last opportunity to drop any kind of breadcrumb for the cartel boss. "Clearly Rafaela Arroyo is as dangerous as I heard she was."

The translator translated, then Nuñez said something, then the translator turned to Crawford and Ott. "He said Malaga told him she tortured and killed a man where you live in Florida."

Crawford nodded and told him the whole story, pausing frequently for the translator to translate.

"Her trip to Florida was kind of like ours," Crawford said. "A waste of time. Her only problem was she went after the wrong brother."

Then, in case he hadn't been clear, he repeated how Weston Paul ended up with fifty-three million dollars.

At the end, Nuñez leaned back in his chair and smiled. "So, why don't you go and have a nice little conversation with the brother?" He paused. "I know I would."

THIRTY-THREE

"You think that diamond earring's gonna end up on Nuñez's wife's ear?" Ott asked Crawford.

They were on an Aeroméxico flight back to Palm Beach.

"Yeah, probably," Crawford said. "Or else he'll hawk it."

"I really liked that country, but Jesus, is *everyone* corrupt?"

"Nah, I just think we saw the really experienced ones."

Ott took a sip of his vodka. "Yeah, but look how they ended up. Dead or in jail."

"Except Nuñez."

Ott nodded and turned to Crawford, who had a half-empty beer on the tray in front of him. "What do you think the chances are?"

"Of hearing from Rafaela?"

Ott nodded.

"Fifty-fifty."

"I'm going with sixty-forty, and maybe Nuñez comes himself," Ott said. "Except he'd have a tough time, not speaking the language and all."

"That's where you're wrong."

"What do you mean?"

"Trust me, he speaks the language."

———————

THE NEXT MORNING, CRAWFORD AND OTT REPORTED ON THEIR trip to Norm Rutledge.

"I figured it was a long shot," Rutledge said.

What? An understanding Norm Rutledge?

"The mayor's been pretty quiet?" Crawford asked.

"Yeah, but now that you're back, I'll be hearing from her again."

Ott's brow furrowed beneath his bandage. "Maybe she'd like to have someone fire an RPG up her ass?"

"What the hell's that?"

"A rocket-propelled grenade. Killed those five people we told you about. Or maybe it was a SMAW, a Shoulder-Launched Multipurpose Assault Weapon."

"How do you know all this shit?"

Ott shrugged. "*Homeland.*"

Crawford suppressed a laugh. "So, what do you want to do, Norm?"

Ott wasn't done. "Maybe *you* want to give it a shot...fly down to Mexico with a couple traffic cops."

"Don't be a dick, Ott," Rutledge turned to Crawford. "Got any ideas?"

"Not really."

Rutledge looked as though the air had been knocked out of him. "That's it? Nothing?"

Crawford just shrugged. "Sorry"—then like he had an afterthought— "But that police chief we mentioned near Zamora—"

"Yeah, what about him?" Rutledge asked.

"Crooked as a—" Crawford couldn't come up with anything.

"Barrel of fish hooks," Ott came to his rescue.

Crawford chuckled. "Thanks, Mort. Plus, my guess is he's got a pipeline to Rafaela Arroyo."

"So, what are you getting at?" Rutledge asked.

"I call him and tell him that I just found out Thorsen Paul's brother embezzled fifty-three million dollars from his brother."

Rutledge was slow but not stupid. "I get it. So, you're gonna play the brother, ensconced at that house your girlfriend Rose finagled."

"She's not my girlfriend."

"Mistress?"

"Enough."

"But why would you call this guy?" Rutledge asked.

"Why do you think? Because in his world most cops have their hands out. So, I tell him I want a pay-off to tell him where to find the brother."

Rutledge was slowly nodding his head. "What if she sends hitters to do it instead of herself?"

"She won't. She's totally hands on."

"What if she comes with a battalion of badasses?"

"She won't. That'll attract attention."

Rutledge glanced at Ott. "So, you think she'll show up with her RPGs?"

Ott rolled his eyes like he regretted ever telling Rutledge what an RPG was.

"Norm," Crawford said. "You do understand that she can't do anything to me until after she gets the money. Or rather when she figures out there ain't no money."

"Yeah, I get that," Rutledge said.

"Which means there aren't going to be any shootouts on Worth Avenue, or whatever it is you're so afraid of."

"Okay, so what do you want to do?"

"Like you said, move into that house on South Ocean and pretend to be a man who doesn't exist."

Rutledge sighed. He seemed out of questions. "Let's do it."

He didn't know they already had.

TWO DAYS WENT BY, WHICH IS A LONG TIME WHEN YOU'RE A homicide cop with a case that has increasingly begun to look as if it's dead in the water. After the second day, Crawford was starting to resign himself to the fact that the Thorsen Paul case might never be solved. It wouldn't be the first time he had ever had an unsolved case but, yes, it would be the first time in Palm Beach. Dropping his average down to an A-, maybe a B+. He had tried to stay busy the last few days. Extra-long workouts at the gym, talking to his ex-partner up in New York about a few cold cases, even slept in the morning before.... 8:15. Wow.

He was about to go to lunch when his phone rang.

"Hello."

"Hello Detective Crawford, it's Pacho Nuñez in Mexico."

What a surprise, the man spoke English. Heavily-accented but still...

Crawford pressed his iPhone up against his ear. "Hello, Pacho."

He dialed Ott's extension on his landline, muting his cell phone when Ott picked up. "Get in here," he said.

"I hope you had a nice trip back, Charlie?"

Now they were Pacho and Charlie, old buddies.

"Yes, thank you—" *Get to the goddamn point.*

Ott walked in and Crawford hit speaker.

"I'm calling because I have a proposition."

Crawford was chomping at the bit. "A proposition?"

"Yes, a two-million-peso proposition. Which translates to a hundred thousand dollars."

Ott waggled his eyebrows.

"Keep going," Crawford said.

"I need information and if you give it to me, I will give you two million pesos—" Of course, Nuñez would assume he would be open to a bribe since it was so ingrained in his culture.

"I'm listening, Pacho."

"I need to know how to contact Thorsen Paul's brother, Weston."

Crawford wasn't about to make it easy for Nuñez to earn whatever Rafaela Arroyo was paying him.

'Why do you want to know that?"

"Because of the money he has that isn't his."

"And why is that your business?"

"Look, Charlie, I called you as a courtesy. I can find out another way, but I would like to include you."

"That's very generous of you, Pacho. I can't help you, though..." Pause. "Wait, hang on, maybe I have an idea."

"What is it?"

"The woman who Weston Paul was having an affair with. Her name is Valerie Rosen, she was high up in Thorsen Paul's company. She could probably lead you to Paul's brother."

"Do you have her number?"

"No, but I might be able to get it for you."

"As soon as you do, I'll get you the two million pesos."

"I'll see what I can do. Call you later, Pacho."

"I look forward to your call, Charlie."

Crawford clicked off.

Ott leaned across his desk and gave him a fist bump. "We're back in the game, bro."

Crawford nodded and smiled. "Yeah, I don't know about you, but I've been having a little problem twiddling my thumbs the last two days."

Ott nodded. "Me, too."

Crawford dialed three numbers on his landline.

"Who you calling?" Ott asked.

"Our very own Valerie Rosen."

THIRTY-FOUR

DOMINICA SAT IN CRAWFORD'S CHAIR BEHIND HIS DESK, HER feet on his desk like she had seen him do so many times. Crawford and Ott faced her, Ott in the wooden chair molded to his posterior, Crawford in a chair he had never sat in before. They had been rehearsing for over an hour.

Dominica held up her hand. "Okay, I got it."

"You sure?" Crawford asked.

"Yeah, it's pretty basic. You give Pacho my number, then either he calls me or the cartel bosswoman does. Or maybe that Castillo guy. Then I give 'em my spiel."

Crawford and Ott nodded. Crawford dialed his iPhone. "Okay, here goes."

Pacho Nuñez answered. "*Hola*, Charlie."

"Hello, Pacho. This is Valerie Rosen's number." He reeled it off.

"Okay," Nuñez said. "If everything goes as planned, I'll get you the two million pesos."

"Wait a minute," Crawford said. "You said you'd give me two million pesos for 'information' and I just gave it to you."

"Don't worry, you'll get the money if everything goes as planned," Nuñez repeated.

"That wasn't our deal," Crawford said, feigning outrage.

"*Adios*, Charlie." He clicked off.

Crawford shook his head. "What a fuckin' sleazeball." He covered his mouth. "Oops, sorry, Dominica."

She laughed. "That's okay, Charlie, I've heard the word before."

———

IT DIDN'T TAKE LONG FOR DOMINICA'S BURNER PHONE TO RING. Twenty minutes later, in fact, while she was still perched in Crawford's chair.

"Hello?"

"Ms. Rosen?" said a man with an accent.

"Yes. Who's this?"

"My name is Alejandro Castillo, Ms. Rosen, and you have something of mine."

Dominica smiled at Crawford, and Ott and sat up straight. "I have no idea what you're talking about, Mr...?"

"Castillo. Fifty-three million dollars. You and your boyfriend Weston Paul have it and I want it back."

Dominica sighed loudly. "First of all, Mr. Castillo, Weston Paul is not my boyfriend and, second of all, good fucking luck."

Dominica shot Crawford a big thumbs-up.

"But, what I heard—"

"I don't give a damn what you heard. The guy screwed me, and he'll screw you, too." Then, like she'd had a revelation. "Oh, wait, you must be one of the investors from Mexico. That LLC. Now I remember."

Castillo was silent.

"You people were large investors in NextRed."

"And we want our money back."

"It doesn't work that way, *amigo*. NextRed's bankrupt."

"Yes, but Weston Paul took the money."

It was Dominica's turn to fall silent.

"Ms. Rosen?"

"I'm thinking," Dominica said, then paused again. "Tell you what, Mr. Castillo, I'm guessing you called me because you want to know how to find Weston Paul, right?"

"Yes, where is he?"

"The answer is going to cost you a hundred thousand dollars."

Castillo sighed dramatically. "Ms. Rosen, we have ways of finding things out."

"Don't give me that," Dominica said. "You have no idea where I live or how to find me. Or, for that matter, that son of a bitch Weston."

Crawford smiled and nodded.

"Okay, we'll pay you a hundred thousand dollars if we recover the fifty-three million."

"No, if I tell you how to find Weston Paul, you pay me."

Castillo sighed again. "All right. I agree to that. Now, where is he?"

"I'll let you know as soon as you wire a hundred thousand into my account."

"Not possible. I have no assurance that we will recover the fifty-three million."

Crawford scribbled a note and held it up: 'Play hard to get.'

Dominica leaned forward and read it. "Then I guess that means your people don't know what the hell they're doing."

"Trust me, they do," Castillo said.

"Okay, we're done here unless you wire me the money."

"I bet you were a very good Chief Financial Officer, Ms. Rosen. It's just a shame that NextRed isn't around anymore. Where are you working now?"

"If that's your way of trying to track me down, it's not gonna work. Let's just say I'm in between opportunities at the moment," Dominica said. "It seems that when prospective employers see

NextRed on my résumé, they jump to the conclusion that I had something to do with its downfall."

"So just leave it off," Castillo said.

"Believe me, if I need career advice from you, I'll be sure to ask." Another long pause. "I've got an appointment to get to. Call me when the money's been wired. I'll give you my ABA and account number."

She read the numbers and hung up.

"Good job," Crawford said.

"No," Ott said. "Fan-*tastic* job. Played that dude like the proverbial fiddle."

Dominica smiled and shrugged. "What did you expect?" she said. "Oh, and thanks, Charlie, but I didn't need your little note."

"I know you didn't," Crawford said with a smile.

Ott turned to Crawford, "No offense, man, but the girl's a better negotiator than you."

"Hey, I admit it," Crawford said with a shrug. Then to Dominica, "You did great. He took the hook, now all we gotta do is reel him in."

THIRTY-FIVE

"You believe it?" Dominica said, her eyes saucer-size. A hundred thousand dollars had landed in a Palm Beach Police Department account an hour ago.

Soon after, Dominica had called Alejandro Castillo and had given him Crawford's burner phone number.

She was back in Crawford's office. This time he was in his normal chair with Dominica and Ott facing him.

"I think we put in the suggestion box that part of that hundred thou goes to SiriusXM in all the Crown Vics," Ott said.

"I second that," Crawford said. "And a new coffee machine."

Dominica nodded. "Are you worried she won't come?" she asked. "Just send some of her guys."

"No way she'd let anyone else handle this," Crawford said. "Or trust 'em with that kind of money."

Ott nodded his agreement. "Yeah, definitely. Plus, the broad loves stickin' cigarettes in guy's faces."

"Come on, Mort," Dominica said, "'broad?'"

"Chick?"

Crawford leaned forward in his chair. "Hey, as I don't need to tell you, the fact that we lured Rafaela here is a secret we all take to our graves."

Dominica leaned across Crawford's desk and bumped fists with him. "To the grave."

Ott did the same. "Hey, one last question," he asked, "how do we know when she gets here?"

"How do you think?" Crawford said, pointing at himself. "Her first call's gonna be to Weston Paul."

AT NINE THAT NIGHT, JUST AFTER HE'D GOTTEN HOME, Crawford received the call he'd been waiting for on his burner phone.

"Is this Weston Paul?" a woman with a Spanish accent asked.

"Yes, it is, who's this?"

"My name is Rafaela. We have business to discuss." The woman's command of the English language was even better than Alejandro Castillo's.

"Business? What are you talking about?" Crawford asked.

"It's about money of mine that you have. I reckon you know exactly what I am referring to."

"I have absolutely no idea," Crawford said.

"Does the name Valerie Rosen ring a bell?"

"Sure. Used to work for my brother. What about her?"

"Used to be your girlfriend, too. She told a friend of mine you have fifty-three million dollars that belongs to me."

"Oh, did she now?"

"That's my money."

"I don't have fifty-three million dollars. But if I did, how do you figure it's yours?"

"Because I invested in that NextRed scam. Your brother cheated me, and I want my money back."

"My brother's company was no scam," Crawford said, trying to sound insulted. "It just had some problems."

"That's rubbish. We were not told about any problems when we invested."

"Look, Rafaela—what's your last name?"

"Rafaela's enough."

"Did you have something to do with my brother's murder?"

She laughed. "If I did, do you really think I'd tell you?"

"Look, we're done with this conversation. I have no idea what you're talking about, so don't bother me again."

"You leave me no other choice. I'll be coming to see you. I'd suggest you get your checkbook ready."

CRAWFORD LOOKED AT HIS WATCH TO SEE WHAT TIME IT WAS IN Mexico City, then called Ott.

"Got a call from Rafaela," Crawford told Ott.

"Oh, yeah? What did blondie have to say?"

"She wants money."

"What did you say?"

"'Can't help ya.'"

"Uncooperative son of a bitch."

"Yeah, that's me," Crawford said. "Hey, can you get Fernandez on a three-way?"

"Sure, hang on a sec," a half a minute went by. "You there, Camilo?"

"I'm here."

"Hey, Cam," Crawford said.

"Hey, Charlie."

"So," Ott said, "how'd you leave it with Rafaela?"

"She's gonna be paying me a visit. Can you get Ignacio Puig on the phone, Cam?"

"Hang on," Fernandez dialed the number and reached Puig right away.

Through Fernandez, Crawford asked Puig several questions about Rafaela Arroyo. The Mexican cop had answers to most of them.

"One last question," Crawford said. "She used several British-sounding figures of speech when we spoke. Did she ever spend any time in England?"

Fernandez translated the question and waited for the answer.

"No, not that I know of," was the Mexican detective's response.

Crawford thanked him and hung up. "And thanks, Cam. Appreciate all your help, man."

"You're welcome. Hope you catch her but be careful."

"I will."

"You still there, Mort?"

"Yeah," Ott said, not his usual bubbly self.

"What's wrong?"

"Like I said before, I'm worried," Ott said. "You putting your life on the line, I mean. Seems like a big fuckin' risk."

Crawford sighed. "Aw, that's so touching, Mort. Don't get me all teary now."

"I'm serious. As we found out in Mexico, she definitely ain't someone to fuck with."

"Don't worry, I'm gonna be very careful." Suddenly, he had a thought. "Hey, I got an idea, maybe you want to play Weston?"

Ott laughed. "Sorry, too late. She already knows your voice."

THIRTY-SIX

THE PAIR RECEIVED A LOT OF CURIOUS LOOKS ON THE FLIGHT from Mexico City to West Palm. Rafaela knew how to clean up but her right-hand-man Alvaro Diaz did not. La Bestia, or 'the beast' as Diaz was known, wore a sleeveless black T-shirt, black jeans, and boots, a sleeve of tats covering both arms, his face, and shaved head. A big number five was tattooed onto his forehead directly above the bridge of his nose, and blue-black teardrops below his left eye. A little girl had asked La Bestia, as he was waiting for a bathroom on the plane, why he was crying. He'd simply grunted and looked away. Skinny and short, La Bestia was wedged in his seat between a corpulent woman and a young man in a U.S. Army uniform. Not surprisingly, he hadn't said a word to either one of them.

Rafaela, on the other hand, had put some effort into her appearance, looking like a young woman whose parents had told her they expected her to dress up when she traveled. She wore a modest white dress, sensible brown flats, and light make-up. As befitting her status as leader of Zamora Cinco, she flew in first class, which was all right because La Bestia didn't seem to know the difference between first class and coach, where he'd been seated. Though when he saw a flight attendant hand Rafaela a white wine shortly after taking her seat, he immediately hit his call button and demanded a Dos Equis. The flight attendant politely told him he would have to wait.

A half-hour later, La Bestia had downed two Dos Equis and was suspiciously eying the plastic lunch tray the cheerful flight attendant had put in front of him. Instead of digging in, he reached down into his backpack and pulled out a Burger King bag. He'd ordered it six hours before, at a Zamora Burger King owned by a retired Z5 kingpin. He told the flight attendant to take away whatever it was that lay on the tray in front of him, which she did promptly. Then he spread out the Jalapeño King Burger, Rodeo Chicken sandwich, and two orders of large— by now, lifeless and cold—French fries.

La Bestia dug in and, ten minutes later, nothing remained on his tray except a few pickles.

Up in first class, Rafaela had just consumed a much healthier lunch: a wrap, fruit, cheese, and a small container of peach yogurt.

Rafaela flashed back to similar lunches when she'd been a student at Edron Academy, which billed itself as The Leading British American School in Mexico City. She and her older sister Constanza had graduated from there, after which she'd attended Stanford and her sister the University of California at San Diego. Their father was a Senior Vice President at Arca Continental, the third largest Coca-Cola distributor in the world, with a market value of $11.3 billion.

Rafaela had been happy at Edron and a stand-out in athletics—to please her father—and academics—to please her Ph.D. mother. In college, she'd walked on to the Stanford women's soccer team, made the cut, and became the team's leading scorer.

After the third game of her first season, Rafaela had attended a frat party at Kappa Alpha, where she'd drunk to excess and passed out in a changing room for the frat's pool. There, two members of the fraternity found her and, one by one, raped her. In a daze, Rafaela had limped back to her dorm room and never mentioned what happened to anyone. But two weeks after it happened, having suffered harrowing dreams at night and flashbacks during the day, she'd abruptly quit school and gone back to Mexico City. She told her parents that the Stanford classes were too academically rigorous for her and she couldn't keep up. Promising to get her special tutors, her parents urged her to go back, but with the trauma still fresh, she'd refused.

Several months later, she visited a friend from Edron, who went to a college in Zamora, and Rafaela ended up staying there and attending the Universidad del Valle de Atemajac. While there, she did social work in the local barrio and became active in a left-wing party.

A little after 6 p.m., Rafaela and La Bestia's plane touched down in West Palm; fifteen minutes later, they rendezvoused at the gate inside the terminal.

"How was it?" Rafaela asked La Bestia.

"Okay, if you like fat people and soldiers." He explained who'd been sitting on either side of him.

"I don't think you're going to complain about the hotel," Rafaela said, describing the Breakers and telling him it was on the ocean.

He nodded as he took in the people around him. A lot of older, well-dressed passengers with tans. Rafaela and La Bestia had only carry-on bags, so she followed the signs to the rental-car area as La Bestia cast withering looks at people who stared at him. Rafaela had reserved a yellow Corvette Stingray at Enterprise. She had always wanted to drive a Corvette ever since seeing one in a movie when she was a kid.

A wide smile crossed La Bestia's face as the attendant drove the Stingray up to them, freshly washed and glistening.

"I like your taste in cars," La Bestia said, walking around to the driver's side.

In a flash, she elbowed him in the ribs. "You ride shotgun, my friend."

AT THE OPENING OF A LONG, TREE-LINED DRIVEWAY, A MAN SAT in a car, ready to shoo curious motorists away from the exclusive Breakers. The yellow Corvette clearly caught his attention. He sat up straight and eyed Rafaela and La Bestia as she drove up alongside his vehicle.

"Where do I park?" she asked through their open windows.

The man eyeballed La Bestia disapprovingly. "You are staying at the hotel?"

"Yes. Where do I park my car?"

The man pointed to a valet. "He'll take it for you."

La Bestia eyed the approaching valet, who was young, blond, and eager-looking.

"He's gonna steal it," La Bestia growled at his boss.

"Just because you would," Rafaela said with a chuckle.

Rafaela made a quick decision not to let the valet take the Corvette. Not because she thought he'd steal it, but because checking into a fancy, five-star hotel with a man who looked like he was about to kill you might raise some eyebrows. She asked the man in the car where they could go buy men's clothes.

"For him?" the man asked skeptically.

"Yes."

"Well, ordinarily, I'd say Maus & Hoffman on Worth Avenue, but your friend here...looks more like a Salvation Army kinda guy?"

"What's that?" Rafaela asked innocently.

The man in the car gave her directions to the Salvation Army in West Palm Beach.

A half hour later, Rafaela and La Bestia walked into the Breakers. He was wearing a frayed, white button-down Brooks Brother shirt, baggy grey flannel pants, brown tie shoes one size too big and a straw hat pulled down low on his forehead to hide the number five.

THIRTY-SEVEN

Rafaela's room had a view of the ocean, La Bestia's of the parking lot. He looked down and, to his surprise, saw the Stingray parked and waiting. It had not been stolen after all.

He took a long shower, not accustomed to the elegance and grandeur of his bathroom, nor the surging water pressure of the shower. He remembered as a kid how his father had punched a handful of holes in a bucket, suspended it in a tree, then filled it with water. That was the family shower...until the water ran out. La Bestia also had never dried himself with thick, fluffy, white towels like the ones hanging on the Breakers' heated towel racks. A few paper towels had been more like it.

He dressed in the same clothes he'd worn on the flight from Mexico City, and went down to meet Rafaela in the lobby.

She wore white slacks and a white collared shirt. She looked him over. "I guess you like those clothes."

The sarcasm was lost on him. "Those things you made me wear smelled bad. Like dead guys. I'm thirsty. Let's get a drink."

Rafaela nodded. "I found a Mexican place for dinner. I know you hate *gringo* food. Except maybe that crappy fast food."

"I hate gringo just about everything, except money," La Bestia said.

"Yes, but wait until you hear the name of the restaurant."

"What is it?"

Rafaela smiled. "La Michoacana."

La Bestia smiled back at her. "No shit."

"I know," she said. Michoacan was a state in Mexico and Zamora its third largest city.

BEFORE GOING TO LA MICHOACANA, RAFAELA DROVE THE Stingray around the island of Palm Beach. La Bestia was so dumbstruck that at first, he seemed incapable of speaking.

"I saw that TV show once, *The Real Housewives of Beverly Hills*," he said finally. "I thought it was fake. Everyone had a Ferrari and a million-dollar house."

Rafaela patted him on the shoulder. "The houses here cost a lot more than a million dollars, *mi amigo*."

"Really?"

"Yeah, like ten million for ones that are nothing special and fifty for ones on the ocean."

"*Increíble.*"

Rafaela drove them down Worth Avenue and pointed out the shops. "You want a thousand-dollar sweater? Or how about a pair of three-thousand-dollar alligator shoes for your girlfriend?"

"You're kidding," La Bestia said. "Everything is so clean and perfect here."

Rafaela nodded, slowed the Corvette, and pointed at something. "See that?"

It was a brightly colored, rectangular ceramic basin on the sidewalk outside of a store. Above it was a metal faucet under a sign that read, "Dog Bar."

"What's that?"

"In case their poodles get thirsty," Rafaela said, and on cue, a well-dressed woman led her long-haired Lhasa Apso up to the basin.

La Bestia's mouth dropped as he watched the small dog take sips of water. "Now I've seen it all."

Next, they drove up to the north end of Palm Beach on North Ocean Boulevard.

"What are those little signs?" La Bestia asked.

"They're for-sale signs."

La Bestia pointed at a massive, Mediterranean-style house with a sign in the yard. "How much do you think that one costs?"

Rafaela slowed down. "Well, it's a big house on a big lot, my guess is fifty million."

La Bestia's head jerked around to her. "No, it can't be."

"*Si.*"

He pointed at the for-sale sign. "Call that number."

Rafaela pulled alongside the sign at the curb, then took out her iPhone and dialed.

Someone answered. "Hello, this is Christian, may I help you?"

"Yes, hello, can you tell me the price of the house at"— she looked for the number "—1071 North Ocean Boulevard, please?"

"Yes, ma'am. The house is thirty-eight thousand square feet, with eight bedrooms on a two-acre double lot, with two hundred forty-two feet of ocean frontage. It includes a grand salon, dual ocean balconies, a massage room, a pub room, a library, a game room, and an eight-car garage. We're offering it on an exclusive basis for fifty nine point nine million dollars."

"Is this a recording?" Rafaela asked.

"No, this is Christian; can I schedule a showing for you?"

"No, thank you, I need, ah, nine bedrooms," Rafaela clicked off and turned to La Bestia. "I was pretty close."

"How much?"

"Fifty-nine-point-nine million."

A police car, driving slowly, came around a corner.

Rafaela left the curb, accelerated, and waved at the cop as they passed.

La Bestia chuckled. "Friend of yours?"

"All *policia* are friends of mine."

They drove a little farther north until Rafaela saw the sign for Dolphin Road. She slowed down, pulled over, and pointed toward the ocean. "This is where they found that poor man buried in the sand."

La Bestia smiled as he scanned the beach and the ocean beyond. "Poor man."

AFTER MUCH PLEADING ON HIS PART, RAFAELA LET LA BESTIA drive the Stingray to the La Michoacana.

The problem was, La Bestia wanted to drive the sports car fast and he wasn't a good driver. He didn't even have a license, having grown up in a family that never owned a car. On Dixie Highway, he got it up to seventy before Rafaela yelled at him to slow down and threatened to pull the handbrake. Obviously, she told him, it would be a bad idea to get stopped for speeding or, for that matter, anything.

La Bestia drove the speed limit the rest of the way, hanging a right on Belvedere. Rafaela pointed at the sign for La Michoacana. It turned out to be a take-out place.

"It's an ice-cream stand," Rafaela said. "Just like in Mexico."

La Bestia nodded. In Mexico, La Michoacana ice cream parlors were as ubiquitous as Baskin-Robbins or Carvel shops in America. The brand had been around forever and offered a variety of customer favorites, such as Esquimals, milk-based bars covered with chocolate and topped with shredded coconut. Another favorite was something called Pico de Gallo Paleta, a water-based confection containing mango, cucumber, and lime juice, plus chili powder.

Rafaela had her iPhone out and was scrolling down looking for actual Mexican restaurants. "Okay. Let's try this place called Torero's," she said. "Then we can come back here for dessert."

La Bestia nodded as Rafaela gave him directions to an address on Village Boulevard, slightly north of them.

The only available parking spots at Torero's required parallel parking. La Bestia reluctantly admitted that he had no idea how to parallel park, so he pulled over and traded seats with Rafaela, who did a commendable job of fitting the Corvette in between two SUVs.

Rafaela turned off the ignition, glanced at La Bestia, and chuckled: "The only thing you really know how to do is torture and kill people."

He smiled. "Yes, but I'm very good at it."

She nodded her assent.

If they were awarding stars, Torero's would have earned 3.5 out of 5. La Bestia had the carne asada and two margaritas, while Rafaela chose the fajita salad and a couple of glasses of wine.

"There was a maid at the hotel who was Latina," La Bestia said, finishing off his second drink. "Know what she told me?"

"What?"

"That lots of movie stars and famous singers stay at the Breakers."

"Oh, yeah, like who?"

"Well, like Elton John and Gwen Stefani. And someone called Alex Baldwin. I don't know who he is."

"An actor. But I think it's Alec."

A rare smile lit up La Bestia's face. "Also, she said, Cameron Diaz. She's Mexican, I think."

Rafaela laughed. "No way. She's American."

"Well, she's got a Mexican name."

Rafaela cocked her head. "So, is Ted Cruz Mexican too?"

"I don't know who that is."

"An American senator. From Texas."

La Bestia waved her off. "Meh, who cares about politicians?"

She smiled and toasted him with her wine glass.

La Bestia was by nature not a subtle man. "How would you like it if I came to your room later on?" he inquired, as if he was asking her the time.

"I wouldn't," she replied matter-of-factly. "Ours is a business arrangement."

La Bestia gave her what he considered to be his most seductive smile. "Yes, but sometimes business can turn into pleasure."

"Not this time."

La Bestia frowned. "Is it true what they say about you?"

"I don't know what they say about me."

"That—" he wasn't quite sure how to express it. "That you do not have sex with men? Any men at all?"

"I'm not comfortable with the direction this conversation is taking...but I'll give you an answer if it'll shut you up."

"I'm all ears."

Rafaela smiled. "Okay, it's true. I do not have sex with men."

"With women?"

Rafaela laughed. "Not with men, women, dogs, or goats. I do not have sex, period."

"Why not?"

"Because I tried it and didn't fancy it. And that's enough on that subject."

La Bestia smiled and a gold tooth molar shined. "Maybe I could change how you think."

Rafaela laughed derisively and shook her head. "Typical man. Think you're God's gift to women."

"You'd be surprised."

Neither spoke for a few moments. "So, I have a theory," La Bestia said.

"About what?"

"You want to hear it?"

"I'm kind of a captive audience."

That concept of a captive audience flew over La Bestia's head. "My theory is that killing people is your sex."

Rafaela thought for a few moments. Her first reaction was to say, *You're not as dumb as you look.* But she didn't dare give him the satisfaction.

"Be careful, my friend," she said. "Too many theories and your head will explode."

THIRTY-EIGHT

THE NEXT MORNING, CRAWFORD'S BURNER PHONE RANG shortly after he arrived at the station.

"Hello?"

"Mr. Paul, it is Rafaela from Mexico, except now I am in Palm Beach."

"What do you want with me?" he said in his most world-weary voice.

"You know perfectly well. My fifty-three million dollars."

Crawford groaned. "Then I suggest you go to a bank."

"If that's a joke, it's not funny."

"It wasn't meant to be." He hung up.

She called back immediately. He let it go to voicemail, then listened to the message when he received the notification.

"I don't appreciate your rudeness," she said in her message. "You can either be cooperative or not. My mate and I have had a lot of experience with men who are uncooperative, and we have many ways of making them cooperative."

Rafaela dialed a different number.

"Hello?" Dominica answered.

"Valerie, it's Rafaela. I need the address for Weston Paul."

"Oh, hello, Rafaela. Well, that's going to cost you more money."

"Look," said Rafaela, her temper rising, "all you had to do was make one phone call to get a hundred thousand dollars. Just one phone call. So that's all you're going to get."

"You need to add another fifty thousand."

"You're starting to irritate me, Valerie. You really don't want to do that. Or my associate and I will find out where you are and come see *you*."

"All right, all right," Dominica said with a sigh. "He lives at 1098 South Ocean Boulevard."

"Thank you."

"You're in Palm Beach already?"

"Yes."

"You work fast."

"Yes, I do, but I'm homesick already."

Dominica called Crawford right away. "I gave you up, Charlie. So be on the lookout for Rafaela and her 'associate'."

"Is that what she called him? Called him her 'mate' when I spoke to her."

"Be careful, Charlie. I worry about you."

"That seems to be going around," he said. "I'll be fine. I got my Sig, my ankle piece, and my Ka-bar—" he said, referring to his knife "— not to mention Mort and the boys, locked and loaded. We're ready."

THIRTY-NINE

A CRIMINAL GANG CALLED TOP SIX USED TO TERRORIZE WEST Palm Beach and Lake Worth. At least until the RICO act and the crushing brawn of the West Palm Beach Police Department drove their members into the shadows. The definitive statement as to law enforcement's take-no-prisoners approach had come a few years back, when Top Six's leader was given a sixty-five-year prison sentence, later upheld on appeal, for racketeering, conspiracy to commit racketeering, and possession of marijuana and ecstasy. The message of the verdict was clear to all: Crime doesn't pay in West Palm. Or if it does, not for long. West Palm Beach went from the thirteenth most dangerous city in the nation to...still treacherous but much less so than before.

Top Six, which was made up of other gangs like Fade Squad and G Block, hadn't disappeared entirely; they'd only became a lot less visible. One of the crimes they still committed on a regular basis was selling drugs on the mean streets across the Intracoastal from Palm Beach. They dealt mostly cocaine, meth, and marijuana, provided by, among others, Z5. And where there are drugs, there are weapons. Lots of them.

Rafaela Arroyo and La Bestia needed weapons and didn't exactly know where to find them. They drove— Rafaela at the wheel— in the yellow Corvette until they found a poor neighborhood in the city of Lake Worth. The depressed neighborhood led into an even more blighted barrio, and Rafaela knew she was getting warm.

They were stopped at a light amid ramshackle houses with trash strewn in their yards, old junkers beached in their yards, and people sitting on their porches, drinking forties and smoking joints.

"A little different from Palm Beach," La Bestia said.

Rafaela nodded and, when the light turned green, pulled over to a group of black guys in their teens and early twenties, shooting hoops at an improvised basket on the street.

They stopped playing at the sight of the yellow Corvette and the Amazon princess with blond hair piled on top of her head.

In a few seconds, they'd surrounded the car, seven men in all.

"Nice wheels," said one, noticing the tattoo on La Bestia's forehead. "What's the five stand for, homey?"

Rafaela answered for La Bestia. "Zamora Five. It's an...organization in Mexico."

"Oh, yeah? Never heard of it."

Another came up to Rafaela and ran his hand through her hair. "You mean, like the Girl Scouts?"

Rafaela slapped his hand away. "Don't do that," she said with a hard edge to her voice.

"Why not?" said the man who had a tattoo on his arm that read *Ghost.*

"'Cause I said so." Rafaela guessed tattoo-boy was the leader.

He leaned in closer to her. "What you want, girlfriend?"

"Guns," she said, reaching into her purse and pulling out a thick wad of hundreds. "And I figure you chaps might just know where we can get them."

Ghost chuckled. "Chaps, huh?" He looked around at the others, who were smiling. "Don't b'lieve we ever been called 'chaps' before."

"We need two pistols and two automatic rifles," Rafaela said. "My particular favorites are either an HK416 or HKMG4, or maybe a F2000 or a M192."

Next to her, La Bestia muttered something in Spanish that included the words Uzi and Kalashnikov. "Yes," Rafaela added. "We would also be happy with an Uzi or AK-47. As far as pistols, maybe a Glock 18 or a Kel-Tec PMR 30."

La Bestia mumbled something more.

Rafaela nodded. "Or a Sig Sauer. You chaps look like you might be...what's the word? Strapped. You have anything that fits the bill?"

"You're a piece of work," said Ghost, smiling. "What if we just took your money and put a bullet between your eyes?"

Rafaela stared him in the eyes. "That would be extremely unwise," she said, taking out her iPhone. She scrolled down it and stopped. Then she motioned to Ghost to take a look at something on her device.

He and another man looked down at her iPhone. It displayed a photo of Rafaela and La Bestia in the foreground, with about twenty hardcore cutthroats clustered around them. Behind them in the background were three shirtless men hanging from a bridge, ropes around their necks.

Rafaela pointed to the men around her in the photo. "These are what I think you call my 'homeboys.' Members of our *organization.* See, if anything were to happen to us, they'd come after you and not rest until you were hanging like these men in the photo."

Now all seven men had come over to Rafaela's side of the car and were staring down at the photo.

La Bestia glanced up at Ghost. "*Comprendes, muchacho?*"

The leader pointed to a black Challenger parked in a driveway. "I think we might be able to do some business."

Rafaela looked over at the car. "You have something in the boot?" she asked, looking up at Ghost while shading her eyes.

"The what?"

"The boot," she said, pointing. "Maybe you have another word for it."

Ghost nodded. "You mean the trunk. I'm gonna drive it in the garage and you can have a look. Ain't good to do business in broad daylight."

"That's fine," Rafaela said. "No tricks, though. My friends in the photo will find you wherever you are."

The leader smiled. "I believe ya," he said. "We just gonna have a nice little transaction. Got a few other things you might be interested in, too."

GHOST'S TRUNK, OR AS THE BRITISH SAY, BOOT, WAS NOT expansive, but it was plenty big enough for an Uzi, a F2000 automatic rifle, a Glock, and a Sig Sauer P226. In addition, Ghost sold Rafaela three hand grenades. Rafaela had no idea what she'd use them for but Ghost gave her a good price. That done, Ghost offered Rafaela something she'd never used before but it looked like fun. Might come in handy at some point.

Rafaela said goodbye to her new friends and drove back to the Breakers, almost ready to pay Weston Paul a visit.

FORTY

FOR A HOUSE ON THE OCEAN IN PALM BEACH, IT WAS PRETTY basic. No comparison to the house that Adriana Palmer's father had given her. Or to Rose Clarke's British colonial, which she had spared no expense in renovating. No, this house was just plain pathetic. Rose said that the owner, a man named Walter Kehoe, had built it as a "spec house," meaning as an investment that he planned to sell as soon as a live buyer with a fat wallet came walking through the front door. But everything about the house was cheap. It looked like a Home Depot special, built by a builder who specialized in tract-housing. According to Rose, instead of paying the going rate to build a new house in Palm Beach, somewhere in the five hundred dollar per square foot range, Kehoe had spent a hundred seventy-five dollars per square foot. And it showed. Everywhere.

The tiles were porcelain instead of stone, the windows bottom-of-the-line Andersons as opposed to high-end Marvins, the kitchen appliances Sears Kenmore instead of Viking or Wolf. The problem with all that was that people looking to buy a twenty-million-dollar house knew the difference and wouldn't settle for cheap.

So, in the ten months the house had been on the market, no one had made any sort of offer. Not even a lowball.

Rose had suggested that Kehoe "stage" the house, meaning spend some money to furnish it and make it look appealing. But, of course, the owner had cheaped out again. Instead of signing up for Trend Interiors' "gold package," Rose's suggestion, Kehoe had opted for their "bronze package," which was better suited to half-million-dollar condos in Jupiter or Palm Beach Gardens.

To no one's surprise except Kehoe's, the house had languished on the market while real-estate taxes and maintenance costs mounted. So, what did Kehoe do next? He dropped the price from $14,900,000 to $14,750,000, a surefire way to get buyers stampeding into the house.

Not.

Then Kehoe had another brainstorm. An old girlfriend had once mentioned that if the house had a good place for her to work on her tan off of the upstairs bedrooms, she'd be tempted to spend more time there. He never got around to adding the second-story sun deck, and she was soon his ex-girlfriend. So, when Rose approached him about lending his house for a "sting operation," Kehoe decided maybe the mayor would look favorably on his variance request and quickly agreed to lend it out. As far as getting a key to the city, Kehoe didn't much care about that.

CRAWFORD WAS AT KEHOE'S HOUSE ON SOUTH OCEAN Boulevard. He had just zapped a Papa John's pizza that had been delivered lukewarm by a guy in a fifteen-year-old Mazda with bald tires and a bumper sticker reading, *Don't Believe A Word The Liberal Media Says.* Crawford wasn't convinced the bumper sticker was the key to getting a decent tip in this town, but, hey, to each his own.

A slice in hand, he opened the refrigerator. Its entire contents consisted of Walmart house-brand catsup, mustard, mayo, and a twelve-pack of Sierra Nevada Torpedo beer that Crawford had bought that morning. He pulled out a Torpedo, popped the top, and sat on a kitchen bar stool.

Ah, heaven...Papa John's and Torpedo.

It really didn't get much better than that.

———

ACROSS THE DRIVEWAY, ON THE SECOND FLOOR OF THE HOME'S equally cheaply built and unfurnished garage apartment, Mort Ott and Bill Strohman waited. Strohman worked undercover in robbery. Crawford and Ott occasionally teamed up with him when they needed an extra man. Strohman had one of the greatest collections of Hawaiian shirts in southern Florida. He also had a protruding gut that peeked out beneath the hem of his sartorial masterpieces.

Ott was looking down at the front door of the South Ocean Boulevard house, while Strohman sat in a wooden chair they'd salvaged from the garage below.

"This is like watching grass grow," Strohman said, taking a hit from his Dasani water bottle.

"Did you think law enforcement was going to be a glamorous life?" Ott asked, not shifting his gaze.

"Well, catching killers is more glamorous than catching guys who jack cars."

Ott shrugged as he heard a car roll over the Chattahoochee pebbles of the driveway. A yellow Corvette convertible crawled to a stop, a woman with a haystack of orange-blond hair at the wheel.

"What do you know," said Ott. "It's our girl."

They watched Rafaela get out, followed by a small, hard-looking man in a black T-shirt and jeans, tattoos sleeving both arms. He looked to Ott like a guy who might have fleas buzzing around his head.

"Nasty-looking dude," Strohman said as the two walked toward the front door below.

"Come on," Ott said, moving toward the door.

———————————

RAFAELA STEPPED ONTO THE PORCH, PUSHED THE DOORBELL, and started tapping her toe. She had spelled out her plan with La Bestia that morning during breakfast at Hardee's. The plan had three phases to it, but she hoped only one would be necessary.

The first phase, the one they were now embarked on, was to confront Weston Paul face-to-face and, acting reasonably but forcefully, convince him of the wisdom of using his computer to wire fifty-three million into an account of hers.

"You think he'll just agree to go ahead and do that?" La Bestia had asked skeptically.

"I do if he's got a gun to his head," Rafaela had said. "On second thought, we shouldn't have any weapons on us since we have no permits, but there's nothing illegal about those bolt cutters you bought last night."

A big smile had rippled across his face. "Or my knife. But aren't you worried about the bank questioning such a large deposit?"

"Not in the Grand Caymans."

"Where?"

"An island four hundred miles east of Cancun. They are only too happy to take my money, no questions asked."

"And what if Weston Paul doesn't cooperate?"

"I have a backup plan for tonight."

"And what if—"

"I have a backup plan to the backup plan."

"And what if he doesn't have the money? All we have is the word of this woman from his brother's company that he does."

Rafaela reached over and patted his arm. "That's a very good question. If he doesn't have it—" a smile lit up her face "—we will take his house and sell it."

"What do you mean, 'take it?'"

"Very simple. Just like any other real estate transaction, except the seller will be in a great deal of pain when we both sign a contract. Him as seller, me as buyer, then in a month or so we close. I'll be back in Mexico by then and have a real estate agent sell it. And he'll be..." She shrugged. "Dead."

"I like it, Rafaela, very creative."

"Thank you. From what I found online, the house is worth about fifteen million dollars. So, I end up losing money, but it's better than nothing. And I still believe we're going to get the fifty-three million from him. That woman was very believable."

CRAWFORD CAME TO THE DOOR, WEARING A FROWN. "ARE YOU that woman I spoke to?"

Rafaela smiled at him. "Yes, I am Rafaela and this is my friend, La Bestia. We spoke yesterday."

Crawford started to close the door but La Bestia put his foot in the way.

"Listen, Mr. Paul," said Rafaela, "I believe the English expression is, *this is getting old.*" She glanced at her partner and shrugged. "It's really very simple: you give us our money and we disappear."

"Yes, I agree," Crawford said, "this *is* getting old. As I told you before, I don't have your money or anyone else's."

Rafaela took her iPhone out of her pocket and scrolled down. "It's about time you took us seriously." She held up the phone so Crawford could see the photo of her and La Bestia in front of the three dead men hanging from a bridge. "This is what happens to people who don't take us seriously."

Crawford blanched and wasn't faking it.

Rafaela heard a noise behind her and turned. Ott and Bill Strohman had their Glocks pointed at them.

"Palm Beach Police," said Ott, showing his ID. "Is there a problem here, Mr. Paul?"

Crawford smiled. "Not anymore."

Ott locked eyes with Rafaela. "What are you people doing here?"

Rafaela paused for a moment, searching for the correct words. "We are debt collectors."

"Mr. Paul owes you money?" Ott asked.

"Yes," Rafaela said.

"No," Crawford said.

"Are you a U.S. citizen, Ms..."

"Arroyo. No, I'm not, but what difference does that make?"

"Well, in this country, if you think someone owes you money and won't pay, then you need to go through the courts."

Rafaela took a step closer to Ott. "Everyone?"

"What do you mean?'"

"Everyone goes through the courts? Because I heard that if, say, someone owes the mafia money, that's not the way they do it."

"That may be true, but you look like a nice law-abiding citizen." He took a long look up and down La Bestia. "Your friend, I'm not so sure about." He signaled to Strohman. "Search 'em for weapons, Bill."

Strohman sheathed his Glock in his shoulder holster, then thoroughly patted down La Bestia. Nothing. He turned to Rafaela. "Ma'am, put your arms up, please. I'll go slow and careful."

Rafaela raised her arms and shrugged. "That's very nice of you, but you're not going to find anything."

He did go slow and careful. Again, nothing.

Ott turned to Rafaela. "Hand him your keys," he said, motioning to Strohman. "He's going to go search your car."

Rafaela handed Strohman the keys. "Be my guest."

Strohman walked over to the Corvette and looked under the seats and in the glove compartment. Nothing. Then he opened the car's trunk, reached in and pulled something out. He slammed the trunk and walked over to the others.

Ott turned to Rafaela and pointed at the bolt cutters in Strohman's hand. "What are these for?"

Rafaela smiled. "To trim my nails with. What difference does it make? Is it illegal?"

There was nothing more Ott could do.

"Okay," he said to Rafaela, "you and your friend need to leave now."

Rafaela nodded "Okay," she said to Crawford. "I guess we'll just have to see you in court, Mr. Paul."

FORTY-ONE

Rafaela, of course, had no intention of seeing anyone in court. So it was on to Plan B, which she had decided was best executed at night. That meant that she and La Bestia had the afternoon off. Normally, when La Bestia had time off he invariably visited one of his favorite *casa de putas*, but since he had no idea where to find hookers in Palm Beach, he'd have to find some other way to kill time.

Once again, Rafaela pulled out her iPhone. This time she typed in, *What to do in Palm Beach?* After studying the options, she decided that she'd go to the Henry Morrison Flagler Museum, the Mounts Botanical Garden, and, to satisfy her historical curiosity, Peanut Island. Peanut Island, she read, was an eighty-acre island off the northern tip of Palm Beach that housed a bomb shelter built for President John F. Kennedy, in case there was a Russian nuclear attack while he was staying at the Winter White House at 1095 North Ocean Boulevard. As she read on, she was disappointed to see that it had been shuttered in October of 2017 because of the discovery of mold, and the fact that the bunker was in dire need of a complete restoration.

For his part, La Bestia had zero interest in a museum or botanical garden. He asked Rafaela to read through the other attractions in and around Palm Beach. Two things caught his interest. One was the Rapids Water Park, which claimed that guests screamed at the top of their lungs as they experienced the Big Thunder ride and "the thrill of zero-g." That totally captured La Bestia's fancy, along with the Palm Beach Kennel Club, known more commonly to its patrons as "the dog track."

Rafaela was not about to let La Bestia drive the Corvette, so she scribbled down the phone number for Yellow Cab, as well as the addresses of the two places he wanted to go. She repeated the names of both attractions several times so he knew what to say when he called the cab company.

Rafaela spent two and a half hours alone, wandering the grounds of Mounts Botanical Garden. She particularly enjoyed the Rainbow Garden and the Butterfly Garden. The park offered a guided tour of the rose garden, which she tagged along on. As she was inhaling the fragrance of a hybrid yellow rose, the tour guide turned to her and said, "In Victorian times, the yellow rose symbolized jealousy, but nowadays it represents friendship, joy, and caring."

Rafaela smiled at the woman and said simply, "It's beautiful and smells so nice."

When Rafaela met up with La Bestia at the HMF bar at the Breakers later on, he pulled out a wad of five and ten dollars bills and told her that four of his greyhound picks had won their races. "Those dogs can run like the wind," La Bestia said, then added, "and those rides, *dios mío.*" He smiled and shook his head, speechless.

"Maybe you should move here," Rafaela said. "You won't have to work for me if you win every race at the dog track."

FORTY-TWO

CRAWFORD AND OTT WERE IN THE LAUNDRY ROOM AT 1098 South Beach Road. It was seven at night. Crawford was sitting on the counter and Ott was leaning against the oversized dryer. It seemed the safest space to occupy, since there were no windows in the room. Even though Crawford knew it made no sense for Rafaela or La Bestia to take a shot at him. But better safe than sorry.

Bill Strohman and another undercover, Al Lutz, were in the guesthouse with the lights out, keeping an eye on the grounds around the main house with night-vision goggles.

Ott pushed away from the dryer and paced the tiny room for the hundredth time. "What do you think they're gonna do next?"

Crawford shrugged. "No clue. If you asked me that before they buried Thorsen Paul in the beach, I never would've guessed. That whole thing this afternoon was their way of asking me nicely. I got a feeling next time's not gonna be so nice."

"Yeah, I agree," Ott said. "Next question: Why do you think they're driving around in the flashiest car they can find and staying at the most visible hotel in town?"

"That's another good question."

Ott stared at him, exasperated. "That's it. You got no theories? You being the theory man and all?"

"Not really. All I know for sure is we ain't see the last of 'em."

"Yeah, no shit," Ott said.

"I'm thinking tomorrow morning we tell Rutledge about Rafaela."

"Yeah, I agree. Just to be on the record."

Crawford nodded.

"Well, I might as well go join the boys in the garage apartment. Where are you gonna sleep?"

"In here," Crawford said. "Got a sleeping bag out in the car. Haven't used it since I went camping up in the Adirondacks a million years ago."

Ott slapped Crawford on the shoulder as he walked past him. "All right, then. You know where to find me."

RAFAELA SMILED AT THE WOMAN BEHIND THE RECEPTION DESK. "We're checking out now."

The woman's surprise was obvious. It was eight o'clock at night. Not the usual checkout time. "Okay, I'll total up your bill. Did you use anything in your mini-bar today?"

"No, nothing."

"How 'bout you, sir?" she asked La Bestia, who had finally changed outfits. Well, at least his shirt. He now wore a white, sleeveless tee with a Puma logo.

Rafaela translated and La Bestia shook his head.

"He didn't have anything," Rafaela said.

The receptionist gave him a look like maybe she didn't believe him. Like he was the kind of guy who could scarf down everything in the mini-bar in one sitting.

"Here you go," she said, at last, handing Rafaela her bill.

"I'm paying for both," Rafaela said.

The woman printed out the bill for La Bestia's room.

Rafaela scanned them and handed her a black Amex card.

THEY WERE BACK IN LAKE WORTH, HAVING DOWNGRADED FROM a five-star hotel to a two-star roach motel. The Blue Moon on Federal Highway claimed to be "Hollywood-themed," which turned out to mean there was a blown-up, framed photo of Sandra Bullock in La Bestia's room and Bradley Cooper in Rafaela's.

The Blue Moon was twenty minutes closer to the Miami Airport than the Breakers had been, but Rafaela had chosen it because they'd be a lot harder to track down here. After leaving the Breakers, they'd also returned to Enterprise and traded in the yellow Corvette for a white Corolla, figuring there must be ten thousand white Corollas in south Florida. Rafaela had also decided it would be wiser to fly back from the Miami Airport than Palm Beach. First of all, there were a lot more flights to Mexico City, and second, if the Palm Beach cops managed to track down their transactions, they'd see she had tickets for a flight out of Palm Beach Airport three days later.

Rafaela felt satisfied that the changes would make apprehending them pretty close to impossible. They checked into the Blue Moon at a little past nine, left their bags there, and headed directly back up to Palm Beach.

"This is a real piece of shit," La Bestia said, slapping the Corolla's dashboard disdainfully.

Rafaela took the high road. "It's a means of transportation," she said. "Inconspicuous, too."

La Bestia looked as though he had no clue what inconspicuous meant.

"Shitty radio, too," he said, cranking up 93.5 FM, a Spanish station that seemed to specialize in Latin salsa tunes with bouncy beats.

Rafaela crossed the Southern Bridge to Palm Beach, then, slowing, pointed north at Mar-a-Lago. "See that, that's Trump's place. It's called Mar-a-Lago."

La Bestia took a long look at the tall tower that rose up above the main building. "I want to be a billionaire."

Rafaela thought for a second, tapping the steering wheel of the Corvette. "Well, then, first thing you gotta do is get that 5 off your forehead."

By 10:30, Crawford had settled into a club chair that he'd moved from the living room into the laundry space. He had his computer in his lap and was watching the Netflix series, *Narcos*. Pablo Escobar had once again made a bold escape from a rival drug gang's ambush and was in a Medellin, Colombia, safe house. His men had been bombing one of his rival's legitimate businesses, a drugstore chain.

BOOM! A huge explosion reverberated throughout the house.

Crawford drew the Sig Sauer from his shoulder holster, bounced to his feet, and crept next to the doorframe in a crouch.

His cell phone rang almost immediately. "Yeah?"

"You okay?" It was Ott.

"Yeah, I'm fine."

"A guy was on the roof. I saw him jump off and head for the beach. Strohman and Lutz went after him, but he had a pretty big head start."

"I'm going out to see what it was."

"I'll be right down," Ott said.

Crawford clicked off and dialed the station. A woman in dispatch answered. "This is Crawford. Send every available uniform down to the area around 1098 South Ocean Boulevard. Looking for two suspects: a tall, blonde woman and a short, dark-haired man. Possibly driving a yellow Corvette. Tell 'em to be careful, both are armed and dangerous." He clicked off.

Crawford smelled a sharp, acrid odor as he walked through the kitchen and into the living room. He flipped on the light and saw smoke billowing out of the fireplace as Ott came in through the front door.

"Dropped something down the chimney," Ott said to Crawford as they approached the fireplace. Much of the mantel had toppled to the floor, a pile of bricks and debris littering the bare floor in front. A nearby hi-hat light fixture dangled halfway to the floor by a strand of electric cord.

Cautiously, they moved from the living room into an enclosed sun porch. It had a fireplace that backed up to the one in the living room. Splintered kindling was scattered around the room, along with two twisted andirons.

Crawford spotted something and dropped into a crouch. He picked it up. Ott, on the other side of the room, looked over. "Whatcha got?"

"Looks like the handle and firing pin of a hand grenade. Fragmentation-style's my guess."

Ott walked over. "What the *hell*, man?"

Crawford started to say something, then heard a shout from the other side of the house. "Hey, where are you?" It was Al Lutz.

"In here!" Ott yelled back.

Lutz and Strohman ran through the house to the sun porch.

"No luck?" Ott asked.

"Nope. Dude was gone, plus it's pitch-black," Strohman said.

Ott chuckled. "Plus, you don't do the hundred in ten seconds anymore."

Crawford stood, the grenade parts still in his hand. "Get in your cars. You—" he said to Strohman "—head south. Lutz, go north. They'll still be in the yellow Corvette unless they ditched it."

Strohman and Lutz hurried out the front door.

Crawford flashed to Rose Clarke. What would he tell her about what had happened to the house her seller had so graciously lent the town. And what she'd tell Walter Kehoe. *Nothing too serious. Just a vicious cartel member from Mexico who dropped a hand grenade down your chimney. But don't worry, I've already contacted an excellent chimney contractor...*

La Bestia yanked open the car door of the Corolla a half mile south of the South Ocean Boulevard house. Rafaela, wearing a floppy hat to hide her distinctive hair, stepped on the gas, heading back up Southern. She told La Bestia to get down so he couldn't be seen.

She heard a siren to the north, then saw a car pull out of the Weston Paul residence, heading south. Some hundred yards away, a fire engine suddenly came around the corner, lights flashing, siren wailing.

"You didn't torch the place, did you?"

Still hunched, La Bestia shook his head. "Just what you told me to do."

Another police car blew past her, racing south. She took a left onto Southern and waved her hand. "*Adios, gringos.*"

FORTY-THREE

CRAWFORD AND OTT WERE IN NORM RUTLEDGE'S OFFICE FIRST thing the next morning. Not that they wanted to be there, but because Rutledge had called them both in the middle of the night after hearing about the bombing of the South Ocean Boulevard house. Crawford had assured him it wasn't that big a deal, but Rutledge hadn't been convinced.

He was no more persuaded now, although he was eyeing Crawford strangely.

"Did I miss the memo about it being casual Tuesday?"

Crawford was wearing blue jeans and a sports shirt because he hadn't had a chance to go to his house in West Palm and put on a jacket and tie.

So typical of Rutledge to focus on something minor. Crawford fought the frequent urge he got around Rutledge to groan or roll his eyes.

"Between adhering to the dress code and hearing your pearls of wisdom, I decided to choose the latter—" this time Rutledge rolled his eyes "—and I know you're going to put the kibosh on the op taking place here."

Rutledge feigned shock. "Put the kibosh on it? Are you fucking kidding me? We had a bombing in one of the most exclusive sections of Palm Beach last night. Yeah, okay we didn't have a shootout on Worth Avenue, but pretty damn close. I want you to go arrest these Mexicans, put 'em in a cell, and throw away the goddamn key. Then we'll extradite them the hell out of here."

The man was not only panicking but coming up with a solution that was totally unworkable.

"Yes, it was an explosion and, yes, it caused some damage, but all it really was, was Rafaela Arroyo trying to soften up Weston Paul," Crawford said. "Her way of scaring the shit out of me so I'd give her the money."

"Yeah, but what if they had abducted you or something? Or tortured you?" Rutledge asked,

Crawford shook his head. "Look, she knows Weston Paul has police protection. Ott and Strohman showed up right after they came to the house yesterday."

Rutledge nodded.

"Another thing," Ott added. "You know what they'd say if we arrested 'em? Had 'em in custody?"

"What?"

"'Hey, we're just two people on vacation, why are you hassling us?' Then we'd have to let 'em go."

Crawford nodded. "He's right."

"You didn't get any shots of that guy dropping the grenade?"

"It was pitch-black, and the guy was wearing a hoodie," Ott said

Rutledge leaned back in his chair and put his feet up on his desk. His official "let-me-cogitate-on-this" pose. Also known as his vacuous look. Thirty seconds later, as Crawford eyed an email he had just received and flashed it to Ott, Rutledge leaned forward. "I still think we should bring in the FBI or the DEA."

"How 'bout the Texas Rangers and the Royal Canadian Mounted Police, too?" Ott said.

"Funny. Your usual wiseass response to a logical suggestion," Rutledge snapped. "This is too big for us alone."

"There're only two of them," Crawford said. "We can handle 'em. No offense, but a clusterfuck is usually the worst possible solution." He held up his iPhone. "I want to show you something, Norm. So, yesterday morning I got my guy Mel from Sun-Tech Systems to rig up a couple of cameras on the outside of the house on South Ocean Boulevard."

He handed the iPhone to Rutledge. "Mel just sent me this. As you can see, it shows Rafaela Arroyo's sidekick in action. First, putting a magnetized bug on the Caddy's bumper, then going around to the back of the house, climbing up on the roof, and dropping that grenade down the chimney."

La Bestia had attached the GPS tracker to the homeowner Walter Kehoe's blue Cadillac, which had been parked in the driveway.

"So, you just remove the bug," Rutledge said.

Crawford eyed Ott, who was shaking his head. "That's exactly what we *don't* want to do. I'm with you that we gotta take the action away from Palm Beach. God knows what else they have in their arsenal. But there are plenty of places out west where there're more gators than people. We can stage round three out there."

Rutledge scratched his head. "My fishing camp's out that way."

Crawford caught Ott's eye. "Well, there ya go."

"'There ya go' what?"

"I'll hide out at your fishing camp, with half the department layin' low," Crawford said. "Our Mexican friends will follow me out and—"

"Whoa, whoa, I just finished paying the place off. I don't want a couple of wetbacks blowin' it to smithereens."

Crawford tapped the arm of his chair. "Here's how I see it playing out: I go to wherever—" glancing at Rutledge "—your fishing camp, or if not, somewhere else out there. Sooner or later, they'll follow me. Probably sooner because they seem eager to get the show on the road. They confront me with hand grenades or chainsaws or whatever they got, but we have our guys hiding out. Then it could go in a lot of different directions. Somehow, I get 'em to confess to doin' my brother 'cause I'm wired. Or we take 'em down for attempted murder, then try to get 'em for the Thorsen Paul hit. Or, who knows, maybe we kill 'em."

"I like that option," Rutledge said.

"And, as I said, we got the cavalry dug in wherever this takes place."

Rutledge sighed. "So, nothin' happens to my camp?"

"Maybe a couple bullet holes. Hey, adds character," Crawford said. "Plus, you're in on the take-down. You need a little excitement in your life, Norm."

Rutledge lapsed back into ponder mode, looking out the window this time.

"What are you thinking?" Crawford asked.

Rutledge glanced over. "I'm thinkin' we already got these two on attempted murder— the grenades. I think we could make that stick. Maybe that's good enough."

Crawford shook his head emphatically. "You say we got 'em, but we don't. They're in the wind, remember? Disappeared after the little grenade caper. They checked out of the Breakers and, I have no doubt, got rid of the yellow 'vette. So, it's not like we can take 'em in any time we want. Maybe we'll find 'em, maybe we won't. My guess is, if we did nail Rafaela Arroyo, she'd give up the mutt who dropped the grenade in a New York second. Which means we'd have nothing on her. So, we get the mutt and Rafaela heads back to Mexico. She failed in her mission, we failed in ours. How's that work for you, Norm?"

Rutledge sighed and looked out the window again.

"Just curious...what do you catch at that fishing camp of yours, Norm?" Ott asked.

Rutledge turned and a wide smile lit up his face. "Best trophy-bass fishing anywhere. And crappies, you won't find any better crappie fishing on Lake Okeechobee."

Crawford chuckled. "Wait. There's a fish called a crappie?"

"Yeah, speckled perch. Also, call 'em specks."

Crawford shook his head. "Not real sure I'd want to eat a fish called a crappie," he said. "Hey, back to what we were saying...if you don't want to use your place, I'm sure we can find somewhere else."

Rutledge thought for a few moments. "No, I'm good with it—" he shrugged— "I mean, what the hell? What's a couple bullet holes?"

FORTY-FOUR

So, Rutledge was on board. Crawford knew the primary reason was that he'd sold him on being in on the actual bust. Hiding out with Ott and the other men somewhere around the camp and taking in Arroyo and LaBestia. Getting a big slap on the back from the mayor. Maybe even a raise.

In case the plan blew up, however, Crawford and Ott wanted to be able to locate Arroyo and LaBestia. Crawford was pretty sure that they had ditched the Corvette, but just to be sure he and Ott split up and went to eight rent-a-car places until they got a positive ID at Enterprise. The woman at the desk said that a six-foot-woman with "distinctive hair"—as she called it— and a short man with a big number five inked on his forehead had traded it in for a white Corolla, license plate LE9435.

Rafaela and La Bestia were at the IHOP on Lake Worth Road in Lake Worth at just before ten in the morning.

"He's either still at the house on the ocean or left in another car," Rafaela said.

"Or maybe someone gave him a ride," La Bestia said.

"Could be," Rafaela said. "In any case, I want to wait until it's dark again to go after him."

La Bestia nodded as he took a bite of his pancakes. "Which means we've got another day off."

Rafaela nodded as she took a sip of her third cup of coffee and watched La Bestia wolf down his Breakfast Sampler. It consisted of two of just about everything under the Florida sun: two eggs, two bacon strips, two pork sausage links, two pieces of ham, two fluffy buttermilk pancakes, and a small mountain of hash browns. At the rate La Bestia was plowing through the stuff on his plate, Rafaela wouldn't be surprised if he ordered seconds. She had a suspicion that he was making up for a childhood in which there'd never been enough food for the boy and his four sisters and three brothers.

"Do you know how far Orlando is?" La Bestia asked, eggs, sausage, and bacon bits now seemingly stitched into his mustache.

"I don't know," Rafaela said. "North of here is all I know."

La Bestia pulled out his phone and started scrolling with one hand while still shoveling in food with the other.

"Why, what are you thinking?"

"Looks like about three hours," he said, looking up at her. "I was thinking about going to Disney World."

Rafaela laughed. "But that's for kids."

La Bestia looked stung. "Grown-ups go too."

"If it's three hours, then that would be a six-hour round trip. You'd only have an hour or so there."

"That might be enough."

"Barely enough time to say hello to Mickey and Minnie?"

"Don't forget Goofy," La Bestia said. "They just opened something called Toy Story Land too."

"You mean, after the movie?"

"Yeah, it's supposed to be fantastic."

"I'll bet," Rafaela said. "Woody, Slinky Dog. Buzz Lightyear. The whole gang."

"Are you making fun of it?"

Rafaela smiled. "Never." She could see he really wanted to go. "Tell you what...when we're done here, we'll go up there. Spend a whole day. Then we can fly out of Orlando. That way you can take your time and see all of them: Woody, Slinky, Buzz, Mickey, and Minnie."

"You forgot Goofy again."

THEY ENDED UP DRIVING OUT TO A PLACE CALLED LION Country Safari, way out west of the Florida Turnpike in a town called Loxahatchee. It took them an hour to get there and they opted for something called the Drive-Through Safari, which meant you drove your car around in the simulated pampas or bushveld, and got to see whatever animals you ran across. Rafaela was initially hesitant, wondering how the Corolla would hold up against a charging rhino with its horn lowered, but she was reassured when a family in a small Chevy Geo drove out from behind a stand of trees.

They first came across a flock of ostriches. La Bestia was snapping away with his iPhone camera. "Can those things fly?" he asked.

"Don't think so, they look pretty heavy. That's a big load to get off the ground."

Shortly after, they spotted a mother and baby zebra. La Bestia showed no interest in them. "Just horses with stripes."

The next thing they encountered were two wooden huts elevated ten feet off the ground that had ropes connecting them, and eight chimpanzees swinging on the ropes. La Bestia shrugged and said. "I hate that racket they make."

Rafaela drove on.

Next came wildebeests. "How do those skinny little legs hold them up?" La Bestia wondered. Then a giraffe, which they watched chew on leaves high up in a tree. Rafaela was reading a brochure: "Says here their tongues are up to eighteen inches long."

"Almost as long as—"

"Don't you wish," Rafaela interrupted, weary of his macho humor.

Finally, they came across the kings of the jungle. The lions were kept in a separate preserve that visitors couldn't get too close to. Seeing the big cats was somewhat anti-climactic, anyway, because they were all sleeping. No roars—which the brochure claimed could be heard five miles away. No mauling a lesser animal for lunch. They just lay there and snored.

After the lions, they came across a muddy pond and didn't see anything in it at first. Then something moved and they could see a large, dark animal with rounded, sharp horns emerge from it.

"What's that?" La Bestia asked.

"A water buffalo, I think." It got larger as it surfaced from the pond. Much larger. "Wouldn't want to get gored by one of those horns."

It was lumbering in their direction. "Jesus, how much you think it weighs?" La Bestia asked.

Rafaela's eyes got big as she read the brochure. "A ton." She wasn't exaggerating. It looked to weigh all two thousand pounds and it kept coming at them. Fifty feet away, now.

La Bestia reached into his jacket, pulled out his Glock, leaned out the window and fired two shots.

"Jesus! What are you doing?" Rafaela cried, jamming the Corolla in reverse and flooring it. The Corolla kicked up mud as she hit the brake, U-turned, and stomped on the accelerator.

Not until they had driven out of the Lion Country Safari main gate did Rafaela look over at La Bestia. "Are you out of your fucking mind?" And she slapped him so hard his head slammed back into the window.

He put his hand up to the side of his head to see if it was bleeding. It was.

He put on a macho front. "Maybe we should have gone to Disneyland."

FORTY-FIVE

A FEW MINUTES LATER, IT HAD BLOWN OVER AND THEY WERE debating whether La Bestia had hit the water buffalo or not.

"I think the bullets bounced off of him."

"I think you missed."

Shooting things with guns—and hitting them—was what La Bestia did for a living. He clearly didn't want Rafaela to think he was deficient at his job. "I'm sure I hit it. I heard they have really thick hides."

"Oh, did you now?" she said skeptically, as her iPhone started flashing. She looked down at the GPS function. "Aha! Our friend is on the move." She handed La Bestia her phone. "Dial Ramon Tamayo's number."

La Bestia hit ten numbers then handed her back the phone. Ramon Tamayo picked up after the third ring.

"Hello, Rafaela."

"Ramon, I need you to drive up to Palm Beach with two men. I don't know exactly where we're going yet but I'll keep you informed."

"Okay, we can be on our way in ten minutes."

"See you in a few hours." She clicked off and switched to the app tracking Weston Paul. "Looks like he's leaving Palm Beach. About to go over one of the bridges."

OTT, NORM RUTLEDGE, AND FIVE OTHER MEN HAD JUST arrived at Rutledge's fishing camp, Ott and Rutledge in one car, the others following. The cinderblock, two-bedroom house was down a dusty dirt road that had deep mud puddles scattered along it. The house was lime-green and had scraggly vines growing up the sides, a few which had burrowed into the roof and lifted up several shingles. A red Jeep, circa 1995, protruded out of a garage that had no door.

Ott could almost picture an odd-looking kid up on the porch, strumming a banjo.

"A little slice of heaven you got here, Norm," he said, pulling into the driveway.

"Thank you, Ott," Rutledge said. "And don't say it reminds you of something out of *Deliverance*."

"Furthest thing from my mind," Ott said. "You use this place for hunting, too?"

"Yep. Crossbow," Rutledge said as the other car pulled in beside them.

"No shit. I didn't know you were into that. What do you shoot?"

"You name it. Deer. Wild boar. Black bear. Gobblers."

Ott cocked his head as he opened the car door. "Gobblers would be wild turkeys, I'm guessing."

"Attaboy."

Ott walked around to Rutledge's side of the car. "Know what's amazing to me?"

"What's that?"

"That there are real, live bears forty-five minutes from Palm Beach."

"Why's that amazing?"

Ott shrugged. "I don't know. Just is."

Rutledge turned to the other five men. "All right, boys, let's walk around, get the lay of the land. Figure out where to station you."

A stand of trees behind the house created an obvious place for one of the men to position himself. Better yet, Norm informed them, he had a blind up in the grove. His "blind" looked more like a basic treehouse—a platform, really—twenty feet above the ground in a gumbo limbo tree. Rutledge explained that he used it to shoot deer from. The beauty of it was you couldn't see the blind unless you were looking for it—hence, the name—and it sat high enough to give you a good view of everything around the small property. The only drawback was that if someone did see you, it left you totally exposed.

Off to the left side of the house stood a fort made of logs that Rutledge explained he had built for his two sons. It had no roof, but was five feet high and a natural place to position two or three men.

The group considered digging a trench for the remaining cops to hide in on the right side of the house, but because of the high-water table decided against it.

All seven men gathered around the chief in front of the house.

"So, I'm thinking one guy in the blind, two in the fort, and the rest in the house," Rutledge said.

Ott glanced around. "What about one in the Jeep?"

"Yeah, that'd be good," Rutledge said. "So, three in the house."

"Plus, Crawford," Ott said.

Rutledge nodded. "When's he gonna get here, by the way?"

"He called a little while ago. I'm guessing about a half hour," Ott said. "And his Mexican friends hopefully not far behind."

CRAWFORD, HAVING TAKEN A WRONG TURN, ROLLED UP TO Rutledge's camp about forty minutes later. There were no cars visible because Rutledge and Ott had parked them down the road behind an abandoned camp that, Rutledge had explained, was owned by a man now in prison for cooking meth on the premises.

As Crawford pulled in, Ott greeted him from the porch. "Welcome to the middle of fuckin' nowhere."

"Jesus," Crawford said. "Feels like we're in Mississippi or Louisiana."

"I know."

"Where's—" At that moment, Rutledge walked out.

"Well, well, Weston Paul," Rutledge said. "Welcome to Camp Rutledge."

"Thank you, Norm, it's good to be here. I like your paint color, reminds me of key lime pie."

"Or puke," Ott mumbled.

Rutledge didn't hear him. "So, let me catch you up on where we are so far. Knowing you, you'll probably want to kick in your two cents' worth."

"Knowing me, you're probably right," Crawford said as Rutledge and Ott took him on a tour of the property.

"I like the blind," Crawford said. "What've you shot from up there?"

"A couple deer. Missed a bear."

"Jesus, you got bears out here?"

"Lots of snakes, too," Ott chimed in.

Crawford groaned. "Thanks for *your* two cents, Mort."

"So, what do you think of how everyone's positioned?" Rutledge asked.

"Seems good to me."

"I also got plated body armor for you," Rutledge said.

"So, what do we do now?" Ott asked, indicating the five other men.

Crawford nodded hello to the officers.

"Get in position and wait," Rutledge said. "I got Evans five miles away, on lookout for a white Corolla with a big blonde either driving or riding shotgun."

Crawford nodded. "All right then, let's do it. I'll take that armor off your hands now." He turned to Ott. "Where you gonna be, bro?"

"Up in the tree."

Crawford patted him on the shoulder. "Sure those branches are strong enough?"

FORTY-SIX

Rafaela Arroyo was paying Ramon Tamayo and his gun thugs ten thousand dollars apiece, but she would have paid them a lot more. It was her second job with Tamayo. Tamayo and his men followed La Bestia and her in a Ford F150 club-cab pickup truck down Route 27, which was the most direct route but also a bumpy two-lane highway that probably hadn't been repaved in a decade.

"Jesus, I had no idea America was so damned rural," La Bestia said after they hadn't passed a car for ten miles.

"Then you've never been to Texas or Arizona," Rafaela said.

"Never been to America period," La Bestia said. "How do you see this working, anyway?"

"Simple. We put a gun to Weston Paul's head. That doesn't work, we cut off a few body parts until he's ready to wire the money."

La Bestia gave her a fist bump.

She checked the GPS on her phone and saw they were only a few miles from where Weston Paul's car had stopped.

On the side of the road, in a silver Chevy Caprice, two Palm Beach cops, Dean Evans and Lou Batcheldor, watched the Corolla speed past, followed closely by a Ford F150.

Evans dialed his phone.

Rutledge answered. "See 'em?"

"Yeah, just went past. Can't miss her. There was a black club cab pick-up right behind her. I'm guessing they're together."

"How many in all?"

"At least four. Hard to be sure. The pickup's got tinted windows."

"Okay, stay there and be ready in case they come back that way."

"Copy that."

Rafaela estimated she was three miles from the target. She pulled over on the side of the road. Ramon Tamayo stopped behind her, got out of the F150, and walked up to her on the driver's side. She hit the button and the window rolled down.

"We're close now," Rafaela said. "Here's the plan: I want to drive by his location and eyeball the place. Then go about a mile past and pull over again."

"You got it, *jefe*," Tamayo said turning and walking back to the truck.

Rafaela pulled back onto the road with Tamayo close behind, following her GPS app until a greenish hovel came into view. Rafaela pointed at it with her arm out the window and slowed down a little, then, just as quickly, sped up and drove on for a mile, finally pulling over opposite an open field, Tamayo right behind her.

Rafaela, Tamayo, and La Bestia got out of their vehicles and gathered in front of the Corolla.

"Did you see anything in there?" Rafaela asked Tamayo.

"I'm not sure. Maybe someone looking out a window."

"What about you?" Rafaela asked La Bestia.

He lit a cigarette. "Pretty sure I saw someone move."

"Yeah, that's what I saw, too," Rafaela said. "Like maybe waiting for us."

"So, what do you want to do?" Tamayo asked, scratching his beard.

Rafaela started walking around the car. "I got something in the boot. Come back and have a look."

She walked around until she was facing the trunk and hit a button on her key.

CRAWFORD, RUTLEDGE, AND THE TWO MEN IN THE HOUSE WERE in the living room. "It was definitely her car," Crawford said. "Blonde at the wheel."

"Yeah, plus she slowed down," Rutledge said.

"And brought company..."

"What do you think we should do?" Rutledge asked.

Crawford shrugged. "All we can do is wait. It would be a mistake to go after her."

"Why?"

"Because we don't have anything to arrest her on."

Crawford dialed Ott. "Did you see 'em?"

"Yeah."

"You think there was any way they might have spotted you?"

"No way. I was totally hidden."

Crawford thought for a second. "Well, if they did spot any of us, they're probably gone. But something tells me they'll be back."

"I agree. Just wonder what kind of artillery they'll be packing this time."

"I know," Crawford said. "One thing's for sure, they won't be tossing any grenades. Can't risk killing the golden goose."

"Good point," Ott said. Then: "What the hell is *that*?"

"What's what?"

"That noise."

Now Crawford heard it—the metallic whir of a hiveful of hornets —and recognized it right away: "A goddamn drone. Get down! Hey, yell to the guys in the fort to get out of sight!"

But it was too late. All three had already been spotted by the Sony IMX camera aboard the Halo Stealth Pro Drone.

"THERE'RE MEN ALL OVER," RAFAELA SAID, PITCHING THE remote control to the ground. The drone would crash-land in a few moments with no one at the controls, but it had done its job. "Let's get the hell out of here." She opened the car door as Tamayo bolted for his truck.

Rafaela put the key in the ignition and hit the accelerator. Dirt kicked up, spraying the pickup behind them, and both vehicles raced down the country road as fast as they could.

AFTER CLIMBING DOWN FROM THE DEER BLIND, OTT JOINED ALL the other officers in front of Rutledge's house.

"Let's go," Crawford said. It was their only choice now, he thought, maybe they could get them at least on gun possession.

Even though Kehoe's car was a Cadillac, space was tight for seven, mostly large men. Crawford floored it and pulled up to the abandoned house, behind which they'd left their cars.

Six officers jumped out of the car, and Crawford hit the accelerator again, burning rubber on the narrow blacktop road. Within a minute, Ott had caught up to him. He was driving a Crown Vic Interceptor with a 4.6 liter, modular V8 engine. The Vic was five years old but could still fly. Ott passed Crawford and quickly put distance between them. Crawford looked over his shoulder and saw the other Vic with four officers coming up on him. A moment later, it passed him on the left.

He called Palm Beach Police dispatch, which was no easy trick doing close to 90 mph.

"John Landry," the dispatcher answered.

"Landry, it's Crawford. I need you to call PBSO district eleven —" PBSO stood for Palm Beach Sheriff's Office "—see if they've got any officers down south on Route 27. If so, I got a late-model white Corolla tag number LE9435 and a black Ford F150 club cab pickup coming that way at a high rate of speed. Tell 'em to set up a roadblock or put down stop sticks but only if they've got five or more guys. Too dangerous otherwise."

"Copy that...so, whatcha doin' out there in the boonies, Charlie?"

"Hunting bear."

THE COROLLA COULDN'T GO MUCH FASTER THAN 95 MPH; Tamayo's pickup was hugging its rear bumper from behind. Rafaela feared that the house had been full of cops. That Weston Paul had gone to the police and that the whole thing was a set-up. If so, the police vehicles would catch up soon.

Or maybe Paul had simply hired a bunch of trigger-happy goons with guns.

She saw a dirt road ahead that angled off the paved road. She slowed to sixty, then forty, and turned the wheel hard so the Corolla went bumping cross-wise down the dirt road.

Tamayo followed closely behind, snapping limbs along the narrow path.

Rafaela drove about a mile down the road, then saw a house coming up on her left. It had a barn behind it and cows grazing on both sides of the road.

Rafaela pulled into the driveway and Tamayo followed. She reached under her seat and pulled out the Ruger she'd bought from the gangbangers in West Palm Beach. La Bestia already had his pistol out. A man in blue overalls and a plaid shirt came out of the barn at the same time that two children, a boy and a girl, walked out of the house.

Rafaela opened the car door and stepped toward the man, her Ruger trained on him. "Put your hands up."

The man stopped walking and his hands shot up. "Don't shoot. Please, don't shoot."

She could use a few hostages in case the cops showed up.

"Nothing's going to happen if you do what I say."

By now, Tamayo and his two men had caught up to her.

"Who else is here?" Rafaela asked

"Just my wife inside," the man said.

"Go get her," Rafaela told La Bestia, who ran into the house.

Rafaela turned to Tamayo and his men. "Put the cars in the barn or behind it," she ordered. "Fast!"

She looked down the dirt road, fearful that the police, or whoever they were, might have seen her dust trail, but now the dirty cloud had settled and she saw no cars coming.

"Okay," she said to the farmer. "We're all going to go into your house. Just cooperate and do everything I tell you, and there'll be no trouble."

The man nodded.

Four hours later, at eleven at night, they collected the family's cell phones, took all four sets of keys to the car and truck, and left the small farm behind.

FORTY-SEVEN

CRAWFORD GOT TO THE STATION EARLY THE NEXT MORNING. Ott was right behind him at 7:15. He went straight to Crawford's office.

"Whatcha doin'?" Ott asked.

"Put in a call to Belle Glade PD near Rutledge's camp. I want to find out if there're any cameras that might've picked up the tag number of the truck. Haven't heard back from 'em yet."

"Good idea," Ott said. "Where do you think those other guys came from?"

Crawford's MacBook Air was open in front of him. "Been doing a little digging and it looks like Z5 has some gangbangers down in Miami."

"Along with a whole slew of Colombians, right?"

Crawford nodded and took a pull on his Dunkin' Donuts extra-dark coffee.

"You think Rafaela and the mutt might give up and go home? Figuring it's not worth the risk?"

Crawford tapped on his desk. "If I was in her shoes, I'd think the job just got a little harder. But hey, fifty-three mil is fifty-three mil, and you know how well Dominica sold it."

"Yeah, she sure did."

Crawford's cell phone rang before he could respond.

"Hello."

"Detective Crawford?"

"Yeah." Crawford hit speakerphone.

"Hey, this is Sergeant Johnny Ortiz, out in Belle Glade. Got your call from earlier and I don't have a tag number on that F150 yet, but I got something else for you."

"What's that?"

"A car was boosted from a farmer's house in South Bay near here," Ortiz said. "And the people who took it were driving a black F150 and a white Corolla. They left the Corolla behind and took off in the farmer's 2016 Chevy Equinox. It's green and the tag number is TS1117."

"Thank you, Johnny, that's a big help," Crawford said as Ott wrote down the info. "Do you have the name and number of the farmer?"

"Well, that's the problem...the crew that boosted his car also took all their car keys and cell phones, so you can't call them. But I got the farmer out in my lobby. Want to speak to him?"

"Yeah, I sure do. What's his name?"

"Hector Brown. I'll go get him."

"Thanks. Hey, by the way, how'd he get to your station?"

"Drove his tractor into town."

CRAWFORD SPENT FIVE MINUTES ON THE PHONE WITH HECTOR Brown. He found out that Rafaela, the mutt, and three other "Hispanic" men had shown up with guns drawn, then had gone into the house and watched *Law & Order: Special Victims Unit* re-runs in the living room with the Brown family for the next three hours. They finally left, after cleaning out a good portion of the refrigerator's contents. Because they spoke in Spanish the whole time, Brown had nothing else of interest to report to Crawford.

But just knowing about the car switch was critical.

FORTY-EIGHT

NORM RUTLEDGE, FRUSTRATED OVER THEIR FAILURE TO apprehend "the Beaners," as he'd taken to calling them, had just authorized the deployment of twenty Palm Beach police officers to drive in a fifteen-mile radius of Palm Beach, looking for the 2016 green Chevy Equinox.

Crawford and Ott were in Rutledge's office. "A fucking drone," Rutledge said, shaking his head. "They pretty much outlawed 'em here."

Crawford nodded. "'Cause of that Knight Mulcahy thing?"

Rutledge nodded.

Knight Mulcahy, also known as The Mouth of the South, was a talk-show host who made forty million dollars a year on his nationally broadcast radio program. He lived up on the north end in a fifty-thousand-square-foot house, where he'd also run his state-of-the-art studio. *Run*— past tense—because he'd been murdered by a Palm Beach patrician who'd been maliciously smeared by Mulcahy on his radio show, a show that was heard by roughly half the country. Mulcahy's murder had been Crawford and Ott's third case together and maybe their toughest...until this one came along.

"What Knight Mulcahy thing?" Ott asked.

"Some guy with a drone was buzzing Mulcahy's house," Rutledge said. "Turned out he thought Mulcahy was banging his wife. Turned out he was right."

"So, the town got tough on drones," Crawford explained.

"Gotcha," Ott said.

"While the uniforms are out looking for the Equinox," said Rutledge, "you guys should try to find out where the beaners are staying."

"We plan to," Crawford said. "But how 'bout *the Mexicans*, Norm, instead of *the beaners*."

Rutledge held up his hands. "Oh, sorry Mr. Politically Correct."

Crawford just shook his head. Guy was hopeless.

Ott stood and turned to Crawford. "I'd say there's virtually no chance they're on the island here."

"Yeah, definitely," Crawford said. "Why don't I start up in Palm Beach Gardens and work south, you start at the northern tip of Boynton Beach and go north."

"That's hundreds of motels and other fleabags," Ott said.

"Yeah, I know," Crawford said, turning to Rutledge. "Is there any chance you can get your pal Sarah to lend us a few guys?" He was referring to the police chief of West Palm Beach. They had about ten times as many cops as the PBPD.

"I'll try," Rutledge said. "She owes me a favor. If she says yes, I'll give her your phone numbers."

"While you're at it, you think she'd go for us borrowing her SWAT team?"

A frown cut across Rutledge's face. "Jesus, I don't know, that's a big ask. We're talking about vicious killers here."

"We sure are," Crawford said. "It would be a real feather in their caps, though, if they helped on this bust. Lots of good press, plus a helluva deterrent for the badasses of West Palm."

"All right, I'll see what she says."

"If not, it'll have to just be PBPD," Crawford said. "Which is cool, we can handle it."

Rutledge was nodding vigorously. "Damn straight we can. With all the vigorous training I've put you boys through."

Crawford racked his brain but didn't remember any training at all Rutledge had put them through.

"Another thing, Norm," Crawford said. "Why don't you give us four extra uniforms to check out the motels? Ott's right, there are a million holes-in-the-wall within fifteen minutes of here."

Rutledge tapped his pen on his desk. "Jesus, you got a long list of shit you want, Crawford." Then, after an expansive sigh, "All right, you got it. I'll let you take your pick of who you want."

TWO HOURS LATER, CRAWFORD, OTT, AND THE FOUR UNIFORMS were beating the streets. Ott had given each of the uniforms nine-by-twelve glossies of Rafaela Arroyo and La Bestia, then mapped out a grid-pattern search between Palm Beach Gardens and the northern part of Boynton Beach.

The other uniforms already out on the lookout for the green Chevy Equinox had instructions that if they sighted the SUV, they should call Crawford or Ott immediately. No playing cowboy.

Crawford pulled into the two-star Knightsbridge Motor Lodge in North Palm Beach, which billed itself as a, "laid-back motor inn offering simple rooms, some with furnished balconies, plus an outdoor pool." Crawford looked up at the second floor and noticed a few guests taking advantage of those furnished balconies. A bearded man in a wife-beater T-shirt was stretched out in a pink plastic Adirondack chair with the stub of a cigar, probably not a Cuban, hanging out of the side of his mouth. An overweight woman in a bright yellow sundress leaned over her balcony railing, iPhone in hand. Crawford estimated that if the woman weighed ten pounds more, the railing might have met its match.

Crawford walked past a pair of big Harley-Davidson motorcycles with leather saddlebags. It looked to be a matching set, except one was panther black and the other flamingo pink.

The office featured a vacancy sign on the door that looked permanent. A man with a Fu Manchu and ZZ Top T-shirt sat at the reception counter, playing video poker on an old Hewlett Packard laptop.

"Morning," the man said, even though it was 12:45 in the afternoon.

"Hello," Crawford said, flashing his ID. "Detective Crawford, Palm Beach PD. Looking for a couple—a tall blonde woman and a short Latino male with long, dark hair. The man's got a tattoo right here—" Crawford pointed to his forehead. "Ring a bell at all?"

The man clicked something on his keyboard, then looked up. "Yeah, I got a couple that may fit the bill. The tat there, in particular. Up in 223."

Crawford put his hands on the countertop. "Do they speak Spanish to each other?"

"Never heard him talk. But she speaks good English."

"When they checked in, what were they driving? You probably have that in your registration book, right?"

"Hell, no, man, we don't care. This couple paid in advance."

Crawford was getting the idea that the Knightsbridge operation was loosey-goosey at best, indiscriminate in its guest selection at worst.

"Do you know if they're in their room now?"

"I haven't seen 'em leave. Saw 'em out at the pool yesterday."

"And you have no idea what kind of car they're driving?"

"Can't help you there."

"Okay, which way's the pool?"

"Just go outside, first left, go straight and you'll run right into it," the man said, then gave Crawford an uneasy smile that revealed a missing upper front tooth. "Not going to be a shoot-out out here, is there?"

"Nah, just want to see if it's my people or not."

"What did they do?"

What didn't *they?* "Digging a hole in the beach without a permit."

"You need a permit—"

"Just kidding," Crawford said, turning toward the front door. "Hey, thanks for your help, appreciate it."

"No problem, man."

Crawford opened the door and turned left. For now, he intended to see whether it was Rafaela and the mutt or not, but not take any immediate action. If it were them, he'd call in the troops. He heard splashing and stopped. He guessed the pool was to his right. He peeked around the corner and saw three kids in the pool, a woman in a one-piece bathing suit peering down at them from the pool's edge.

On the other side of the pool, a large blonde woman held a sun reflector up under her face. It was not Rafaela. She looked a little rough, a pouch of skin hanging over the bottom half of a bikini that revealed more than most would want to see. Crawford made her for the pink-Harley biker chick. The guy next to her in cut-offs was indeed short, and had long dark hair in a braid. But instead of a number five on his forehead, he sported a Charlie Manson-style swastika.

Crawford turned and hustled back to his vehicle.

On to the next dump.

FORTY-NINE

Rafaela Arroyo wasn't happy.

From the camera on the drone, Rafaela hadn't been able to tell whether the men were real cops or rent-a-cops Weston Paul had hired. It didn't matter because she didn't have a dime to show for all her efforts. She was in her room at the Blue Moon Motel, watching a silverfish bug skitter across the stained maroon carpet. She wore a pair of blue vinyl gloves in the room at all times, including when she slept. La Bestia was next door watching something on the Disney Channel called *Hannah Montana*. He had absolutely no idea what they were saying but clearly enjoyed the sight of all the pretty young girls on the show.

Rafaela saw that the silverfish seemed to be carrying something now. Like maybe a crumb from the pizza she had just wolfed down.

"Got it, Mort." The uniform cop, Randall Folsom, had just called Ott on his cell phone. "The green Chevy Equinox, tag number TS1117, is sitting in a parking lot at a place called the Blue Moon Motel."

"Halle-fucking-lujah," Ott said. "All right, I'll call Crawford. You stay there, one of us will get back to you shortly. If anyone gets in the Equinox, just follow it...at a safe distance. But don't lose 'em, whatever you do."

"Copy that."

Ott clicked off and hit Crawford on speed dial. "Found the Equinox," he said.

"Where?"

"Federal Highway and Tenth Ave, Lake Worth. Place called the Blue Moon Motel."

"Meet you there in fifteen. Outside the place, though—don't drive in."

"Gotcha."

Crawford called Norm Rutledge as he headed south on Route 1.

"Yeah, Charlie, what's up?"

"We located the car. Did you talk to the West Palm chief?"

"Yeah, no-go on the SWAT team. They're up in Jacksonville doing some kind of training exercises. Where's the car?"

"A motel in Lake Worth," Crawford said. "Can you ask Chief Toomey if she can spare Red Noland and Jesse Garza?" Two solid West Palm Beach homicide detectives who Crawford had worked with before.

"Sure. I'll call her now and get back to you."

"Okay, later."

While the Palm Beach Police Department had lots of good men and women, Noland and Garza were seriously battle-tested warriors. A plan began to form in Crawford's head as he drove south to the Blue Moon Motel. His gut told him that a small insertion team was the way to go, especially given Arroyo and the mutt would be in close proximity to guests and staff in and around the motel.

Five minutes later, he saw Ott's unmarked Crown Vic pulled

over to the side of Federal Highway, the hazard lights on. He pulled up behind him, got out, walked around to the passenger side of Ott's Vic, and got in.

"I had Folsom drive around in the motel parking lot. No sign of a black F150, so my bet is the Z5 Miami guys drove back home."

"That's good," Crawford said. "And the Equinox hasn't gone anywhere?"

"Nope."

"All right, let's you and me go talk to whoever's at the desk here."

Ott started to get out. Crawford grabbed his arm. "Hold on a sec, don't forget those two might recognize us."

"Oh, yeah...Hats and shades, right?"

"Exactly. Whatcha got?"

Ott turned and looked at the back seat. "Well, I got my Cleveland Indians ball cap or my fedora...and, of course, my trusty Foster-Grant wraparounds."

"Go with the fedora, since all I got is my Yankees cap," Crawford said. "We don't want to look like twins."

"Fat chance of that."

Ott grabbed the dark brown fedora, donned it, then pulled a pair of sunglasses out of the glove compartment and put them on. "How'm I lookin'?"

Crawford slapped him on the back. "Like a fuckin' stud." He got out and went back to his car, then came back wearing his Yankees cap and Ray-Ban Aviators.

Ott, standing next to the Vic, chuckled at Crawford's Yankees cap. "Isn't that the team that just lost to the BoSox sixteen to one in the playoffs?"

"Don't go there," Crawford said with a shake of his head. "All right, let's do it."

His cell phone rang.

"Hello?"

"Charlie, it's Red Noland. Me and Garza are ready to rumble."

"Beautiful," Crawford said, pumping his fist. "Get your asses down to the Blue Moon Motel on Federal in Lake Worth. If you can, get a hold of a flash-bang or two. We could use 'em."

"You got it," Noland said. "Give us twenty minutes."

"Look forward to workin' with you again, Red."

Crawford and Ott walked up to the office of the Blue Moon Motel and went in. The man at the desk reminded Crawford of Mr. Rogers from the old TV show. He even had a snazzy grey cardigan sweater.

They flashed their IDs and introduced themselves. The desk clerk, Earl Knott his name was, did the same.

Crawford took off his Aviators. "We've got two persons of interest staying here. They were driving a white Corolla, tag number LE9435. Now they got a green Equinox SUV."

"Very tall blonde-haired woman," added Ott. "Short man with a dark complexion, braided ponytail—"

"And a big number five on his forehead."

"Can't miss that duo," Knott said. "They're in 204 and 205."

"Are the rooms on either side and below them occupied?" Crawford asked.

Knott looked down at his registration book. "Nobody in 203, but a couple in 206. Below them there's a guy in 104, but he works and doesn't get back here until late, and a woman in 103 who I haven't seen all day."

"Okay," Crawford said. "First thing I need you to do is call the couple in 206 and ask them to come down here. If they balk, tell them it's an emergency situation and they'll understand when they get here."

"Now?"

Crawford nodded. "Yeah, please."

Knott dialed the room. The couple didn't seem to have a problem with what they were being asked to do and said they'd be down shortly.

Knott hung up. "What else?"

"Two men are gonna check in to 203 and 206."

"They're police officers," Ott clarified.

Knott nodded. "Okay," then after a beat, "what else?"

"You don't happen to have a spare bathing suit, do you?" Crawford asked.

"Bathing suit?"

"Yes."

"I might have one or two," Knott said. "From guests who left 'em behind. Got 'em in the lost-and-found back there," he said, pointing to a door behind them.

"Can I take a look?"

"Sure. Come on back."

Crawford and Ott followed him back to a room that had a box of clothes, cleaning supplies, and several vacuum cleaners. Knott went over to the box, reached down in, and pulled out two bathing suits. One looked to be very large and had a flashy floral print. The second one was red and appeared to belong to the Speedo family.

Crawford looked at them both dubiously.

"Don't worry, I had one of my cleaning ladies wash and disinfect all this stuff."

Ott looked bewildered. "What do you want it for?"

"My tan needs a little work," Crawford explained. "Thought I'd hit the pool."

Ott nodded and smiled. "Got it."

Crawford took the bathing suit with the floral print from Knott and saw its label.

"Forty-four," Crawford said, shaking his head. "About ten sizes too big."

"What are you?" Ott asked.

"Thirty-four," Crawford said, eyeing the Speedo-type suit skeptically. "I guess it's got to be this one—" then seeing the label— "thirty-two."

"Gotta suck it in a little, Chuck."

It was bright red and had about twenty percent as much material as the other suit. Crawford nodded, then noticed something hanging on a hook. "What's that?" he asked Knott, pointing.

"The maintenance man's uniform."

Crawford reached over and lifted a grey pair of pants and a grey shirt off the hook. A name was stitched in on the upper right side of the shirt.

Wayne.

He turned to Ott. "How do you feel about playing Wayne for a while?"

Ott nodded. "It's a good cover if it fits."

"So, try it on."

Ott took off his pants and shirt and hung them on the hook. Then he tried on the maintenance man's pants and shirt. The pants were many sizes too small. The shirt was even worse.

Crawford shook his head. "Guess you're gonna need to lose a quick fifty to be Wayne."

"Shit, I always wanted to be a janitor."

A bell jingled and the three walked back into the office as a couple entered.

"Oh, hi, Mr. and Mrs. Raskin," Knott said. "This is Detective Crawford and Detective Ott." The Raskins looked a little freaked at being introduced to a pair of detectives.

Crawford smiled and shook their hands. "We're just going to need to borrow your room for a little while." He glanced over at Knott. "Where can you put Mr. and Mrs. Raskin?"

"Other side of the building. We call it the Burt Reynolds Suite," Knott said. "He stayed here once when he was just starting out—"

"Hope that works for you," Crawford said.

"Sure, I mean, I guess," Mr. Raskin said.

"Great," Ott said. "Mr. Knott will take you there."

Crawford turned to Knott. "We're expecting a few guys any minute now, so we'll just man the desk until you come back."

Knott was clearly a little overwhelmed with everything swirling around him, but at the same time seemed amped up by it. He led the Raskins out the front door.

No more than a minute later, Red Noland and Jesse Garza walked in, each carrying a suitcase.

"Hey Red...Jesse," Crawford said, shaking their hands. "Thanks for coming—" then pointing to Noland's suitcase "—plan on staying a while?"

"As long as it takes. Brought my toothbrush and a few other necessities," Noland said, shaking Ott's hand. "So, what's the play? Toomey was kinda sketchy."

For the next five minutes, Crawford filled them in, including the fact that they were going to check in to the rooms on either side of Arroyo and La Bestia.

"You got body armor in those suitcases, by any chance?" Crawford asked.

"We got body armor, flash-bangs, high-powered weapons, the works," Noland answered.

Knott came back in and was introduced to Noland and Garza.

Walking back behind his reception desk, Knott said, "I forgot to tell you something. Every once in a while, the guy in 205 comes out onto the balcony to have a smoke."

"So, the rooms are non-smoking?" Crawford asked.

"Yeah, what happened was, when they were checking in, he pulled out a cigarette and started to light up. I told him no smoking here or in any of the rooms."

"I love it," Ott said, shaking his head. "Breaks every law in two countries but obeys the no-smoking rule."

"Gives me an idea," Crawford said.

"Okay," Noland said. "You told us everything except where you guys are gonna be."

"Saved that for last," Crawford said, then eyed Garza more closely. "Hey, Jesse, you look about the right size. How would you feel about playing the Blue Moon's maintenance man?"

Garza shrugged. "Uh, what?"

"Just step right over here into the changing room," Ott said, gesturing to Garza to follow him.

Garza followed Ott into the lost-and-found area, Crawford and Nolan were right behind them. Ott handed him the maintenance man's pants and shirt.

They fit like a glove.

Crawford straightened Garza's collar. "If you're okay with it, you're gonna play the janitor here, positioned on the ground below the suspects' rooms. Sweeping the sidewalk, emptying the trash, whatever it is you guys do."

Garza nodded. "Sure, I'm good with that."

"And me, I'm going to be a sunbather out by the pool," Crawford said, turning to Noland. "You and Mort are gonna go up to the rooms on either side of the suspects. So, we'll all be in position surrounding them, except for the backs of the rooms, which are solid walls. I'm gonna have a throat mike, you will, too, so it'll look like I'm just talking to a buddy on the phone—"

"—and we wait for the guy to come out for a smoke?" Noland asked.

"Exactly," Crawford said. "Then one of you takes him down and cuffs him. So, all that's left is Blondie. At which point—" he turned to Garza "—you toss a flash-bang through the window. How's your arm?"

"Pretty good. Third baseman at Forest Hill High for two years."

"Good," Crawford said, turning to Noland, "Ready to rumble?" Noland smiled and nodded. Crawford turned to Garza. "How 'bout you?"

"Let's do it," Garza said.

"All right. Suit up then."

"You, too," Ott said to Crawford.

"Hold on. Couple last things," Noland said. "What if they come out together? Like they're leaving."

"You and Mort take 'em from either side. Me and Jesse backing you up in front."

"What if the mutt doesn't come out for a smoke?" Ott asked.

"We'll be communicating," Crawford said.

Ott poked Crawford in the chest. "Okay, buddy, time for you to go squeeze into that ball-hugger."

FIFTY

Ott burst out laughing when he saw Crawford in the red Speedo. Then he took a picture of him on his iPhone. "Your lady friends're gonna want to see this."

Crawford put on his Yankee hat and Aviators. Then Noland went up to room 203, followed a few minutes later by Ott to 206. Garza had changed into the janitor's outfit.

"All right," Crawford said to Garza. "Time for you to go clean up this place, Wayne."

Garza smiled and walked out the door.

Crawford looked out the window at the pool. Nobody was out there. He walked out the door after putting on his headset and throat mike. He was carrying a canvas beach bag. In it were his Sig Sauer P226 9mm pistol and two twenty-round clips. He casually strolled over to a blue chaise beach chair. He picked it up and walked it over to the edge of the pool. His plan, if shooting broke out, was to jump into the pool and hunker under its lip.

"All right," he said into his throat mike, "everybody set?"

Ott and Noland both said "ready" in unison.

Garza, who was rolling a big green garbage can nodded. In it was his HK MP5 10mm submachine gun and two flash-bangs.

———————

A HALF AN HOUR LATER, AS THEY ALL WAITED IN PLACE, A woman came out of a ground-floor room. Number 109. She was around thirty, wore a white bikini, and was medium-height and pretty.

"Shit," Crawford said, pushing up from the chaise and walking toward her.

She gave him a smile as he approached. At the same time, the door of room 205 above them opened and La Bestia walked out. He had a pack of Marlboros in his left hand. He looked down at Crawford and the woman below.

"Hi," the woman said to Crawford, flicking her head at the pool, "been in yet?"

Crawford smiled and spoke sotto voce: "I'm a police officer. Do exactly as I say. Pretend we're just having a normal conversation." Out of the corner of his eye, he saw La Bestia light a cigarette.

The woman's expression didn't change. "Okay," she said, then with a smile. "What do you want to talk about?"

"Beautiful day," Crawford said, louder than before. "You oughta get some good color." He kept the brim of his cap between his face and La Bestia, above, praying that the Mexican assassin wouldn't recognize him.

"Charlie," he heard Ott say in his earpiece. "I'm gonna take him."

"Go," Crawford said quietly.

"What?" the woman said.

"Talking to someone else," he said, now seeing Garza directly under Room 205.

Ott's door flew open and he tackled La Bestia, who went down hard with a sharp yell then crashed into the railing. La Bestia swung at Ott's head with his left elbow and caught him just above the ear. Then, he spat at Ott. The unexpected gesture enraged Ott, who reared back with his right knee and slammed it into La Bestia's jaw. Then he did it again. Then he did it a third time. La Bestia was unconscious, blood streaming out of his mouth.

Crawford pushed the woman into the deep end of the pool. Her head popped up a second later, surprised.

"Get under the lip and stay there!" he shouted, then looked up to see that Ott had cuffed La Bestia and was dragging him into his room with one hand while aiming his Glock at the door of Rafaela's room with his other.

Garza, from the ground below, had heaved a flash-bang grenade that crashed through Rafaela's window and exploded with a loud boom, followed by a brilliant, blinding flash of light.

Smoke belched out through the shattered window. Garza lowered into a crouch, MP5 machine gun in hand, staring up at her door. Red Noland was peeking out of his room's doorway, gun in both hands, his eyes on Rafaela's door.

Crawford heard coughing from inside 204, as another thick plume of smoke billowed out. Then he heard a second loud explosion and, right after it, a third.

He yelled up at Red Noland. "What the hell's that?"

"Fuck if I know," Noland said, inching toward 204 as Ott followed.

Noland looked in through the blown-out window, then swung around to Crawford. "She blew a hole out the back and jumped."

Grenades, Crawford knew, as he sprinted around the side of the two-story building, rounding one corner, then slowing, not wanting to give Rafaela a shot as he got to the other side. Holding his Sig high, he peeked around the back side of the building in a crouch, wishing he had his plated ballistic vest instead of the too-tight Speedo.

He saw her run around the side of a house. Fast. Like she was no stranger to the hundred-yard dash.

He had no time to think about his un-cop-like appearance and took off in pursuit. He ran to a corner of the house Rafaela had just disappeared behind, then slowly looked around it. He saw her a block away, running like a sprinter down the center of a street. Crawford bolted after her and saw her turn and glance back. He closed the gap a little, but she was not slowing down. He flashed to running down the field in the Dartmouth-Princeton game his junior year, the end zone in sight.

"Stop!" he yelled. "Or you're dead."

It had worked one time before, but not this time. Instead, Rafaela turned and, with two hands steadying her gun, squeezed off three shots. There were people on both sidewalks and cars behind him and a slow-moving blue VW up in front of Rafaela. She didn't care if she hit a bystander, but he did. He might be able to take her out with a shot, but what if he missed...

His mind jumped to Rutledge worrying about a shoot-out on Worth Avenue. This wasn't Worth Avenue, the busiest commercial street in Palm Beach, but you never knew about a stray bullet.

Rafaela suddenly dodged to her right. It was mid-block, and Crawford was starting to feel his legs get heavy. He willed himself not to slow down as he got to where she had gone right. He darted across a sidewalk into a grass backyard. Then, no more than a hundred feet away, he saw Rafaela aiming her automatic at him. He dove to the ground as she fired off another burst.

She missed.

Then she turned and started climbing a chain-link fence behind her. She was wearing tight black jeans, Nikes, and a torn white T-shirt. On the other side of the fence, Crawford saw two little girls, oblivious to what was going on, splashing in a shallow plastic pool. Their parents, who had been sitting at a picnic table and had clearly heard the shots, scrambled toward their daughters in the pool.

Crawford's mind raced ahead, picturing Rafaela with two small children as hostages.

Not gonna happen.

"Rafaela Arroyo!" Crawford shouted, his Sig pointed at her. "Drop the gun and get down on the ground."

She turned and, without hesitating, fired four shots, one of which ripped into the ground between his legs.

He raised his Sig in both hands, took aim, and squeezed off three shots.

FIFTY-ONE

CRAWFORD'S FIRST CONCERN WAS COVERING RAFAELA'S BODY SO the little girls wouldn't be traumatized by the sight of it. But the parents were way ahead of him. They covered the children's eyes and rushed them into their nearby house. Hopefully, the girls would never know what had happened on the edge of their backyard.

Ott had a sore shoulder from crashing into La Bestia but was still capable of Mirandizing the suspect. Ott charged him with the murder of Thorsen Paul while Red Noland looked on and Jesse Garza acted as translator. When La Bestia understood the charge against him, his eyes bugged out and he started talking a mile a minute. Garza calmed him down, then listened as La Bestia claimed he'd been thousands of miles away in Zamora, Mexico, when Thorsen Paul was killed. His alibi asserted, La Bestia couldn't give up Ramon Tamayo down in Miami fast enough. He said that Rafaela Arroyo came to Palm Beach alone and recruited Tamayo to help with the torture and murder of Thorsen Paul.

A half hour later, Crawford and Ott had a location where Tamayo lived. They drove immediately to the big city and, with three Miami cops in tow, arrested Tamayo without a shot fired. By day's end, Tamayo occupied a prime basement cell in the Palm Beach Police Department Building.

———

THE NEXT DAY, CRAWFORD AND OTT, ALONG WITH NOLAND AND Garza, convoyed over to Walter Kehoe's house on South Ocean Boulevard, the same residence where La Bestia had dropped the hand grenade down the chimney. Rose Clarke's chimney-repair crew had already been there and the chimney was as good as new.

Crawford and Ott were hosting a celebration of the bust of Rafaela Arroyo, La Bestia, and Ramon Tamayo. Everyone in attendance had had some role in solving the case except for David Balfour, who Crawford felt bad about ever suspecting in Thorsen Paul's murder. Crawford had also recruited the bartender from his favorite bar, Mookie's Tap-a-Keg in West Palm, to keep the cocktails flowing. Everyone had gathered in the large, enclosed sun porch. The only downer was the presence of Norm Rutledge. They coped by plying him with drink after drink, knowing he was probably only a half-hour away from passing out in one of the unoccupied couches.

Crawford and Balfour had just gotten refills at the bar and were standing in a corner of the sunroom, Crawford having just recounted Ott's all-star tackle and takedown of La Bestia.

"La Bestia," David Balfour said to Crawford, "doesn't that mean *The Beast* in Spanish?"

"Sure does," Crawford said. "And, trust me, he is."

Balfour laughed. "What's going to happen to him?"

"He'll probably get seven to ten years."

"That's all? For attempted murder?"

"Well, my guess is he'll probably have a decent enough lawyer to make the case that dropping a hand grenade down a chimney isn't the most effective way to commit murder."

"Gotcha, so it'll get pled down to something else?"

"Exactly."

"Wow," Balfour said. "All this going on in our peaceful little town." He shook his head.

"Yeah, you never know when the cartel's gonna move in next door."

Balfour looked out a window. "Probably better than the old battle-ax next to me."

"The one who accused you of poisoning her cat?"

Balfour shook his head at the memory. "Yeah, what a whack job."

Rose Clarke sidled up to them. "You're not talking about me, I hope?"

"God, no, Rose," Balfour said. "If we were talking about you, it'd be...*the beautiful goddess* or *the smokin' hot babe*."

Rose kissed Balfour on the cheek. "I'll take either."

She and Balfour walked toward the bar, Balfour's arm around her shoulder.

Norm Rutledge weaved up to Crawford.

"Charlie, Charlie, Charlie..." The last one sounded like Sha-lee. "You did it again, motherfucker. Made the department proud."

This was the first compliment to ever emerge from Rutledge's mouth in the entire four-plus years Crawford had worked in Palm Beach.

"Well, thank you, Norm. I appreciate it."

"But you're still kind of a dick." The chief roared with laughter. "Jus' kiddin'." Then he got right up to Crawford's ear. "Hey, ya think your fren' Rona likes me?"

Crawford laughed. "How could she not? But her name is Rose. And, 'case you forgot, you're married."

"A mere technicality, Sha-lee."

"Charlie."

"Thaz whud I said."

Crawford spotted Camilo Fernandez a few feet away. "Hey, Cam —" he motioned him over.

Fernandez walked over. "What's up, Charlie?"

Crawford pointed to Rutledge, who was doing his best to stay on his feet. "Do me a favor, I need you to translate what this guy is saying."

Rutledge raised his arm. "Fuu-fff off," he said, and followed it with something totally unintelligible.

Camilo Fernandez got close to Crawford's ear. "Gibberish," he said.

Crawford laughed then veered over to where Ott was chatting up Dominica. Ott had a paper plate full of ribs in one hand, a drink in the other.

"How do you eat," Crawford asked, "with both hands occupied?"

Ott smiled. "Very simple," he said. "Here hold this, will you —?" he handed his drink to Crawford, grabbed a rib, and started eating.

Dominica laughed. "Ask a stupid question, right...?" She raised her drink. "I want to say congratulations, Charlie."

Crawford raised his drink. "Couldn't have done it without you...*Valerie.*"

Dominica laughed. "Yeah, well, you know me, always ready to jump in on one of your juicy murders."

Ott snatched his drink from Crawford's hand and raised it. "You done good, Dominica."

"Thanks, Mort."

Ott handed his drink back to his partner, reached into his pants pocket, pulled out his iPhone, and looked around the room. "Okay, everybody!" he said, raising his voice. "Gather 'round. Got something to show you all."

Everyone came over and huddled around Ott.

"Whatcha got, Mort?" asked Dominica.

"This was taken at the scene of the crime yesterday. Just before the shoot-out at the Blue Moon Motel. It shows our fearless leader and courageous hero, Charlie Crawford—"

Oh shit. Crawford couldn't believe he hadn't seen this coming.

Ott raised the phone screen for all to see. "And here he's about to...wade into action."

There on Ott's phone, an embarrassed-looking Crawford stood uncomfortably in his borrowed, undersized, red Speedo.

Crawford's protests were smothered in laughs, hoots, and catcalls.

Three-sheets-to-the-wind Rutledge stepped closer to get a good look, then turned to Crawford. "Got a kielbasa in there, Charlie?"

"Oh, nice, Norm," Dominica said, glancing at Rose. "And with ladies in the room."

"How crude, Norm," Ott chimed in, then to Crawford. "You could make a Christmas card out of that."

"Yeah," Rose said. "Or post it on match dot com. Have every chick in southeast Florida after you."

"Okay, okay," Crawford said to the room. Then, to Ott: "Fair warning. I'm gonna get you back if it's the last thing I do."

Ott laughed. "You're never getting this chubby body into a Speedo."

"I'll get you some way, trust me."

Dominica got between them and put a placating hand on each man's shoulder. "Okay, okay...so, you boys going to take a little time off now?"

"Funny you should ask," Charlie said, and flicked a glance at Ott. "You got it, right?"

Ott stashed the phone and reached into his breast pocket. He pulled out a piece of paper and handed it to Dominica. She read it aloud:

"I am hereby pleased to authorize an all-expense paid trip to the hard-working Detective Charles Crawford and the always-enterprising Detective Morton Ott for a one-week fishing trip to Cabo San Lucas. Hope you boys snag a marlin. Meanwhile, I'll be out at my camp reeling in crappies."

Dominica smiled and looked up. "Crappies? What the hell is that?"

Crawford cocked his head. "You know, I can't even remember."

"It's a fish that's a hell of a lot smaller than a marlin," Ott said.

"Got it," said Dominica. "And Norm signed this, I see."

"Yeah," said Ott, grabbing his drink back from Crawford. "And all it took was five margaritas."

THE END

To find out when the next Charlie Crawford Mystery is available, sign up for Tom's free newsletter at **tomturnerbooks.com/news**.

KILLING TIME IN CHARLESTON (EXCLUSIVE PREVIEW)

I am pleased to bring you two chapters from the first book in a new series set in one of my favorite cities: Charleston, South Carolina. It's entitled *Killing Time in Charleston*.

Killing Time introduces Nick Janzek, a hero/anti-hero—you be the judge. He's a man with a tragic past and an uncertain future in a town that doesn't always throw out the welcome mat for Yankees. Nick, a homicide cop, hooks up with new partner, Delvin Rhett, who's fresh out of the ghetto and a recent graduate of hard knocks university. Right off the bat they have a murder, and while that body is still warm, another stiff turns up. Never a dull moment for Nick and Delvin...and you as well!

Killing Time in Charleston will be released in 2019. To find out when it's available, sign up for my free newsletter at
tomturnerbooks.com/news.

ONE

A YEAR AFTER WHAT HAPPENED IN BOSTON, JANZEK FLEW DOWN to Charleston, South Carolina, for his college roommate's wedding. It took him about five minutes to fall in love with the place. Beautiful old houses, five-star restaurants on every block, streets crawling with killer women and, best of all, no snow in the forecast. What was not to love?

He had wandered off from his friend's wedding reception with Cameron, the twenty-eight-year-old sister of the bride. Together they discovered the culinary gusto of an out-of-the-way spot called Trattoria Lucca then followed it up with some jamming music at a quasi-dive he figured he'd never be able to find again. Last thing he remembered was teetering down a cobblestone street, arm around Cameron's shoulder, looking for a place that had either Lion or Tiger in its name. That Cameron, what a handful she turned out to be.

The day after the wedding he canceled his return flight to Logan Airport, then on Monday morning walked into the Charleston Police Department on Lockwood Street. The résumé he had knocked out in his hotel room that morning had a typo or two in it, but that didn't seem to bother the chief of detectives, who hired him on the spot.

Now, three months later, he was coming down the home stretch: Interstate 26, just north of Charleston. The first half of the trip down had been a little dicey, since the day he had picked for the move had turned out to be especially cold and windy. He was driving a U-Haul, his car on a hitch behind it, and had been wrestling the steering wheel of the orange-and-white cube the whole way down. A few miles before Wilmington, Delaware a gusty blast blew him into the path of a rampaging sixteen-wheeler, which roared up on his bumper like an Amtrak car that had jumped the tracks. It was a close call, but things quieted down after he hit the Maryland border.

He had the window down now and was taking in the warm salt air, which reminded him of the Cape when he was a kid and life was easy. He was looking forward to the slow Southern pace of Charleston. Kicking back with a plate full of shrimp and grits, barbeque and collards or whatever it was they were so famous for, then washing it all down with a couple of Blood Hounds, a bare-knuckled rum drink bad girl Cameron had introduced him to.

He was thinking about how he might get his lame golf game out of mothballs, psyched about being able to play year-round. One thing he'd miss would be opening day at Fenway, but he'd heard about Charleston's minor league baseball team and figured it would be good for a few grins. One thing he'd never miss would be staring down at stiffs on the mean streets of Beantown.

The ring of his cell phone broke the reverie. He picked it up, looked at the number, and didn't recognize it.

"Hello."

"Nick, it's Ernie Brindle. Where y'at?" Brindle was the Charleston chief of detectives, the man who had hired him.

"Matter of fact, Ernie, I'm just pulling into Charleston. A few miles north. Why, what's up?"

Brindle sighed. "Looks like it's gonna be trial by fire for you, bro. I'm looking down at a dead body on Broad Street... it's the mayor. The ex-mayor, guess that would be. How fast can you get here?"

Janzek had figured he'd at least get a chance to unload his stuff from the U-Haul before his first-day punch-in.

"Thing is, Ernie, I'm driving this big old U-Haul with all my junk in it. Can't I just drop it—"

"No, I need you right now. Corner of Broad and Church."

Janzek stifled a groan. "Is Church before or after King Street?"

"Two blocks east. Just look for a guy under a sheet and every squad car in the city. Not every day the mayor gets smoked."

"Okay, I'm getting off I-26. I see a sign for King Street."

"You're just five minutes away," Brindle said. "Welcome to the Holy City."

"Thanks," Janzek said. "Kinda wish it were under different circumstances."

Janzek rumbled down Meeting Street, breathing in the fragrant scent of tea olive trees. He got stuck behind a garbage truck and his first instinct was to lay on the horn, but something told him you didn't do that in Charleston. Up ahead he saw a horse-drawn carriage jammed with gawkers. The garbage truck and the carriage were side by side—like blockers—creeping along at ten miles an hour. The smell of horse manure wafted through his open windows and replaced the sweet tea olive smell.

Janzek finally saw an opening, hit the accelerator, and slipped between the truck and the carriage. Broad Street was just ahead. He had never seen that many squad cars except at an Irish captain's funeral up in Southie. Ernie Brindle was keeping an eye out for him, and when he saw the U-Haul pull up he directed Janzek past the long line of black-and-whites to a spot in front of a fire hydrant. Janzek got out and walked over.

Brindle, a short, intense guy with hair he didn't spend much time on, eyeballed Janzek's transportation. "Jesus, Nick, not just a U-Haul, but dragging a sorry-ass Honda behind it?" Brindle shook his head. "Thought you were s'posed to be a big-time homicide cop."

Janzek glanced back at the car that had served him long and loyally. "I'm not much of a car guy, Ernie."

Janzek looked down at the body sprawled half on and half off the sidewalk. Brindle pulled the sheet back. The late mayor was dressed in an expensive-looking blue suit, which was shredded and splattered with blood. A crushed gold watch dangled loosely from his wrist.

"So, what exactly happened?" Janzek asked, looking around at the cluster of cops, crime scene techs, and a man he assumed was the ME.

"According to a witness," Brindle said, "he was crossing the street when a black Mercedes 500, goin' like a bat out of hell, launched him twenty feet in the air."

"So... intentional then?" Janzek said.

"Yeah, for sure. Guy said he saw the driver aiming a gun."

"In case he couldn't take him out with the car?"

Brindle nodded. "I guess."

"Pointing it out the window?"

"Uh-huh," Brindle said.

"So he was a lefty," Janzek said. "Guy say whether he fired it or not?"

"He didn't think so. Didn't hear anything, anyway."

"How'd he know it was a 500?"

"He's a car salesman," Brindle said. "On his way to the bank."

Janzek knelt down next to the body to get a closer look. It was clear the mayor had landed on his face. His nose was shoved off to one side, and his forehead and cheeks looked like a sheet of salmon.

The guy he figured for the ME, who'd been talking to two men nearby, came up and eyeballed him with a who-the-hell-are-you? look.

"Jack," Brindle said to the man, "this is Nick Janzek, new homicide guy." Then to Janzek, "Jack Martin is our esteemed, pain-in-the-ass ME."

"Good one," Martin said, crouching down next to the body then looking up at Janzek. "So how come you caught this one, Nick?"

Janzek didn't know the answer.

"'Cause I liked his sheet," Brindle said.

"Who you got him with?" Martin asked Brindle.

"Delvin."

Martin shook his head and glanced over at Janzek. "Urkel? Good fuckin' luck." Then he noticed the blue parka Janzek was wearing. "You plannin' on goin' skiing or something, Nick?"

Janzek glanced down at his coat. "Just drove down from Boston. Weather was a little different up there."

Martin nodded and kept looking Janzek over.

"Hey, Jack," Brindle said, "how 'bout examining the mayor 'stead of Janzek?"

Martin ignored him. "Boston, huh?"

"Yeah," Janzek said. "Massachusetts."

"Yeah, I've heard of it," Martin said, looking over Janzek's shoulder at the U-Haul. He shook his head, shot Brindle a look, and muttered, "Just what we need down here."

"What's that?" asked Brindle.

"Another fuckin' wiseass Yankee."

TWO

PICTURE TWELVE OAKS IN *GONE WITH THE WIND*, A TWO-STORY
Greek Revival-style house with enough piazza and balcony space for
a small platoon of soldiers to do marching drills. Leading up to it was
a long, perfect allée of live oak trees and, in between, a smooth tabby
driveway. A black butler in a dark suit, white shirt, and a tie with the
logo and coat of arms of Pinckney Hall on it watched from the porch
as Ned Carlino pulled up in his Tesla Roadster.

Carlino got out, stretched, and looked around as Jeter, the butler,
walked down the last few steps to greet him.

"Hey, Mr. Carlino," Jeter said, his bushy white eyebrows arching,
"welcome back to Pinckney."

"Thanks, Jeter. Good to be back."

Ned Carlino, fifty-four years old and a stocky five eight, was not a
man you'd ever mistake for Rhett Butler. Born in a socially unaccept-
able suburb of Philadelphia, he had gotten a scholarship to Villanova
then another one to Harvard Law, and quickly became one of the
best ambulance chasers around. Back then, his card read *Personal
Impairment Attorney*, but everyone knew.

His first big case came at age twenty-six when Hector Nunez, the hotheaded, power-hitting Philadelphia Phillies right fielder, lost it after a called third strike in the fifth game of the playoffs and flung his bat in disgust. It clanged off the metal railing in the boxes to the left of the Phillies dugout then bounced off the head of an out-of-work cleaning lady from across the river in Camden.

Turned out to be the best thing that ever happened to her.

Carlino, who was watching the game in a bar because he hadn't paid his cable bill, beat it over to Thomas Jefferson Hospital—where he figured they'd take her—in just twenty minutes. Practically beat the ambulance. He crept up to a woman at the nurses station in the ER and told her he was a cousin of the woman who had been hit by the bat, even though she was sixty and Hispanic. The nurse looked at him funny, but Ned was not about to be deterred.

Long story short, the former cleaning lady, Ned's new client, got four million dollars when his expert witness convinced the jury that she would have constant migraines, and possibly life-altering seizures, for the rest of her life. The expert witness was convincing, and Ned, even more so. Half of the four million went to the woman and the other half to Carlino's firm, Suozzi and Scarpetta—or Sleazy and Sleazier as one TV news reporter dubbed it. Carlino managed to wangle nearly a million for himself. He immediately paid off his cable bill, bought a BMW, and moved to the Main Line. After five years of following his sensitive nose to massive settlements— including one where he represented the widow of a three-pack-a-day smoker and wangled twenty million dollars out of National Tobacco Company—he decided to seek legal respectability and become a trial lawyer.

That was thirty years ago and, surprisingly, a few of the big Philadelphia white-shoe, establishment firms pursued him despite his low-born Italian heritage and somewhat unsavory reputation. Because—unsavory or not—Ned Carlino was a winner. Along the way, in the great tradition of all American success stories, Carlino decided he needed to burnish his image and erase all hints of his past. He first became a prodigious collector of modern art, outbidding a

Connecticut hedge fund owner on a Jim Dine and several Jasper Johns. Then, in addition to his townhouse in Rittenhouse Square and his Nantucket beach house, he bought a third house on the Intracoastal in Palm Beach and a fourth on Sullivan's Island, outside of Charleston. Three years after that, he sprang for the five-thousand-acre Pinckney Hall plantation, forty minutes south of Charleston. Lastly, he became a philanthropist and sat on the boards of a hospital and a library in Philadelphia, to which he had just donated nine million dollars for a twenty-thousand-square-foot wing. *The Edward G. Carlino Research Library* was etched elegantly into the building's limestone facade.

"Jeter, grab my bag in the trunk and take it upstairs," Carlino said. "I'm going over to the guest house."

Jeter smiled wide, and his teeth looked like a freshly painted picket fence. "William is waitin' on you there, sir."

Carlino walked across the driveway then down the antique-brick path to the guest house, where he pushed open the massive mahogany door, which he'd shipped over from a tumbled-down manor house in England. He walked into the vast living room, painstakingly decorated piece by piece by Madeline Littleworth Mortimer herself. He waved at William across the room and gestured that he needed a drink. William nodded eagerly and reached for the Myers's rum bottle.

The first girl he saw was Ashley. Twenty-three, give or take, she was wearing black-and-silver spandex tights, a gypsy top, and red jellies—teen dream, circa 1994. She was shoving quarters into an antique slot machine, which was lined up next to a collector's item Gottlieb pinball machine on the far wall. She looked up and gave him a Marilyn Monroe pop of the lips and a fluttery smile.

Justine was sitting in a pudgy leather couch facing a huge fireplace with a mantelpiece from a Normandy castle. She was wearing a miniskirt with pin-striped tights, a white silk top, and Tory Burch flats. Under the tights was one of the best pairs of legs in South

Carolina. The look was girl-who'll-do-anything-to-get-ahead, circa 2018.

"Hey, Mr. C," she said, her hoop earrings jiggling beneath her Jennifer Aniston haircut. She came up to him and gave him a prodigious kiss on the lips. "So glad you're back, lover boy...I missed you *desperately.*" She knew exactly what he wanted to hear.

He kissed her back then reached down and cupped her remarkably perfect breasts. She smiled up at him and pretended to like getting pawed.

"Missed you too, honey," he said, marveling at how tight her stomach was, "but I told you, lose the Mr. C, it makes me feel old."

"Sorry...Ned," Justine said with a wink. "I got the sheets all turned down."

"Hold on, girl, I haven't even had my first drink yet."

Martha was sitting on a barstool as Carlino approached. She turned to face him. William, behind her, was adding a lime wedge to his drink. Martha, twenty-five and runway-model striking, was dressed in a short tartan skirt. Her legs were spread, a few inches beyond discreet, revealing a black thong and light coffee-colored thighs. Bad girl cheerleader, circa... hard to tell.

"Welcome home," she purred.

Carlino walked over and kissed her on the lips.

"Oh, *baby,* can't wait for you to rip my clothes off," she whispered and winked at William, who pretended not to be listening, "and do all those naughty things you do." She was the one who talked dirty, but in such a refined way.

William was a six-eight former basketball player from Clemson who blushed easily. He set a drink down in front of Carlino. "Good to see you again, sir," William said. "Hope you enjoy the drink."

Carlino took a long sip and wiped his lips. "I always do, William." Looking back at Martha, he said, "You know something? I'm thinking about changing your name. You're way too hot for Martha."

"What's wrong with Martha?" she asked, ratcheting up the smile.

"It's just not sexy. I mean, Martha Washington, Martha Stewart... Martha Wiggins."

"Who's Martha Wiggins?"

Carlino chuckled. "My old neighbor growing up. Two hundred pounds, three chins, five-day growth. I'm thinking of—I don't know—Willow or Miranda, or maybe Vruska."

Martha laughed. "What? I'm Russian now?"

He nodded.

"Of course," she said. "Whatever you want me to be."

Ned's cell phone rang. He punched the green button. "Hello, Rutledge," he said, smiling at Martha. "Yeah, I'm looking forward to seeing you and Henry down here tonight. Got a couple of girls just dying to meet you."

He looked away from Martha and listened. "Yeah, I know, terrible thing that was." He chuckled. "People just gotta be more careful how they drive in Charleston. But, hey, the good news is I got the perfect guy lined up to fill his shoes."

END OF EXCERPT

Killing Time in Charleston comes out in 2019. To be the first to know when it's available, be sure to sign up for my free newsletter at **tomturnerbooks.com/news**.

ACKNOWLEDGMENTS

First, I'd like to thank my beta readers, Gordon McCoun, Nick Manno, Len Morrison, Michael McTaggart and brother John, for their excellent, incisive comments and suggestions. I appreciate all your input and you truly helped make this a better book.

My thanks, also, to my friend John Randall, lawyer nonpareil and the heroic man who saved my life (so he thinks anyway).

Many thanks to Nick Johansen, who makes it all possible...I'm going to miss you.

Also, to the gang at the dog park, who, oddly, always seem to give me ideas, inspiration and perspective. So thanks to a giant of a man, John Willard, and one of the most generous woman I know, Karen Feeney, then, in no particular order, Tim, Florian, Carol, Robin, Les, Hugh, Eric, Jeff, Ann, Blake, Pat, Tanis, the two Jerrys, the three Kathys, Tina, Steve et al.

Lastly and forever, to my beautiful, smart, kind, and extraordinarily talented daughters, Serena and Georgie, who are always in my corner.

ABOUT THE AUTHOR

A native New Englander, Tom dropped out of college and ran a bar in Vermont...into the ground. Limping back to get his sheepskin, he then landed in New York where he spent time as an award-winning copywriter at several Manhattan advertising agencies. After years of post-Mad Men life, he made a radical change and got a job in commercial real estate. A few years later he ended up in Palm Beach, buying, renovating and selling houses while getting material for his novels. On the side, he wrote *Palm Beach Nasty*, its sequel, *Palm Beach Poison*, and a screenplay, *Underwater*.

While at a wedding, he fell for the charm of Charleston, South Carolina. He spent six years there and completed a yet-to-be-published series set in Charleston. A year ago, Tom headed down the road to Savannah, where he just finished a novel about lust and murder among his neighbors.

Learn more about Tom's books at:
www.tomturnerbooks.com

 facebook.com/tomturner.books

ALSO BY TOM TURNER

CHARLIE CRAWFORD MYSTERIES

Palm Beach Nasty

Palm Beach Poison

Palm Beach Deadly

Palm Beach Bones

Palm Beach Pretenders

Palm Beach Predator

Palm Beach Broke

STANDALONES

Broken House

Made in the USA
Coppell, TX
29 November 2021

66672525R00173